Before the Dawn

ISBN: 1-4392-6214-4
ISBN-13: 9781439262146

Before the Dawn

The First Book of the Satya Yuga Chronicles

Paul Colver

2009

As Vorguld reached to retrieve the dagger his malevolence filled the Hall of Justice like a rancid stench.

"Thank you young Prince," he hissed. "I owe you dearly."

Chapter 1
Blue Dust

The sun would rise soon.

Silent in the shadows, a horseman mounted on a towering horse watched an oddly matched pair walk past a wide stretch of neglected buildings. Secure within his armor the Swike could see that one of the fallen buildings created a recess in the rubble. There he would trap these who dared transgress the Founding Edicts. How long had it been since any of the Company of the Lords had found someone foolhardy enough to brave the streets of Harnell after dark? He rubbed the criss-cross of scars on his right cheek as he considered this thought but he could not remember.

Presently he flashed a brief glance at his footman who had been waiting expectantly. They would herd these two malcontents into the corner and then the fun would begin.

Fun, the Swike thought. *There is so little fun in this forsaken land. When was the last time we Swikes were allowed to thunder through the night striking terror into the Sluds? Our lust for life has cooled with the passing of time—and the tedium of ritual and meetings. But my capture of these two will fill my comrades with the sweet juice of life.*

The Swike and his footman waited in silence but with much anticipation.

In the faint haze of the early light, the oddly matched pair might move faster. The leader, a youth, not yet a man in size, walked with his long upper body bent forward as though ready to fight. He turned to look behind him at a figure cloaked in a sand-colored blanket, rags and other swaddle: a figure he had guided since midnight. Though the red haze of predawn faintly illuminated their way the rag bundle continued to walk with the slow pace of a person without a worry in the world. Not for the first time, anxious to be within the safety of his father's Keep, the boy hissed at his charge, "Faster!"

During the last year, much to his grief, he had watched his father's life ebb away. Once strong and vigorous, the man's flesh, as well as his zest for life, had slowly evaporated. The boy searched the small kingdom of Harnell for any healer, each a man as was required by The Edicts, who professed to have the powers of Calli. In desperation he presented these odds and sods to his father but every last one of them failed to provide a cure. Now in hopelessness, he had taken a great risk. Against the Protocols of the Founding Edicts, and certainly against his father's wishes, he escorted a woman to the King's court. Though old and shrunken and nondescript, she was a woman and an affront to the Edicts.

This foolishness was his mother's and grandmother's doing. They had begged and badgered him to fetch this crone who now followed him at much too slow a pace. "A great Sybil," Grandmeer had gushed with a tone of reverence in her voice, "A great, wise healer." While his mother instructed him in what to say in the presence of the The Sybil, his grandmother whispered again and again: "Wise women; protectors of our very life," much similar to what she had drilled into him when he was a child.

He had objected to the women's plan, but his mother had been her most forceful self: "Jessyl, your father is dying. Will you bring in Broken Charlie to sing his nonsense as you have brought forth your other wastrels?"

Jessyl had argued, but she interrupted resolutely and with finality. "You must choose between the Edicts and your father's life. Have you another hope than The Sybil, or will you sit on your hands, a sad, moping boy, only to witness your father's death?" Her anger and sarcasm increased as she spoke. "And then what? Spend the rest of your life swallowed up in remorse because you failed to act? Be bold, Jessyl: be a man!"

Throughout his early life both women had filled his young head with stories of the wisdom and power of The Sybil. His father spoke an entirely different tale, as had the boy's grandfather.

Growing up, the Prince loved both men dearly. When he was not sitting beside his father, listening to him resolve a dispute or dispense justice, he would often seek out his grandfather and cajole him into telling stories of the old kingdoms.

Now, in the morning silence, nearly at the entrance and the safety of his father's Keep, he recalled, as he had many times during his youth, a memory of his grandfather that often came into his mind when he followed the counsel of his mother.

The young prince and his friend Ennar had been exploring the vast fortress of his father, as they often did when Ennar was allowed to visit. The fortress had been built by a rich and powerful kingdom now forgotten—even by his grandfather—long before the great wars. His father's court occupied only a small portion of the countless rooms and halls, and next to nothing of the towers and turrets and battlements.

One early morning, soon after breakfast, Jessyl and Ennar climbed the precisely built stone stairway that led to their favorite room high in a turret top. The boys had used this room as their lookout. It had likely been just that, a watchtower in the ancient days when a messenger, or indeed an army, might come from a neighboring land. In those times it had been necessary to keep a watch posted. But during all the hours of all the days he and Ennar had spent gazing out hoping to see a rider, or an army, or anything out of the ordinary, all they had seen, other than the visions created by their imaginations, were the never-ending dunes covered with brittle ashen-green scrub that faded away in the distance. True, in the west there were mountain walls that rose like pale blue tombstones out of the scrublands, but the gray green of the dunes faded into nothingness at their base.

As they had done so many mornings throughout their young lives, Jessyl and Ennar scampered up the stairs arriving breathless at the top landing. Jessyl boldly flung open the door of the lookout. To his shock there sat his grandfather, eyes closed, a patch of sunlight warming his chest. At the sound of the door, the old man's eyes snapped open and he stood and lunged for the boy. The sunlight brilliantly illuminated his startlingly clear eyes, and what the boy most remembered from those few moments was the fierce blueness of those eyes. Trapped within their depths, Jessyl felt a hand with the strength of steel grab his wrist, and he remembered the slam of the door wrenched shut. Ennar was left outside.

"Look out as far as you can see," his grandfather rasped. "Look out and listen to my counsel. All this before you, as far as you can see even with your young eyes, was once green. All you see—look out at the land boy, not at me—all this you see before you was once lush and green orchards and grain fields."

He turned the boy to face him and looked with tear-filled eyes deeply into his grandson's eyes. "Orchards and vineyards and cattle: wealth. Wealth! Do you understand? That is what a king provides for his kingdom—wealth! Full tables and full larders, and comfort and safety for those loyal to him, and in abundance." He roared out these last words.

"Remember always your lessons. Remember the lessons I have taught you...pass all you have learned on to your son. And remember, Jessyl, the most important lesson of all. What is of most importance my grandson?

He waited but the trembling boy did not answer.

The old man cried out: "But for the meddling of the women, all the land would be green. Remember this greatest of all truths Jessyl: the meddling of women in the affairs of men—most of all the meddling of the Sybils, cannot but end in disaster."

He looked long at his grandson. "In time I will leave our earth: tell me you have learned this one lesson my boy."

Of course the young prince nodded in agreement. Slowly he mumbled the words 'the meddling of women' and the like over and over as his grandfather stood nodding and smiling, tears running down his wrinkled cheeks.

And now as the boy walked in the cool air of dawn, hounded by the frustration and the guilt of having done nothing to help his father—worried to exhaustion that his father would die—he escorted a woman to the court of the King of Harnell. Not just a woman, but a Sybil. Not a Sybil of the True Light, but, as she called herself, a Sybil of the Protective Light—not that her title would make any difference in the least to his father, or to the Company of the Lords.

Great Sur and all you blessed gods, the boy prayed, *let there be a cure for my father within ken of this sorry woman.*

He had left the protection of his Father's Keep the previous day, at the first light of sunrise, intending to return no later than the twilight of evening: certainly before dark. The 'great, wise healer' had dawdled. First, at the time appointed for leaving and later she refused to set out until some star rose in the eastern sky.

"We will be with your father at sunrise," the crone had trilled, wagging a long finger at the boy. Her voice was filled with assurance and when questioned about traveling at night, she showed not a worry in the world.

The horseman waited patiently as he had been trained to do since youth. He breathed in cool morning air and relished the dark mirth that turned the air warm within his chest. Finally, when the time seemed right, with a silent nudge of spurs he prodded his massive horse towards the unsuspecting pair, not at all in a hurry.

The boy, throughout the journey, had urged the Sybil to hurry. About to do so again, his voice froze in his throat as he heard the sounds of a horse. A horse could only mean danger. A Ranger might be bribed. But if one of the eight Lords or their Swikes were to confront them...a couplet from one of Broken Charley's songs sounded in the boy's mind:

"Travelers out after set of sun, the Lords they crave your life.

Travelers out after night's begun; beware the Swike's cruel knife."

The morning air that had felt pleasantly cool now felt like a sickly glue of sweat sticking the boy's clothing to his skin.

To speak would show fear.

The horseman would remain silent in order to establish terror.

Jessyl stopped moving. Without realizing it, he stopped breathing. He listened. The steady rush of air from the nostrils of just one horse, the clicking sounds of one set of hooves on the gravel of the pathway, and the shuffling of one pair of human feet were all that was to be heard. A lone rider would not have dismounted to confront them: two warriors would challenge the boy and the Sybil.

As the horseman had planned, at the corner formed by the two piles of rubble, the pair found themselves trapped. The bundled figure wedged her body tightly into the angle formed by the stones; the boy positioned himself to act as a shield. The horse, its breath steaming in the morning air, came to a stop, its muzzle a hand's width from the boy's face. In a firm, menacing voice, and as deeply as his young voice would allow, the youth said: "I am Prince Jessyl, one day to be king. Pull your horse from my reach."

A dull laugh burbled from within the creaking mound of armor. "To be king," and after a wicked chuckle, "and soon no doubt." Then the voice thundered, "Evil enough that as your father lies dying, you stalk the night streets. In addition, I see you escort some derelict?" The voice then continued in a cajoling tone, "Pray, tell Great Lord Vorguld's humble servant the purpose of your foolishness?"

Of the eight lords of Harnell, Vorguld, through cruelty and guile, had clawed his way to the top to become the Chief Lord of the Kingdom. His First Swike Direoll, who now toyed with the Prince, was nearly his master's equal in malice.

The Prince spoke, again attempting to sound forceful and older than his years. "Move your horse back a pace, Swike Direoll. Perhaps I may speak with you."

As the Prince spoke the word 'perhaps,' Direoll slithered off his horse and landed stiff- legged, his armor rattling. One large stride brought him to the boy. Grabbing him by the throat and lifting him with his left hand, he pressed his victim with the full weight of his body hard against the stone wall, his face guard cutting into the boy's face. With his right hand he pressed the flat of a dagger against his victim's cheek, the point level with a large, terrified eye. The Swike's footman steadied his sword, the point touching the hood that covered the Sybil's head and face.

"Perhaps," hissed the Swike, his breath reeking in the boy's nostrils, "perhaps you are in the streets after dark. Perhaps I say I don't know you from a thief. Perhaps you will now die."

Toying with the boy, he chuckled slowly and darkly. "Although I would like you and I to be at our leisure for that."

Releasing Jessyl's throat as quickly as he had seized it and letting the boy collapse to the gravel, and with his left arm now free, he knocked away his footman's sword and tore back the crone's ragged hood exposing her face. As he raised his dagger and pulled her face close to him, she pursed her lips and blew into his eyes a pale blue mist nearly the color of her skin.

Blinded and dropping his weapon, he roared, "You witch!" and then the pain began. "My eyes!" he screamed piteously as he fought to remove his helmet.

Immediately the Sybil pointed at the footman and commanded in a loud voice, "Sit," as one might command a dog. The footman collapsed, a hand shading his startled eyes which rapidly became dull and then heavy lidded.

Jessyl rolled away from the screaming Swike, snatched up the dagger and sprang up slapping the flat of the blade across the horse's muzzle. The horse reared and ran.

The Sybil flipped up her hood and resumed her sedate pace as though nothing of consequence had happened. She walked, slowly moving her head from one side to the other, looking as though she was on the most pleasant of walks through the most pleasant of vales.

The Prince rapidly looked about him, his face clouded with fear. He walked backwards, in the direction of his Father's Keep, surveying the scene of the Swike of the Chief Lord of Harnell groveling in the dust of the pathway, cursing and fiercely rubbing his eyes. Beside the Swike sat the stunned footman still as a tombstone, both hands shielding his face as though protecting his eyes from blinding sunlight.

Jessyl held the dagger between his thumb and index finger as far from his body as his long arms would allow.

He croaked in panic, "Quickly, to my father's Keep!"

The Sybil, her slanted eyes widened in a look of mock fear, snorted a brief chuckle and continued her leisurely pace.

Chapter 2
The Windriders

In the time it took the Ranger Gelt to gasp a great breath of astonishment, the Windriders—this is what they would come to be called by the people of Harnell—floated over a pale rose colored dune top as silent as ghosts. Behind these apparitions two ancient and elegantly carved stone sentinels looked to be rapidly shrinking ghouls in the first light of morning. Buoyed by red sails the Windriders leaped forty paces to each stride, their colorful clothing rippling in the crisp dawn air. A few more strides and their sails would fill and they would fly.

The Ranger Gelt blew a weather darkened horn that a moment earlier had hung on a slim chain about his shoulder. He had no thought of the Protocol for Outsiders as set out two hundred years earlier in the Founding Edicts. His hand had lifted the horn to his full lips, his wide chest and belly had expanded and contracted, and the horn had sounded. His partner stared in disbelief at this deviation from the Protocol of the Edicts.

Immediately upon blowing the horn, Gelt thought: *What have I done? The Edicts! The element of surprise has been lost...and with Dern as my partner we will fight these two, and hear scarcely a word from their lips.*

The Windrider closest to the two Rangers tilted his sail and drove his left leg into the sand, altering his course towards the sound of the horn. His companion followed flawlessly, the muscles of his leg bulging beneath black skin. When they were ten paces from the Rangers, they flattened the sails to the earth and in one smooth motion unclipped themselves from their harnesses. They held their hands palms forward, fingers pointing down in what appeared to be a greeting; their laughing eyes shone with exuberance.

The Rangers, heavy with mismatched armor and wrapped in sand-colored cloaks, stood legs apart, hands on their sword hilts.

The Ranger Dern, who had stared in disbelief at his partner's transgression, spoke with a sneering tone: "Who are you, and what is it you seek in our land? Since you passed the Stone Watchers you have entered the Kingdom of Harnell."

The two Windriders dropped their hands and each widened his stance.

"We are from far to the south. For the last twenty-three mornings Great Sur has blessed us and we have ridden the winds northward," said the shorter of the pair. "Our business is peaceful. We travel to meet what people we might. To trade. To learn, and to return to our Mothers' Houses with what wisdom we may. Tell us of this Kingdom which, as is your duty, you proudly protect."

Each Ranger had listened intently and the Ranger Dern had, against his will, allowed an eyebrow to lift nearly imperceptibly at the words 'Mothers' Houses.'

The second Ranger, Gelt, who had been silent aside from the sounding of the horn, offered their names. "We are Rangers of the Kingdom of Harnell. I am Gelt of Rawlings." He then gestured towards his companion. "And my partner for this moon's watch: Dern of Rawlings. Forgive our lack of welcome; you are the first to cross our borders during these last eight generations that Kings and the Company of the Lords have ruled the land."

Dern, his long, permanently pained face rigid and expressionless aside from his constant grimace, began speaking again in the same soulless tone he had used when he first spoke. "Our orders are to bring outsiders to our Chief Lord to be questioned."

The Windriders stepped apart from each other. The taller of the pair was occupied scanning the horizon and did not look at the Rangers as he spoke: "In this rising wind, if we pick up our sails, we will be high in the air before you can blink."

As he spoke he thought, *Searching twenty three days this year and what do we find? Sir Humble and his partner with a voice from the grave. When I to empty their skulls on the sand, will there be half a brain between them?*

His partner, whose round face conveyed a sense of joviality no matter how hard he tried to look stern, eyed the Rangers and interjected with warmth in his voice: "This is not to say that we might not join you and visit your Chief Lord. We desire to meet others and learn their skills and knowledge—and to share ours."

The Windrider who meticulously viewed the horizon continued: "We are curious, however, about what 'to be questioned' might mean."

His partner, allowing no room for an answer, interjected in a placating tone: "You must understand that we are travelers alone in a strange land."

The more aggressive of the two Windriders, intent on viewing the horizon and still not looking at the Rangers, arched an eyebrow at the words 'in a strange land' in mockery of Dern's earlier lapse of control. He now finished his scan and knew that he and his partner and these two men were alone in the dunes. Staring deeply into the Ranger Dern's eyes, he said, "You lack bows, and, of course, the arrows that go with them. Should you draw those swords you now grip, Jolar and I will kill you before your weapons may be of use."

Jolar quickly interceded: "Now, now, Leason my friend, not so hasty."

Leason, standing erect, his face impassive, continued speaking and looked hard at Dern. "As you stand on my side, I will take you down." He added, with disdain in his voice, "Consider it just the chance of where you stand." He bowed, but his focus on the Ranger was unwavering.

Jolar, his usual playful grin now nervously broad with encouragement and hoping for peace continued: "Their deaths gain us naught, Leason. These Rangers have a duty. And we wish to learn. Surely there must be a way. What say the Rangers of Harnell?"

Dern, keen for blood, continued his grating manner of speech: "The ridge of the Stone Watchers where you trespassed this morning is our southern border. None have crossed that border in the eight generations that the Lords and the Kings have ruled the land. The Founding Edicts demand that outsiders be questioned."

Jolar replied with exasperation creeping into his voice. "Who is able to guarantee us safe passage to speak peacefully with your King?" *Great gods, man!* He thought as he spoke. *You repeat your partner's words. You live in an island amidst a sea of dunes: are Leason and I going to pick up the kingdom and carry it away? Your brain has suffered from inbreeding.*

Leason continued, "Here, alone with you among the dunes, we have the advantage."

Jolar laughed nervously to himself as he heard Leason speak. *If we don't have the advantage with these two, we will never have the advantage.*

Dern interrupted before Leason's last word was complete. "Advantage!" he scoffed. "You are fools. We have no bows," he spoke with haste, his dull cadence forgotten with the excitement of battle before him. "Women's weapons are not allowed in the Kingdom of Harnell. Throwing knives are quicker than arrows, and you are well within our range. We throw with great accuracy and our knives are sharp. You will come with us or I will set my dagger in your eye!"

His speech was cut short by a sharp pinch of pain much like a wasp's sting, and the last word he spoke extended into a squeal. He quickly pulled a feathered dart from his neck. Embarrassed at his seemingly womanish shriek, he forced a smile as if about to laugh at the delicacy of the seemingly inconsequential weapon but the pressure of his thumb and forefinger had forced the last of the dart's drug into his blood. As he began to feel weak, fear engulfed his face, his eyes rolled back in his head, and he collapsed; his companion fell beside him a moment later.

In unison, the Windriders lowered their arms and each released the end of a flexible silver tube from their lips. They scanned the horizon, each viewing one half; then they cautiously inserted a dart far into the other end of the tube which had been hidden beneath their shirts' cuff. Continuing to move as one, they tucked the other end of their weapon under their collars.

"Enough talk," Leason said spitting into the powdery soil.

"I'd have talked further," Jolar said pointedly.

"My friend, you were not far behind me in dropping your man."

Jolar reluctantly nodded in agreement, "Once weapons begin to fly, let ours be the ones to find home."

Leason agreed with a laugh and said, "By the time they awake, they will be fried eggs."

"No, no, I do not intend to leave them so soon," Jolar replied firmly but with entreatment in his voice. "They are all we have seen in twenty-three days and all we are likely to see in the few days remaining before we must return. When they awake, let us question them."

Chapter 3
Of Lords and Swikes

The eight Lords of Harnell, each with his Swike in attendance, met at the Southern Gate of the King's Fortress and prepared to enter the Hall of Justice for the first of the day's meetings. Each morning, shortly after sunrise the Company of the Lords gathered to enter the Hall in order to make demands or entreaties of the King, and to report on the events of the previous day and night in their respective domains. These meetings, along with numerous others, were set out two centuries earlier by the Founding Edicts.

The Edicts were a feeble spark of sanity after centuries of madness. The few survivors of The Great Wars were all that remained of vast multitudes who died before the Edicts were agreed upon. Millions had been slaughtered until so few people remained alive that it became clear that mankind might disappear from the earth.

As the Lords waited for their Swikes to help them dismount from the horses Lord Rawlings clutched his neck and shrieked a stifled yelp of pain. Nearly falling he struggled off his horse his face ashen and staggered to support himself against the stone wall of the Fortress.

Lord Vorguld—it was his role to speak to such a bizarre occurrence, and the role of none other—spoke sharply to his underling. "Lord Rawlings, will you live?" There were nervous smiles among the Lords and Swikes, though only the Lords chuckled.

"Gelt has fallen," Rawlings gasped, "shot in the neck."

Vorguld in surprised raised his thick eyebrows and looked at Rawlings, momentarily concerned.

"Have you taken up necromancy, Lord Rawlings?" Vorguld replied, chuckling at his wit. None of the Rangers or Swikes dared to laugh, though most would have loved nothing better than to join the Lords who laughed mercilessly at Rawling's discomfort.

Rawlings smiled in deference to the Chief Lord.

"Gather your wits about you," Vorguld continued. "We must enter the Hall and await the King as The Edicts require each of us to be present. Join us shortly, whether or not you have regained your composure."

Vorguld turned to his Swike Direoll: "And our other casualty of the day? How goes it with you, my blinded Swike?"

"The pain is blistering, my Lord, though I am able to see a bit."

"I am not concerned with your pain, blistering or otherwise. You deserve the pain and much more of it to have let a woman, old and tottering, as you describe her, take your sight. We shall see if there may be an opportunity for revenge."

"Revenge, my Lord," the Swike snarled. "Please my Lord allow me to have revenge."

"There may be an opportunity. There may be," Vorguld mused and then added loudly for all to hear: "Pray, do not fall a second time to the damsel's charms."

The Company laughed uproariously, but the boys who stood behind the gathering remained silent though they bit their lips or otherwise repressed their pleasure that someone other than they were being ridiculed.

Mishrup, Rawlings' Swike, had earlier leaped off his horse to join his master and now stood beside his Lord. The other Swikes helped their Lords dismount and all but Rawlings and Mishrup entered the Hall of Justice. "A few moments of rest and all will be well," Rawlings said to his Swike. "Gelt is alive, of that I am sure. You and I, with a host of the lads, will ride to his aid as soon as this morning of banter with the King has ended. Join the others. I will stand with you presently."

Mishrup bowed his head slightly to his master as was required by the Edicts, and turned and walked up the steps, under the portcullis, past the ancient wood doors, and into the Hall of Justice.

Rawlings rubbed his fingers over the criss-cross of scars that adorned his cheeks and muttered to himself, "Gelt down and I must keep my temper throughout another insufferable meeting. May the strength of Mangala be with you, Gelt. I will ride to your aid once the babbling of this morning is finished." Rawlings leaned heavily against the fortress wall and closed his eyes in thought.

Enough of the tedium of these reports in the Hall of Justice: 'The guards saw this, or this slud was punished for...' Great Sur only knew what. Blah, blah, blah, blah. On and on it goes, day after day, year after year. As the Founding Edicts require. Damn the Edicts. Damn whoever wrote us into their trap. They are a trap. A waste of life: a waste of my life.

Rawlings had read the Founding Edicts many times. He had pondered deeply and marveled that the authors had so completely shaped the Kingdom even to this day.

Those who wrote the Edicts knew what they wanted to accomplish...and they have succeeded. To keep the land poor is to keep the land peaceful. We Lords and our underlings live in one vast Keep. Aye, well named: a Keep. We must work together. What we enjoy depends on it. Depends on squeezing as much labor as possible from the Sluds.

The water we believe is ours -it is controlled by the King. Long we suspected this. It was confirmed by the young healer found wandering and lost in the streets after dark. The sorry lad...broken before the night had even begun. Babbling all he knew. A great disappointment to the fools gathered for sport. And what fools they are—each of them a fool. Content with wine and meat and the occasional drunken frolic with some screaming girl. And a bit of torture. What fools. Casualties of the Edicts that they so revere. Not that each of us, me included, isn't a victim of the Edicts. Yes, the creators of the Edicts were clever, no doubt. The King his water and healers and crossbow, to keep us in check. And the weapons and strength and food supply that we control keeps the King in check. And what is left after two hundred years? A handful of mindless fools. Fools with no vision. None of them see as I see. The Edicts are a death trap. Yes, the Edicts keep us from slaughtering each other, but just as surely, they keep us in Hell. When the time is right I will burn The Edicts and anyone who speaks of them.

Rawlings felt the sun warming his face and muttered to himself, "I will enjoy these few precious moments before I must enter the Hall and the tedium begins."

The Lords stood waiting within the vast Hall of Justice. The room's floor, pillars, walls, and arched ceilings, as well as the entire Fortress itself, had been constructed entirely of well crafted stone many centuries before the Edicts, in a time of prosperity now long forgotten.

The Founding Edicts specified that the Lords and Swikes, while within the Hall, were not allowed armor, though each was permitted one weapon: a sword.

Jessyl had entered the fortress through the East Gate and as the Lords waited, he had rested in the courtyard near the kitchens. Now he had wended his way through the King's Passage to the Hall of Justice with the Sybil waddling behind him concealed within her blanket and swaddle. As the odd looking pair entered the Hall, the assembled warriors, warm within their floor-length cloaks, stared boldly at the Prince and the Sybil, disdain and hatred palpable in the air.

Lord Vorguld's voice echoed off the cold stones: "What bundle of rags do you bring to our court and what concessions will the rag bundle beg from the Lords?"

The Lords and Swikes chuckled as Vorguld played with his words. There was little opportunity for entertainment in their dull lives, and trysting with words was well appreciated. Vorguld and the King were masters at it.

"We Lords are as beneficent as Great Sur himself, though if we gave to every beggar we would soon give away our ability to protect our subjects in such a sparse land as ours," Vorguld continued. There was a murmur of assent from his underlings.

"We are here to give a great gift, not to demand one, Lord Vorguld," Jessyl spoke, hoping to somehow silence the man. "Something that these halls have seldom seen," he added, his lips trembling, as he stared at the towering men held apart from him by two lines etched in the stone floor.

Whether he was referring specifically to a 'great gift' he claimed to have, or to the lack of any great gift ever being given in the Hall, the young Prince allowed the Lords to determine—if, in fact, they could understand the subtlety of his speech. "And that gift shall be given presently," he continued. "With your great discipline you will certainly be able to await the presence of the King."

The Sybil remained motionless, and strangely she had been quickly forgotten by the Lords.

So these are the thugs that terrorize the populace of Harnell into submission, she mused. *Big boys all, but none of them would last a minute in a fight with someone who knew weapons and war,* she thought with pleasure.

"I do advise that you will be asked to report on a fray," Jessyl continued, immediately wishing he had remained silent, "in which some of your men were roughly handled. At dawn this fracas occurred. Dawn, the Edicts tell us, is a time when travelers may go about their business without hindrance if they appear to be of good intent. Dawn is not night, as you no doubt have instructed your guards."

He continued, unable to stop: "The report I have from a truthful source is that two guards of the night watch—presumably yours, Lord Vorguld, as the Kingdom's safety after sunset is your duty throughout this moon—accosted two innocent travelers. As proof of their good intent they have asked me to return this, dropped by one of your men."

He retrieved the dagger from his belt.

The Lords and Swikes, who, until the sight of the dagger, had been savoring the confrontation, had not expected to see the weapon again. They now released a collective gasp of surprise.

The Prince, the turmoil of his stomach momentarily forgotten, enjoyed their reaction. "I trust you to punish the owner of this weapon in the fashion he deserves. I pray the Company of Lords will not coddle such irresponsibility with weakness."

A long, long time since I have been in this Hall, the Sybil thought as she surveyed the elegantly crafted room. *This time things will go my way or by Yama I'll send the lot of them to Hell!*

Jessyl began another scrambled speech to control the time while he awaited the arrival of his father. "A weapon being drawn during the day, unless in utmost need, is clearly prohibited by the Edicts. This weapon is of your house, Lord Vorguld?"

He intended to return the dagger with his father present but found that he had said as much as he had rehearsed, and more. The time to return the weapon was now, or he would face the alternative of standing foolishly by as Vorguld twisted his words about, leaving him to wait like a helpless boy needing to be rescued by his father.

"The Edicts forbid that I go to you with a weapon in hand, Lord Vorguld. Please take it from me and return it to its careless owner."

Jessyl had walked to the King's Boundary Line and held the dagger as he had a short time before, between his thumb and forefinger, far from his body as though he held something putrid and stinking with decay.

Vorguld saw that a weapon belonging to his First Swike's was being handed to him by a boy with barely the fuzz of a beard. And he, the Chief Lord of Harnell, was bid to fetch it as though a dog. His forehead had been turning a dark, sickly scarlet; inwardly he frothed with rage.

"I am constrained by the Edicts and allowed no more than my sword in the Hall of Justice. Surely you do not seek to trap me in a breach of the Edicts?" Vorguld questioned, his will entirely focused upon regaining the offensive and dominating the upstart boy.

In these moments as Vorguld plotted how to humiliate the boy, the King, supported by one of his healers under each arm, and a third carrying the King's crossbow, entered the room. It was clear to all who saw him that he was merely a hint of the man he had once been. Though handsome and well proportioned and his shoulders still wide even without the muscle that had long since withered away, he appeared to be a remnant of a once vigorous man. As the Lords nodded a slight bow of greeting, the King held up his hand, palm forward, to silence them, indicating that he would speak.

You are far gone, King Gemar, the Sybil snickered to herself. *Not much left of your body and not much left of your life. You had best latch on to what I have to offer or your son will be trysting with these thugs as soon as the last shovel full of earth covers your coffin.*

"I see my son is playing king. Let 'his eloquence' proceed with this business," the King said sarcastically, unsure and nervous of what his son's plans might be.

"Father, I attempt to return this dagger to Lord Vorguld. One of his guards has become separated from it—who can imagine how other than through carelessness. The Chief Lord rightly states that the Edicts forbid him more weapons than his sword in the Hall of Justice."

The King immediately replied, "Lord Vorguld, Chief of the Lords, I ask you to set your sword outside the doors of this Hall and retrieve this misplaced weapon from my son."

Vorguld quickly handed his sword to his second Swike, Dinar, and bade him set it outside under the watch of the boys who were tending the horses. As the Swike bowed and turned to leave, Vorguld whispered faintly, "Rawlings."

The King missed this communication, for he had turned and, proud of how he had handled the situation, smiled knowingly and wisely at his son.

After barely a few seconds, Vorguld spoke in a loud voice. "Thank you, wise King, and thank you, young Prince, for your thoughtfulness. I owe you dearly." As he said these words, he walked with his great chest and belly swaying from side to side, as far towards Jessyl as allowed by the Lord's Boundary Line that, as required by the Edicts, had been etched in the stone floor two centuries previous. He stretched his arm, hand palm up, to receive the knife. Jessyl, with his arm outstretched above the King's Boundary Line, laid the knife in the palm of Vorguld's hand, giving full attention to every aspect of the man. He could sense the malevolence that emanated from his adversary as though it was a rancid smell.

Jessyl thought, *Pray I never meet this monster when I am alone.*

Vorguld's baleful eyes stared deep into the boy's eyes. Jessyl held the gaze until the Lord turned and walked to his men. Feeling somewhat safe, he walked to his father with quick strides and bowed deeply. During this interchange Dinar had returned to the room. Rawlings followed him, and now stood beside his Swike, Mishrup. The Lords and Swikes, as was required, nodded a bow to Vorguld.

The Sybil surprisingly had been forgotten during this interchange. She did not bow to anyone. Without a sound she lithely moved to stand in front of the King and threw back her hood, exposing her face and head. Her white hair stood on end as though the bristles of a brush and her pale blue face held the expression of a cat that has found a mouse for play. The presence of a woman in the court, not to mention her ragged appearance and, most strikingly, her eyes, startled the King as well as all those gathered. She squinted her eyes closed to near slits, although the pupils could be seen flashing about as she surveyed the Lords and Swikes. Her glance finally settled on the King. Without a bow or even a nod to the King she laughed a mournful, pitying laugh.

"Yes, you would be exhausted, feeding this beast that sucks away at your life. No doubt, no doubt," she mused, appearing truly concerned.

Within their respective groups the Lords and the three priest-healers exchanged knowing but uncomfortable looks.

The King chuckled darkly, "A Sybil." He turned to his son. "Your mother, or your grandmother, and likely both, have had you fetch, to me, King Gemar of Harnell, a Sybil." He breathed in deeply and then out tiredly and with disgust. "You will need more than your eloquence to be king," he said loud enough for all to hear.

The Sybil continued speaking as though the King had been silent. "I suppose, as the true man you are, you will require a look at the leech that suck away at your life with your own eyes?" She stared at the King as though reading his thoughts. His face sagged with fatigue and he slumped slightly forward as she spoke.

"Only I can show you this creature that consumes your flesh," she continued. "Shall I show you?"

She pointed at the King's main healer. "I have walked throughout the night to be here to cure your King. Am I to stand unfed and untended? Make yourself useful. Bring me a chair. Some wine, and cheese, and bread."

The healer looked at the King and received a nod of permission. As he scurried towards his tasks, she shouted after him: "The best wine! Bring three glasses."

She glanced at the Lords disdainfully. "And the great lords. The local thuggery. Mind your manners, each of you. The clown, who suffered so horribly this morning, has a bit of his eyesight back, I see." She curled her lips downward and flashed a mock-filled grin at the Swike. "There are much worse plagues than loss of eyesight," she cackled, "and more painful too."

The tall priest, breathing heavily under the burden of a wide chair, staggered towards the Sybil. The healer who held the King's crossbow rushed to the aid of his floundering companion. As the Sybil looked at the hilarious picture of the healer's staggering approach, Vorguld nudged Swike Direoll and nodded toward the Sybil. The Swike, drawing his sword, strode forward, and in contravention of the Edicts leaped over both the Lord's and King's boundary lines.

"Your head!" he shouted in a hideous snarl. As he continued to stride towards the Sybil, he aimed a sword swing that would encompass a full circle of arc at her neck.

Upon hearing the first sound of his words, she turned quickly to face him. As the sword approached, and when there was no chance of its course being altered, she collapsed into a squat quicker than an eye blink, the backs of her thighs pressed tight to her calves, her haunches momentarily flattened on the stone floor. As the sword passed over her head, she launched her body up and forward. The heel of her left hand was aimed carefully and made a sickening sound as it struck the startled Swike below his right ear. His head snapped sharply back and to one side. In mid collapse, his sword, now loosed from his grip and flopping slowly, much like a child's teeter totter on his rolling belly, slid off and rattled on the floor stones. As his head hit the floor, a muffled snap sounded from his neck much like the whack of a door knocker rapped against a thick wood door.

The Sybil turned and strode towards the Lords, and in three steps she was close enough to do as she wished. Holding her hands much like a young girl about to float an offering of flowers onto a coffin deep within a grave, she cast a mist of blue dust into the air directly in front of the Lords and Swikes. The dust seemed to have a will of its own as it floated with increasing speed straight for their eyes.

Chapter 4

A Message for the King

As the morning grew warmer the Windriders removed Dern's armor. Leason yanked the Ranger's hood back, exposing his head and face to the sun. Jolar objected, but Leason replied sharply: "Sur's rays will encourage him not to dawdle away our time. All cannot be gentle, Jolar."

They struggled with Dern's limp body and set him on his horse. Leason tied the Ranger's feet beneath the horse's belly; Jolar tied the man's hands and then wrapped the reins twice around the knot between the wrists.

Jolar pointed to the criss-crossing of scars covering both of the Rangers's cheeks.

"What might those markings be?"

"A sign that these people, much like ours, have time on their hands to be idiots," Leason replied curtly. He looked long at Jolar, as though an entire book was to be found within this brief observation.

The Windriders began setting up a sail to shade themselves from the rapidly increasing heat. As they worked, each rider scanned half of the horizon at regular intervals. Leason left the work to return to Gelt and removed the Ranger's hood, exposing his face and head. As he began to retrace his steps to Jolar, he stopped, walked back to Gelt, and turned the Ranger's head so that the man's face pointed directly towards the sun.

Leason shouted across the distance to Jolar: "You wish to speak with them Jolar; I will make sure they talk." He left Gelt lying limp on the sand.

Once the work of the sail was complete and shade provided, the Windriders began to drink and eat the food and water they had taken from the Rangers' packs. Jolar broke the silence with enthusiasm in his voice.

"We have met our first people, Leason. Last year on our travels into the snows of the mountains and the year before to the south and into the desert of the east, we suffered greatly and saw little. Ruins. Wastelands. Piles of skulls. We have found people. Survivors, Leason. A Kingdom. Some bit of knowledge, some scrap of wisdom, and all is paid for."

Leason spoke with frustration in his voice. "And the water? What about the water, Jolar? Each year our peoples' water is used up before the snows begin to fall. There are too many of us. Will this be the year we slaughter each other for water?"

Gelt and Dern were moving sluggishly.

"If these two are the top of the crop, there is nothing for us here," Leason concluded.

Gelt turned his face away from the sun, and Dern, though stilled dazed, instinctively turned his horse to face away from the heat of the sun.

"Profit is of little use if we do not return. You focus on the profit, and I'll focus on the return."

Jolar laughed at Leason's joke. "We are well matched, my friend."

The Rangers were nearly awake. Leason sprayed a slight mist of water into their mouths, though he quickly pulled the leather flask away from their lips.

"Not so greedy with our water," he snarled.

Jolar began speaking as soon as Leason had finished.

"Gentlemen, we found Dern to be the more loquacious of you two," he said sarcasm heavy in his voice. "Thus we have chosen him as our messenger. Whomever he speaks to will either quickly agree to our requests or, given the vivacity of Dern's voice, fall asleep or more likely run screaming for peace."

Leason laughed and continued: "Your voice is by far your greatest weapon! Our biggest struggle was to stay awake as you spoke. Only through our magic arts we succeeded. It was a close call," he said, wiping imaginary sweat off his forehead.

Leason could hardly choke out the last words over his very real but mocking laughter.

Jolar, who was biting his lip to keep from exploding with laughter, continued speaking. "What will you say to whomever you choose to visit Ranger Dern?"

"Likely my next stop will be Hell. I'll soon be melted to skin and bone."

"It is doubtful that Hell will have you," Leason jested. "Bad enough they must suffer fire and torment of all sorts. You talking throughout eternity would be more than any man could stand."

Jolar was holding his hands behind his back and bending a finger painfully to keep from bursting into uncontrollable laughter. He flashed a quick glance of disapproval at his partner and continued his questioning of Dern.

"Suppose you survive: how long would it take you to journey somewhere of use to us...and of use to you?"

"This sounds as though I am being questioned."

"If there is any questioning to do, I will take care of that," Leason threatened with a sinister tone large in his voice.

Jolar started speaking immediately, allowing for no time between Leason's words and his own.

"Say that we unhobble the horse, and you leave now. How far would the sun move across the blue sky as you travel to where you might?"

Dern sat on the horse in silence, his face, as usual, implacable.

Leason, with the promise of cruelty in his voice, glared at the Ranger and said, "We can sit under the shade of our sails all day and drink our water—and yours. The breeze you scarcely notice is cool here." With that said he flopped back, using his small pack for a pillow, shut his eyes, and stretched out his long legs his feet pointing at Dern.

Gelt had awoken and listened to the last interchange.

Buddh help my feeble partner. Dullness is a thing to put up with in this life, but Dern revels in it. He has nearly gotten us killed and now he tries a second time. Are there no bounds to his stupidity? "As the sun moved less than one quarter of the distance to its highest point Dern would arrive at the Lord's Keep well past the morning meeting of the Lords and the King. Better though, tied to his horse as he is that he seeks the protection of the King."

As he spoke these last words, Gelt looked intently at Dern, wondering how the man had managed to stay alive all these years.

"Good, good!" Jolar encouraged. "If we continue to water your horse, as we have been doing while you two took your morning nap, Dern would travel to...?" He paused, looking at each Ranger in turn. "...to the King?"

"And," he continued, "supposing our messenger was given, say, a quarter flask of water, or a half flask if he were cooperative, and was yet alive when he reached the King, what message would he deliver?"

Both guards remained mute.

Jolar, his white teeth exposed in the wide smile that usually dominated his round, black face, began speaking as though on stage before a large and grand audience: "Dear King, have mercy on me and my fellow Ranger, worthy Gelt. We were fallen upon by two mighty..." He looked at Leason as though at a loss for words, before continuing. "...Two mighty warrior wizards, the likes of which have never been seen in your kingdom. Even as we ordered them to lay aside their weapons and travel with us for questioning by our trusted? worthy? illustrious? King they cast us into a strange sleep. Under their spell we slept while they questioned us, yet we viewed the scene as though awake.

Though we fought with all our will our sleeping bodies answered their every question.

"They swear on their Mothers' Houses that they travel in peace and bring great gifts, and have knowledge and a message from their Mothers that they wish to share. And though they are masters of all manner of combat, they have no wish to subdue an entire kingdom. They beg you to travel to speak with them, or to send a trusted emissary who will prevent any misunderstanding between themselves and your subjects. They have traveled in the cool season each year for the last three years and yours are the first people they have met. Theirs is a strong desire to present gifts sent by their Mothers and to speak peacefully with the King."

Leason had remained motionless under the shade, his eyes closed, smiling as though spellbound. Now he clapped his large hands as though he had just watched the conclusion of a moving stage presentation. "Bravo! It suits us...a grand message. Well spoken. I would change only the words 'warrior wizards.' Let it be 'wizard warriors.' Call us two mighty wizard warriors. Wizard warriors has a pleasant sound and is an apt description."

Gelt looked at Dern. "Dern, take the half a flask of water and deliver this message to the King."

Leason, his voice laced with sarcasm, questioned, "What are the chances that Dern the Loquacious One may travel elsewhere? Keep in mind, loquacious one that we could put Gelt on a horse, along with your share of the drinking water and keep you here for questioning."

Dern remained silent but Gelt answered, "He will seek the protection of the King, as I shall, when in your goodness you free me. The Lords will not take our lives, for men such as we are valued in the Kingdom of Harnell. Though sometimes death might seem preferable to what our masters might decide."

"Agree to deliver this message to your King," Jolar commanded sharply.

"Agreed," Dern replied in his usual dispirited voice.

With that said, Jolar put the water flask in Dern's tied hands. "A leather of water, a bit more than half full, for you." He flipped up the Ranger's hood to protect his head and face, and pulled the slip knot in the cord that hobbled the horse.

Leason had been watching and thinking: *We have sent the right man riding. To try and work that dull pea brain for information would be like trying to squeeze water from a stone—assuming that there was anything in his skull worth knowing.*

Leason spoke in a matter-of-fact voice from his comfort in the shade: "I will speak slowly for you, oh dull and woebegone messenger: return today and before sunset, or what you will find here will not be a pretty sight."

As Dern turned the horse in the direction he would travel, Jolar, to emphasize the need for haste, slapped the animal sharply across the rump. As he watched the rider disappear over a dune top, he turned and untied Gelt.

"Dear Gelt, join us in the shade. There is much need for us to talk freely."

Chapter 5
Succumon

As though the Lords were magnets for the blinding dust, a mist of ragged blue tendrils inexorably floated towards their eyes. At first contact it clouded their vision, but quickly, all—but for crafty Vorguld—were sightless. They cursed and stumbled about, though there were no screams of pain as there been from Direold earlier that morning. After lofting the dust towards them the Sybil, quick as a cat, had taken three steps back to where she had been sitting.

She laughed above their cursing and railed at them: "Please entertain us by slashing your swords about in manly rage." Then she cackled hideously as her short upper body doubled over with laughter, at times her head nearly touching her knees.

Vorguld roared above the tumult: "Put up your swords." He breathed in an enormous volume of air and thundered again: "Each of you—put up your swords." There was silence in the cavernous room but for the echoing cackle of the Sybil's laughter.

"You ugly witch!" he spat. "Your pack was to be scoured from the Earth. Tortured and killed for the slaughter you brought to the kingdoms of men. King Gemar, she will show us only what suits her evil purpose: slay her or banish her to die in our desert, her face painted red with a hot iron as a warning to any who should meet her."

Yes, Vorguld, the King thought, *that your solution for everything. Maim someone and all will be well. Sur help me. This is the Chief Lord my son will soon inherit?*

The King spoke soothingly. "Silence, Chief Vorguld. Silence, you Lords." He gathered his strength. "My son brings a guest to me and you attempt murder—and fail."

He mused, almost to himself, "Quite comedic to see the men who guard our Kingdom in action." He then continued in full voice. "You Lords and Swikes: Vorguld has commanded you to put up your swords. Obey him and obey me. I command you: Do not touch your weapons!" This last statement was interrupted by his hacking cough.

Vorguld's voice boomed forth in agreement: "On my life, we assent to the King's command."

"On your life, Vorguld! My command will be honored, or as the Edicts allow me this crossbow, one of you will lay skewered and groaning."

Jessyl knew, as did all those assembled, that this was an empty threat that had been invoked many times before. The King handed his crossbow to Jessyl and said aside to him: "Do not do something foolish."

In the meantime, the Sybil had pulled her fallen chair upright and with a push of a foot returned it to where it had been. She sat down with her back to the Lords, facing Jessyl and his father. "Healers, drag the guts here. Here!" she pointed impatiently. "Yes, here at the foot of my chair."

When Direoll was placed as she wished, she casually rested her feet upon his faintly breathing body: one foot on his neck and the other on his chest.

The King groaned inwardly. *Well she lives up to her billing. Eight generations of Kings have not been mistaken: The Sybils are not to be trusted. Had she power she would use us all for furniture.*

He commanded in a growl: "Dark Sybil, the Swike is not your footstool."

Not obeying immediately, she finally pushed against the body and slid her chair back half a pace. "A simple easy prick to the back of my neck and I would be dead, yet Swike Slug shows us a wide swing of sword, a swing so wide and leisurely that a slurring grandfather would have had time for lunch."

She laughed in mockery at the Lords. "You have spoken well, Lord King. Harnell is guarded by a pack of fools.

Great Sur forbid that the Kingdom be attacked by anyone who knows the ways of war."

She rose majestically from her seat.

"I am Sybil Kalla, Sybil of the Protective Light. For two hundred years my sisters and I have watched over your suffering kingdom. It has survived, as was our wish, to be the seed for something better."

As she said this, the bread and cheese arrived, along with the wine. Kalla poured three glasses full and handed two to the tall healer. She breathed in deeply, drawing the smell of wine into her lungs. She closed her eyes, engulfed in the aroma. The healer carried the two glasses and handed the one in his right hand to the King. Transferring the other glass to his right hand, he handed it to the Prince who stood beside his father. The healer returned to the Sybil and held a wooden platter laden with bread and cheese not far from her face. At the smell of it—for her eyes were yet closed— her head snapped upright and her eyes opened wide, disturbed from deep reverie. Looking about as though to see where she was, she waved the healer aside impatiently and raised her glass to the King, and then to Jessyl.

"May your lives be long and full, and may your Kingdom grow and prosper," she said. Then, as she stared with wide, luminous eyes at King Gemar, she drank the top third of the wine from her glass. Her eyelids slowly sagged closed.

"It is so long since I drank wine," she murmured, scarcely to be heard. "There was a wine, ages ago—I drank wagon-loads of it with my two sisters: a purple wine, almost black, though in early morning light it shone dark blue. And sweet it was, not sickly sweet, but faintly sweet, with the pleasant bite of oak cask, and the taste of springtime and rain, and the smell of burdock and heather."

Jessyl, horrified, watched this crazed woman he had brought to his father's court muttering to herself. *What have you done, you foolish boy?* He cursed to himself.

Presently she nodded, awakening from her reverie, and spoke loudly. "You, tall healer, search the house. Look for a wine from Galanth, the grape Merlow. A miracle for the tongue. Glorious stuff. Go. Go, good healer."

"Stay, stay, good healer," the King cried out in mimicry and waited, thinking, until the healer returned to where he stood prior to Kalla's order. *She is truly a Sybil, no doubt. Give her a chance and she would have us all scurrying about. Give her a chance and she would rule us all or, rid the world of men altogether.*

He then said to his Prime Healer Kindeen, "Because this Sybil has thrown about some dust and rested her boots on Swike Direoll, that does not make her a goddess invincible." He looked at Jessyl, delighted with the cleverness of his words.

"I am yet the Lord of this house and this Kingdom," he added.

"Now, Dark Sybil, for I take it you are not of the True Light, why have you undertaken such an arduous and, from my son's report, harrowing journey? What do you want for yourself and your sisters? I take it that you are not alone? You mention 'your sisters.' Certainly you are not here for the good of men. What of ours do you wish to take for yourself?" There was a rumbling of assent from the Company of the Lords.

"I am Sybil Kalla of the True Sybil, and a Sybil and Daughter of the Protective Light. We have nothing to do with whatever Sybil you have mentioned. But yes there is a purpose for my visit: I have a message for the world of men, a message of great import.

She stood, her shoulders thrown back in a dramatic pose, and uttered a single word: "Time." And then in a hushed and devout fashion, she repeated the word: "Time. Time has allowed us only slaughter and want these last thousands of years. Now our great Mother Time affords us a chance...a great opportunity...for progress. We who obey

Time will make a glorious leap forward. But I warn each of you," she intoned as though from a pulpit, "those who drag their feet will live mired in misery."

She drained the last third of her wine; the middle third she had greedily swallowed as the King spoke. She motioned for the healer to refill her glass.

"The time of which I speak is not beginning in years to come. It is today, now and for a huge span of years to come. For as many centuries—yes many, many more than these few thousand years we have lived in hell. Now we have a great opportunity. Mother Time once again will cradle us lovingly in her loving hands."

Vorguld, who, unbeknownst to the rest of the gathering, had been only partially blinded, chortled darkly: "King Gemar, here are the beginnings of a witch's web. I implore you to silence the old woman with an arrow through her lying throat."

Kalla listened to his every word though she gave no indication. *Give me the chance and I will cut your lying throat, Vorguld,* she thought fervently. She continued as though Vorguld had not spoken. "And you, King Gemar, are grievously weakened," she said.

She looked at the King through eyes that she had compressed into slits. "For the King to journey to Yama, the great and fair adjudicator of our lives, and a boy of fifteen summers to be chopped to bits by the local thugs...this would provide a great chance for us to remain chained in hell."

As she talked, she slowly moved to an arm's length from the King.

"Very well, then. Let us have a look at this demon that sucks away your life."

Her eyes snapped open. They shone large and luminous, and brightly as a mirror in noon sun. The King stared blindly into the glare.

Presently, as the brightness dimmed, he briefly glimpsed, reflected in Kalla's shining pupils, a dark cloud peering over his left shoulder. And then an oval shape that was clearly revealed to be an eye appeared within the ugly haze. The eye, at first, was as soft as the eye of a baby at suck, quickly contorted to become as malevolent and greedy as a snake's eye leering at a young duck. Jessyl gagged at the sight of the creature. The King staggered. Jessyl moved to him. Kalla stepped back, her eyes shut to their former tightness. The King collapsed at her feet. Swords flashed; curses were muttered.

"I have harmed him not!" she shrieked. And in a much softer tone: "And who but I, Sybil Kalla of the Protective Light, is able to heal him of this dread Succumon?"

Jessyl, his eyes large with terror, commanded in a loud but shaking voice, "No weapons!" He sank weakly to his knees beside his father, clutching the crossbow to his chest.

Chapter 6
The Windriders Question Gelt

As Gelt shuffled unsteadily into the shade beneath the Windrider's sail, he inwardly scoffed at Jolar's pretence of kindness. He was sure that the Windriders wanted to learn all they could from him. He was also sure that when these two stood against any pair of Lords—if they were lucky enough to stand against only a pair—they would fall. They would be questioned and would quickly make known anything he might tell them. On the other hand, the tall Windrider, and Jolar too, for all his feigned friendliness, would not settle for a talk about the weather.

Gelt had a tightrope to walk.

His entire life had been one long tightrope walk. He had been chosen to join the Company of the Lords at a young age. He was taller, and more muscled and agile, than his fellow youth even though all the children ate the same poor food. One spring day a Ranger rode into the village where Gelt was born, dropped a noose over his neck, and trotted off with him in tow. His mother glanced at him with a flicker of sadness in her eyes though she continued with her work without a sound. The rider wrapped Gelt's leash twice around the pommol of his horse's saddle and rode at a brisk pace. As the boy ran along beside the horse, the Ranger instructed him that with hard work and obedience he might become one of the Company of the Lords.

Gelt remembered the rider had snorted at him: "Just now you are meat. But as the years pass, you may be worth something." The horseman laughed, saying, "The violet color of your eyes gives you away as a close relative of one of our great Lords, Lord Rawlings."

In the years that followed, Gelt had been obedient to his superiors. He had worked hard for them. When it came to his equals and underlings, of whom there were at first only a few, he beat them, took their food, and made them work for him. The Rangers liked him, and Lord Rawlings, whom Gelt resembled in nearly every way—from his large eyes and his thick, dark red hair, to his build and his walk— took an interest in him. The Lords chided Rawlings that the boy was the result of a night of drunkenness that had ended with rape in the village where Gelt was later born. With luck, Gelt too would someday have a son.

Years passed, and Gelt had become a Ranger. Until today he had liked the look of the future, although his sounding of the horn had shaken him. Surely it would be reported by Dern, though the report was not his chief concern. He could stand the punishment of another face scar, and the humiliation, as he had many times throughout his life. What bothered him was that he blew the horn without thinking! But the dire situation currently facing him flashed into his mind, and he knew he must regain control of his thoughts. *So be it...that breach of The Edicts is done. Now I must focus on the mess before me. How will I keep these fellows at bay until help arrives? I have the freedom of a horse, the beginnings of armor, good food, occasionally a woman, all the luxury of being in the Company of the Lords. All is at risk. I must find a way to handle these two.*

As he entered the shade, he was handed a water flask by Jolar for which he bowed his head in the pretense of thanks.

Of one thought I am sure: these two, clever as they are, should have kept Dern and sent me on the horse. If there is a way to cut their throats and drag them through Harnell by their heels, that will bring me great praise.

He sat under the shade as he had been invited by Jolar, and though he was thirsty, he set the flask on his knee.

Jolar laughed: "How brazen our guest is, Leason. He holds the flask as though we return it for him to keep."

Turning back to Gelt, he said, "It is yours. You may keep it. Our water comes from the sails being spread on the sand at night. We are not in need of your water. And your water: has Harnell a stream or a spring, or, praise Chandra, a great lake?"

The questions had started. Gelt had surprised himself when he blew the horn, and now his truthfulness surprised him even more.

"You handled Dern and me quite easily, but you will not have any such luck with the Lords. By nightfall you will be begging Lord Vorguld to be allowed to tell all you know."

Leason spoke: "It is certain that someone in this kingdom is more wily than yourself: otherwise, how would there be a kingdom?"

He was watching Gelt through nearly closed eyes.

"And no doubt for you to subdue us and bring us to your master would merit a great reward. We are not two sluggards who have grown up like dogs on a dirt pile. My counsel is to leave you staked on a dune top to fry like bacon. What could there be for us in a kingdom that dresses its Rangers in rags?"

"What can you give us, Gelt?" Jolar entreated.

"Anything I tell you, you will spill at the feet of the questioners."

"Then I will tell you of ourselves."

Leason sighed in disgust and closed his eyes.

"To the south a great distance, further than anyone could easily travel on foot or horse, is our home. It is a dry land: as dry as this."

He had scooped up a handful of soil and poured it from one hand back to the other, and then returned it to the earth.

"Our fathers, and their fathers, and their fathers' fathers have worked the land ever since Sur's Great Clarity swept over our people ages ago after the centuries of war. Our land is not much different from yours, yet we have made our land rich."

Gelt saw opportunity for a time-consuming argument.

"To make the land useful takes water," he said. "Your fathers must have had water. Give us water and we will have forests to hunt in."

"What would your Lords, or your King, say if we could show you how to get water and store water? Water in your Kingdom must be more valuable than gold. Where does your water come from, but more important, what if we could show you how to find more?"

They waited long, but Gelt would not answer.

"The poor beggar doesn't know what gold is," Leason said in a sleepy voice. He drew from beneath his collar a loop of a gold chain that he wore around his neck and jiggled a gold pendant that held a glistening blue stone. In one quick movement Leason sprung outside the shade of the sail to squat beside Gelt, bumping him with his knees and directing the light sparkling off the sapphire into Gelt's eyes.

"This one I would not part with, but I have gems far more suitable for your King and your Queen."

The quickness of his movement startled Gelt. Leason stared hard into the Ranger's eyes.

"The idea that you will drag us through the streets of Harnell is a foolish idea, Ranger Gelt."

It was evident from the expression on Gelt's face that this statement deeply agitated the man.

"We have weapons you do not see," Leason snapped sharply after staring long into Gelt's eyes. He retired slowly to his seat.

Jolar well knew the game being played. Leason's hypnotic ways would pay off.

Before the Dawn

Sometimes I'd like to throw him to the earth and trounce him—if I could, Jolar thought. *And then he does something far beyond my powers...Ah, Leason, my friend since childhood, the Mothers were wise to train us to travel together.*

Jolar began again to speak, though softly, much of the work done. "If it is reward you seek, surely we all seek reward." His eyes looked warmly into Gelt's eyes. "How would the King reward you for bringing water to the kingdom?"

Gelt blinked. He was coming under the spell of these men.

Jolar pressed on in a breathless, conspiring voice.

"Surely the great Lords will approve of forests for hunting and water for fishing. Surely the gift of water will make you a Lord!"

Chapter 7
Vorguld's Opportunity

When Lord Vorguld saw the Sybil take her first steps towards him with her hands cupped holding the blue dust, he instinctively reached for his sword. Suddenly, without even remembering that his sword had been set outside the Hall, he understood that in the time required to draw and strike out, he would be blind. In a flash far quicker than words he also knew that his men would be drawing their weapons and slashing about in rage. Instantly he thundered: "Put up your swords!"

As he shouted, he squeezed his eyes shut and pressed the heel of each hand against an eye. His eyelids felt a faint prickle of the dust, but he could feel the same sensation more strongly on the backs of his hands as the blue tendrils fought to reach the moisture of his eyes.

"No swords!" he shouted.

Elsewise, he thought, *the hag will have her way and we will hack each other to bits.*

Earlier he had seen the King fall but now his sight, though dimmed and blurry, was returning. He had had time to think. Cautiously, without moving his head, he looked about at his fellows. They stood stupidly, sometimes blinking, sometimes rubbing an eye.

That filthy Sybil has spun her filthy magic, he thought. *So be it. She has forgotten the dagger. A dagger exactly like the one I have thrown these last thirty years. Let her slobber on about time. Let her talk her drivel…*Then, as Vorguld continued to listen to the melodic, sound of her voice, he heard the word 'opportunity,' and it set him pondering. *"Opportunity? After all the years of tedium, here I am with my sight dimmed to blindness. But perhaps I've been given a great opportunity. The Witch babbles on, drunk likely; the King has fallen; the boy holds the crossbow; my comrades are easy prey. No wild sword swings as from my conspirator Swike Direoll. Direoll 'the foolish.' Yes, my conspirator. For all his promise he has twice had a bad go with the hag. No... there will be no wild sword swings from me.*

He chuckled to himself.

Just a light touch of steel to their necks and they will fall silently. And who will remain? Lord Vorguld the Good and with a kingdom properly run, bounty for me and mine. But first the witch: the dagger stuck in her small head, an easy throw, yes, through her right eye. Then take the cross-bow from the beardless boy, but save him and the King for sport. Who will beg to give their pain to the other? The King is weak, not who he once was, though I bet the boy to break long before his father.

Vorguld's pleasing thoughts were disturbed by Kalla intoning, "And who but I can heal him?" She walked solemnly as though in a religious ceremony, her legs stiff, the toe of a shoe touching down before she smacked its heel against the floor stones to the rhythm of her speech.

"Healers, you have been unable to mend your King. Little wonder."

She looked at each of them as though she might spit and then turned to the Prince.

"What did you see, young Jessyl? Have I fabricated a vision to have my way with you and your father, and your beggarly kingdom?"

She chortled and drank another large swallow of wine.

"Little wonder the King wastes away. I will tell you of the leech that sucks away at your father's life. A Succumon. A Succumon from the long ugly war of men. It is not possible to rid your father of this leech during the day—from sun up to sun down. No, it is not possible during the light of day."

She breathed in and then out, dramatically.

"Nor," she slurred after she sipped more wine, "will this monster be destroyed from set of sun to sunrise. It is not possible to destroy this monster at night."

A sardonic laugh rumbled from deep within her belly. "Yet the creature may, as any creature, be destroyed."

Again she drank deeply and then slurred: "but neither during the day nor night. So when, and how? Who can answer these questions?"

She scrutinized each of the assembled, looking at them as though they were pictures in a museum.

"Not in the day; not at night. And who but The Sybil knows how to destroy this monstrosity that sucks away the life of your King?"

As her speech rambled on, she had moved in a semicircle and now stood facing the Lords; the King sprawled at her feet.

"Speak, Prince Jessyl. What did you see?"

Jessyl had stood stunned since his father had fallen. He could not believe he had brought this drunken woman to his father's court. *Great gods in heaven, make this horrid dream stop,* he prayed.

After a silence he replied with a tired, gloom-filled voice: "I saw a dark cloud, thin above my Father's shoulder."

"No more?" she questioned. "Surely you saw more? You must see more. Come. Come. Stand with me. Let us be certain that this is no Sybil's prank to lure away your precious Kingdom."

She laughed and raised her arms out from her sides and upwards, holding her wine glass high above her in her left hand. She lowered her right arm and motioned for the Prince to stand beside her and to take her hand in his.

As Jessyl took the Sybil's hand, Vorguld, consumed with malice and with no room for thought, threw the dagger. Then, after he had pranced nimbly to his fallen Swike, he bent and snatched up the sword that had earlier clattered on the floor stones. With his increasingly long strides propelling his bulk towards Jessyl, he raised the sword high above his head and shouted: "Today you will die!" His blood-freezing scream of hatred echoed through the Hall.

Moments earlier Kalla had seen Vorguld move. She saw the dagger flip in the air, the point headed for her right eye. She turned her face and snapped her head to the left. The dagger sliced her scalp above the right ear. She fell in a heap, her blood quickly staining her white hair and darkening the floor stone on which her head soon came to rest.

Moments before Vorguld's assault, Jessyl had noted as he held the Sybil's hand, that it was hot rather than warm. Presently he turned to look at his father and just then the dagger that had slashed the Sybil's scalp continued its now altered course, ripping across the boy's forehead above his left eye. Blood clouded over the eye beneath the gash and Jessyl felt himself falling backwards. Then he heard Vorguld's scream "Today you will die!" At the sound of the blood-freezing shriek, he felt body meet the hardness of the floorstones but he clutched the crossbow tightly to his chest.

Chapter 8
Blood on the Floorstones

The sun had moved well into the second half of the morning sky. Dern expected that he would find the Hall of Justice vacated by the Lords. He would seek out the King to present his message from the Windriders and then beg protection from the King until the wrath of the Lords abated.

A short time earlier he had left the dunes and now, sparks flying off the horse's iron shoes, Dern charged ahead recklessly, spurring the horse without mercy. A young boy was walking along the roadway using a switch of scrub to swat at flies. Dern yanked with all his strength on the horse's reins, cruelly twisting its head and neck, forcing it to come skidding to a stop. The horse nearly stumbled forward but Dern expertly released the reins in time.

The lad of eight summers looked up at the Ranger and the horse that stood towering over him only an arm's length away.

"Playing in my roadway, boy?" Dern thundered his voice from the grave. "Damn you if you have harmed my horse!"

Through threats of torture, he cowed the boy to untie the cord that tied his feet beneath the horse's belly. Then he expertly slipped off the horse and thrust his tied hands at the boy.

"Run from me, and I'll drink your blood. Untie my hands," he growled.

The boy, nose dripping and eyes watering, fumbled with the knot. The Ranger hissed, "Get your teeth on it, boy."

The King would be at his table, the Lords at theirs, he thought. The knot loosened. His hands now free, he grabbed the boy and threw him face first into the gravel. "Stay out of the road, you stupid slud," he roared as he leaped on his horse and charged off in a cloud of dust and a clatter of stones.

Dern's mind raged. *Bad enough to be stripped of my armor and weapons and groveling before the King. At least I will not be tied to a horse. I have not clawed my way up a long bloody climb to be a tale for the sluds to laugh at for generations to come.*

As Dern approached the King's fortress, he saw the Lord's horses tethered each to their respective hitch posts. The wide double door to the Hall of Justice was closed. *The meeting has lasted this long into the morning!* he cursed to himself. He tied the horse securely. The sleeping boys awakening to see the disheveled sweating Ranger cautiously tip toe up the steps and look through the gap between the thick wood doors.

He saw that the King lay sprawled on the floor, a silent bundle of rags lying beside him. The boy Prince sat, bleeding and stunned, with the crossbow supported on his knee, tilted upward, pointing at Lord Vorguld. Vorguld, a sword in hand, had leaped across the boundary of the Lord's Domain and charged rapidly into the prohibited King's Domain. Dern saw the boy's quavering finger touch the crossbow trigger. He watched, spellbound, as the finger squeezed. The bowstring sounded a sharp snap as it fired the bolt. In the same instant, Vorguld bellowed a shriek of pain and collapsed onto the floor stones, his knees tucked to his chest. He skidded to a stop, an arrow, red with blood, sticking from his back below his belt and a bit to the right of his spine.

Vorguld lost hold of his sword. It rattled across the floor towards the Prince, who, as he reached for another arrow, stopped the slithering weapon with his foot. The fallen Lord laid only a body's length away from the boy.

For Jessyl, all movement had slowed to a near stand-still. Blood covered his right eye and slowly oozed down his cheek as though it had thickened to glue, and then disappeared ever so slowly beneath his shirt collar. He watched, transfixed, as Vorguld's chest heaved as the man painfully sucked in air between gritted teeth.

A flood of calm swept through Jessyl. Anything that moved appeared to be nearly frozen in time.

"Healers," he croaked his throat dry.

The healers jerked awake as if they had been suddenly thawed out of a paralyzing fear. Jessyl's sensation of the slowness ended abruptly, yet he felt as if his blood carrying an elixir to every cell in his body. He notched another arrow to the bowstring and with calm hands readied the crossbow.

Kindeen moved to the King, another healer approached Jessyl, and the third cautiously moved towards Vorguld. Jessyl shook his head at the one who approached Vorguld and pointed to the Sibyl. To the healer who held a cloth to his wound and wiped the blood from his eye, he ordered: "Leave me a clear view." Resting the bow on his knee, he sighted down the arrow at the Chief Lord's slowly heaving chest. He allowed his finger to lightly caress the crossbow's trigger.

Dern, completely stunned by the scene before him, flung open the doors. "Hold, hold, Prince Jessyl!" That the swaying, wounded boy could hit him with an arrow from such a distance was unlikely. And though Dern's allegiance was to Rawlings, he would be able to report that he had tried to save the Chief Lord.

"What has happened here?" Dern shouted, though to no one in particular.

"I'll ask the questions!" Jessyl snapped. "Be silent unless I ask you to speak."

Vorguld painfully pushed himself to a half-sitting position.

"Dern of Rawlings," he gasped,"...to me. Pull this arrow."

"Stay," the boy cawed, waving the point of the crossbow's arrow at Dern and then pointing it back at Vorguld. *Stay, he thought, or there will be two arrows to pull.*

Vorguld sagged to the floor stones with a gasp of pain. *Downed by a boy with a down covered chin,* Vorguld chided himself in his near delirium. *I will find a way to live. Oh yes, I will live, and I will tear him limb from limb. And the witch...*

He abruptly passed out.

"Why are you here and not at your duties?" Jessyl spat the words at Dern. "Without your sword, I see," he added derisively.

"I have ridden in haste from our southern border. Just on our side of the Great Watchers, two wizards hold Gelt of Rawlings. They demand safe passage to speak with the King.

The King was partly conscious and now moving. The healer attending Sybil Kalla had parted her hair on either side of the wound and held a cloth tight to her head. The healer at Jessyl's side pressed a bloodied cloth to Jessyl's forehead with one hand. The thumb and forefinger of that same hand held a curved needle. With his free hand he managed to poke the thread through the eye of the needle after missing at two attempts.

Again time began to slow for Jessyl. Out of the corner of his eye he watched the thread floating at the speed of a drifting cloud as it passed through the eye of the needle. An overwhelming desire to send Vorguld to Hell completely filled his mind.

Any excuse, give me any excuse. As though I wish to banter with Lord Ghoul, day in and day out for tedious year after tedious year to come. Give me an excuse. Here, reach for the sword, Vorguld.

Jessyl kicked the fallen sword towards the Lord. It slid and stopped the handle within Vorguld's reach. Jessyl laughed, hoping Vorguld could hear him. He sat watching the Lord: *If not Vorguld, then I trade wit with some other goblin. Is that it how it will be for me...and for all the Kings of all the days to come?*

"Stay to the side, healer," Jessyl hissed. "Should our Chief Lord spring to life..."

And now for my first stitches, he thought.

He spat blood that had dripped into his mouth and then snarled to Vorguld, "Move again and I will send you to Yama, this time no mistake."

He spat again.

"Water, healers. Water for us all," he barked. "Do I need to tell you your trade?"

He looked towards his father.

"Father, you have heard that there are two wizards at our southern border holding the Ranger Gelt of Rawlings?"

He waited as the King stirred.

"Dern of Rawlings, we note, minus his weapons..."

To the Ranger, the Prince shouted, "Your weapons and armor are taken? Come closer...to the boundary."

Jessyl pointed the crossbow at him.

"Father, the Ranger bears a message from wizards," he scoffed as he said the words.

The healer knelt patiently beside the Prince, holding the threaded needle so that Jessyl would see that he was ready to begin. The boy continued to look towards his father. Without looking at the healer he nodded permission to begin stitching the wound.

The King, though faint, had raised his head slightly off the floor stones and had been surveying the scene.

"Blood and mayhem!" he said, his voice genuinely filled with awe. "Our Kingdom has not seen such a bloodletting for many generations. Great Sur protect us—listening to the advice of women! Observe, young Prince, one day to be king, where your folly has led. The advice of a Sybil is for a weakling, not for a king."

After all my instructions, and those of his grandfather... what has he done to me? He looked with complete disgust at his son and then turned his gaze to the fallen Sybil.

"And our blue friend slashed quite handily above the ear."

And Vorguld, has he lost his mind? To contravene the Edicts—to attempt murder. The hag, yes, that is understandable, but my son and I—it is unthinkable!

He turned towards Vorguld. "And our Chief Lord with a pin in him. Dead or just dying?"

Vorguld raised his hand, his elbow resting on the floor, and waved feebly.

The King again turned his attention to the Sybil.

"Our blue friend tells us that time..." After he had venomously spoken the word 'time,' he again blew the same word, hatred hard in his voice, towards the Sybil. "'Time', you say, 'presents us with a great opportunity'—if I have heard you correctly."

He waited, but Kalla did not respond.

He chuckled, with a large measure of cruelty in his laugh, and then he turned to Dern.

"Tell us precisely, and with haste—for each moment is dear—what it is you have been instructed to say."

To have to listen to Dern, he thought with nervous humor. *Could there be a worse torture?*

"And you, my son," he interrupted, as Dern took a breath to begin to speak. "How goes the small price for your folly?"

As Jessyl turned to look at his father, the healer ceased pulling the thread through the flesh of the boy's forehead.

The King asked, "How many in, Healer, and how many to go?"

"Two in, my Lord, and four or possibly five to go."

"Help me," the King said. "Help me move to my son. He looks as though he will faint. I'll man the bow."

With help he shuffled to his son and began to sum up the situation.

"Our Prince covered in blood, wizards at the southern border, and a meddling Sybil, drunk and ridiculous, telling us that Father—pardon me—*Mother* Time presents us with an opportunity. And that I am lost to a leech that sucks my life away. Let us have your story, Dern of Rawlings. Is it better than the one I have just related, or are you unable to speak since these wizards have tied your tongue?"

The King breathed heavily, glared at Dern, and then slumped to the floor beside his son. He did not take up the bow.

"Hold, hold," the King said with his palm facing outward and silencing the Ranger, who had again taken a deep breath in readiness to speak.

"The Sybil stirs. Does the goddess invincible return to life?" he said to her. "Some wine to clear your head, great Sybil? Or have you bargained with Yama to spare your life by renouncing drink? Look around and make sense of what has happened. Is this part of the 'great opportunity' that your Mother Time grants us? Listen to the guard who has been stripped of his armor and weapons by wizards who seek an audience."

"Dern, speak!" he shouted. "Will you keep us all day awaiting your news?" He turned away from Dern and began haranguing his healers. "Healers! Water for all, and tea, and something fit for a man to eat. Do I need to tell you your trade? Dern, will you not speak, or is your tongue tied by the sight of a few daubs of blood?"

At last Dern began to speak, tentatively at first, resigned to the fact that he would be often interrupted.

"Keep speaking!" the King commanded. "We follow your discourse quite well."

King Gemar was listening intently to every word that Dern spoke, thought he gave no sign of this, nor any encouragement.

To his son he said: "So, wise Son. If your father was not here and you were king, what would you do with this tangled mess?"

The healer pulled the last stitch through Jessyl's skin and neatly tied it off with as gentle a tug as possible. Jessyl winced, his eyes stinging and full of tears.

"Lucky to be alive," the King rasped with disgust in his voice.

"Speak up, Dern, we follow you."

To his son he said: "Do you hear what he says? Do you follow the gist of it? Were I not here, how would you handle this debacle? You are to be king...though a long way from ready...," he coughed, "but maybe not so long from kingship. I'll tell you what we have on our plate this morning on the chance that being stunned by a scratch you have yet to comprehend the situation. There are two men at our southern border playing wizard. Dern is without armor and sword, and Gelt is their captive. Therefore...?" He waited a few seconds.

The healer was wiping congealed blood from Jessyl's wound and face and neck.

"Stay back," Jessyl growled as he pushed the man from him.

"Ergo?" the King persisted, and then waited. "Therefore, these wizards are somewhat wily, my son. When I am no longer of this earth will you go to your mother to figure out such things? Or better yet, call in a Sybil?"

The healer dropped the cloth he had used to clean Jessyl's wound. Jessyl snatched it up and briefly patted the stitches, and then pressed it hard into one eye and then the other.

What have I done? And I am nearly in tears!

"And these Lords?" the King continued. "What would your mother have you do with them? Dern, we hear you: 'These wizard warriors come in peace and wish safe passage to speak with us.'"

Again, he focused on his son.

"Now what would you do with these blind Lords, my wily Son?"

He stared wide-eyed, grinning at his son, mocking him.

"Dern, unclasp the sword belts of these worthy Lords. You Lords, Dern will remove your sword belts. Dern, will you do this, or just stand about as if stricken?" He spoke with a space between each word as though frustrated and yelling at a child. "Take the swords one at a time and hang them on the saddle of that Lord's horse. You know who rides which horse?"

Dern nodded hesitantly: "Yes, Sire."

"You are good for something, then. You will lead this company of the blind to their Keep? Or will you continue to act like an old woman and, in a daze, lead the Lords to their death among the dunes?"

As his father berated Dern, Jessyl thought, *I must find a way to make this right. What a completely useless idiot I have been...to look to a Sybil for help!*

"I will lead them safely to our Keep, My Lord," the Ranger replied.

Dern unclasped the sword belt of the Swike nearest him and walked out of the building to hang it on the horse of its owner.

"Hurry, Dern. Run!" the King shouted.

Though it was a great strain for him, the king continued loudly for all to hear: "Healers, treat Vorguld as though he were myself. If Yama presently requires this great Lord's presence, then let that be Yama's doing. My Son, you and I shall meet these wizards.

"Dern, carry the swords two at a time. Are you a ranger or a slud?

"And you, Sybil Kalla of whatever light you profess to be—of the bloody light perhaps—you will not be here when we return from dealing with these wizards. And you will never return again." King Gemar's face was as pale and gaunt as death.

The Prince stood.

"Father, please remain and guard the Keep. Though I am slowed for the moment, allow me to meet these intruders at our southern border. As to the Sybil, I promised her sisters the safe return of her. Let her remain until I may fulfill my vow, as I must. She has been a fool, but she has shown us a foe that will not be slain with arrow or dagger. In this regard she may be of use to us."

The King replied loudly for all to hear.

"You have missed my instructions yet again," he said, his voice increasingly angry. "The Sybil is of no use to us. Would that your understanding of the ways of women were as well formed as your speech."

Jessyl's shoulders slumped, and he hung his head in shame.

In an attempt to rise, the King turned away from his son and then painstakingly collapsed into a squat and sat. He turned and looked up at his son.

"Jessyl," he groaned, "the women bade you bring a Sybil, to me, King Gemar of Harnell: would you not tell your father of their counsel? Are you not my son?"

The King looked long at the boy, who squirmed beneath his sad and wrathful gaze.

"Foolish, foolish boy. That scratch on your forehead is but a small glimpse of the tragedy Sybils have brought to the world of men. As you awaken on all the mornings of your life, pass your fingers over your wound and let it remind you of all I have taught you of Sybils—and too, let it remind you of the blood spilled when women meddle in the affairs of men."

The King reached out for his healer. Jessyl wrapped his hand around his father's forearm: his father reluctantly allowed his son to pull him to his feet.

King Gemar spoke as though talking to the least of the Rangers: "Travel with Ennar. Take Vorguld's and Direoll's swords and horses. And the dagger. I will require your presence at tomorrow's meeting with the Lords."

He grew silent again, looking darkly at his son for a long time and then continued quietly, but in a voice as hard as flint, "Regarding the Sybil: I grant what you have asked. We may, through extreme guile, squeeze some helpful tidbit from her frozen heart."

"Father...," Jessyl began.

"Go. Quickly! Ahead of Dern and the blinded."

He looked hard at his son. "You will find, as time passes, that a king has few he may trust. He prays that his son will be among the trusted."

The King extended his arm to the healer who had stitched Jessyl's wound, and turning abruptly, left his son standing alone. The main healer hurried to aid the King. Though the King attempted to walk from the room he was nearly carried out. The kit with the curved needle was passed to the healer attending Sybil Kalla.

Jessyl stood beside Kalla. He looked down at her and then stared questioningly at the healer. "She will live, my Lord. Though her head will throb doubly from wine and wound."

Jessyl replied, "After I leave, and all but Vorguld and his Swike have left, bolt and bar the doors."

The healer nodded a bow of assent and returned to his work.

Dern had finished hanging the remaining swords on the horses' saddles. Jessyl crossed over the King's and the Lords' boundary lines.

"Move this riffraff far from me!" he shouted at Dern, pointing at the remaining Lords and Swikes.

He looked hard into the Ranger's dark eyes and pointed to Vorguld's crumpled form.

"Your Chief Lord likely dies a painful death?"

He continued to look fiercely into the Ranger's eyes.

"I will not threaten to use the bow as my father has!" he shouted. Finding himself completely enraged, he struggled to regain control.

Shocked at the intensity of his anger, he stalked quickly out of the Hall of Justice.

Chapter 9
Talk at the Smithy

The sun was well past its zenith: a third of the day remained. As his father wished Jessyl rode towards the home and smithy of Ennar's family. That his father, in the midst of chaos, was able to think of Ennar for his traveling companion was not a surprise to Jessyl. His father had many remarkable abilities: this not the greatest of them.

I have failed him again, Jessyl thought. *This time most miserably of all. I brought a fool to him. A fool who quickly drank herself to drunkenness and blathered on about Time…though she handled the Swike quite well. Twice. And at least for now, the Lords are blinded.*

Jessyl continued to chastise himself: *Easy to rail against the Sybil. I brought her. On my mother's insistence, without the counsel of my father. Not the first time this sort of thing has happened. How could a father trust such a son as you?*

An unusual silence pervaded the Kingdom. Sharecroppers, their children toiling beside them, weeded vibrant patches of green, surrounded by the dun, dry landscape. Older women, each with a leather water container balanced on a hip or a shoulder, walked as a group towards the Keep of the Lords. It would be foolhardy for a lone woman to seek water. And even more foolhardy for a young girl to be a part of the group.

The horse Jessyl rode, though huge, moved agreeably in the direction where prodded. Jessyl looked about. Stone houses with slate roofs leaned drunkenly against one against another. But for the gardens of the croppers, the landscape was dominated by dust and rock and an occasional bent and spare tree and the never-ending scrub.

Yes, Jessyl thought, *Ennar will be welcome. That I would have undertaken this journey alone is just another example of my stupidity.*

Ennar and Jessyl had been born at the same time, in the same building, and on the same table, though of different mothers. Ennar was the son of Klayton, the chief blacksmith of Harnell, and Rebecca his boisterous and mischievous wife. Jessyl's mother had learned that she and Rebecca were due to birth their babies at about the same time, and had proposed that they deliver the children in the same room and, if possible, at the same moment. It was Rebecca who suggested that they use the same birthing table.

The two women joked, "We will see what the healers' astrology tells them of these births."

All this was reported to Jessyl years later by his grandmother. Jessyl had many warm memories of his mother's outrageous and contrary ways.

And he had many warm memories of Ennar. They had grown up together and played as though brothers.

Now Jessyl bounced along on the horse at a faster pace than a walk, though not yet a trot. Earlier at the South Gate of his Father's Keep, he had hung Vorguld's and Direoll's sword belts and the swords in their scabbards, on Direoll's horse. Having scared off the attendant boys with the dagger, he had slipped the knife between Vorguld's horse's saddle and blanket. Then, as he loosened Direoll's horse from the hitch posts, the thought occurred to him that to take Dern's horse would slow the Lord's trip back to their Keep. With both sets of reins in one hand and the reins of Vorguld's horse in the other, he had climbed upward and into the saddle. When seated on the horse his anger seized him again, and with no thought for his safety he spurred the horse forward, kicking and cursing and fell into an uncontrollable rage. His eyes filled with tears: he swore and shrieked, while flailing at the horses and leaving behind a clamor for Dern and the Lords to set straight.

Now he slowed the three horses to a stop at the gate of the blacksmith's smithy and home.

Dern, without his horse will slow them all down, he thought grimly, a flicker of a satisfied smile crossing his lips.

"Ennar!" he called. "Uncle Klayton."

They had heard the sound of horses' hooves and both quickly appeared in the doorway. Klayton, wide in the shoulders but narrow across the forehead, stood filling the doorway. Ennar, a tall, lean, well muscled young man, looked out over his father's shoulder. An instant after the door had opened the blacksmith's wife and daughter and several young children squeezed into the doorframe to stare at the small rider on the towering horse. The family was much relieved that the visitor was not one of the Company of the Lords

"I am commanded to fetch two wizards who dare to cross our southern border. My father commands that Ennar be my companion for this task."

Rebecca, stout but lithe, pushed herself between and past her husband and son.

"What folly is this? Two boys riding to fetch who knows what on horses huge and unruly. My son will not be one of them. And what do I see bristling underneath your hood, Prince Jessyl? Stitches! Have you not had enough blood for one day? Are you again drinking your father's wine?"

"All will be told quite presently, dear Aunt—and for generations to come. Vorguld lies on the floor of the Hall of Justice with an arrow deep in his belly. When I left he was alive, but he may soon travel to his reward. Direoll lies beside him, a sickly blue color, looking as cold as winter snow. I must be at the southern border before sunset if I am to speak with the two men who hold Gelt of Rawlings. Lend me your son, small and frail though he is."

Jessyl tried to maintain a disparaging glare at Ennar, but he smiled at having made a joke to which his friend did not have opportunity to reply.

The blacksmith spoke: "Becky! Water, food, blankets, quickly. You know that our son will travel with Prince Jessyl. Quickly Becky...," his voice trailed off to nothing and he looked at her, ashamed of his curt words. His eyes begged for her to do as he had asked.

"Do you suppose, Uncle Klayton, that you could find a use for the horses' armor? I could say that I left it by the pathside."

Klayton eyed the armor his green eyes flickering like a snake's. Presently he replied to the Prince in a whisper, "Jessyl, it would give me great pleasure to melt that armor to iron and sell it back to the Lords." A large sigh escaped from his huge chest as he ran his finger and thumb up and down each side of this throat.

"Yes, I would love nothing better, but the Lords would go on a rampage for a scrap of missing metal. To pinch a bit—that would be a treat. I will ponder the idea: there may be a way."

"Then guard over it until I return. The Lords will pass here shortly, but they will take no notice of the armor. All except Dern who leads them, have lost their sight for a time. And Dern's horse has followed me here. Might he wander to the shade of the north side of your smithy if he found some water waiting?"

"Yes, he might," the blacksmith replied, his thoughts of how to pinch some of the Lords' metal interrupted but not far from his thoughts.

Klayton pointed at one of his young sons and directed him to place the water where the Prince had suggested.

"What a day! What a day! Praise Mangala the Fierce," the blacksmith said looking about warily as though someone of the Lord's Keep might hear him.

"I will watch over this armor on your command, Prince Jessyl. Please stay and eat and rest with us. You have time for that and then time in plenty to be at the southern border before Great Sur tucks into bed for another night."

"Thank you, Uncle. The Lords come this way. I do not wish to see them again today."

"Nor they you," the blacksmith chuckled.

As they talked, Klayton adjusted the horses' stirrups to suit the legs of the boys. Ennar stripped the armor and piled it neatly, almost reverently in front of the gate.

The blacksmith shouted out: "Neighbors, I am commanded by Prince Jessyl to watch over this armor. As the Edicts allow me to command on behalf of our King: I charge you in the name of our Lord King Gemar to watch over this armor with me."

At the words 'I charge,' the neighbors began to scurry for the safety of their hovels. They had no interest in being caught up in an affair involving the Lords.

Rebecca came from the house with two rolled blankets. Ennar's sister handed the blankets and food to Ennar who had found his way into the saddle of Direoll's horse.

The blacksmith directed two of his sons to fetch and partly fill the large leather waterbag, and to sparingly allow the horses a few gulps each. Rebecca stared in dismay at her husband; appalled at this use of her water bag.

"If you must gallop the horses, then walk them before you come to a stop," he said to Jessyl and Ennar. "Especially at night, after the cold descends. They will need water, but sparingly, or you will be the ones walking. Only the Lords have food for them."

From the direction Jessyl had only recently arrived, muffled curses and the faint clatter of hooves sounded from within a large cloud of dust. Upon closer scrutiny, those gathered at the smithy saw a lone figure walking and holding the reins of the first horse in a long procession.

Rebecca began sobbing.

"Foolish, foolish boys, return to see your mothers again!" she wailed.

Klayton's face was stern as he twisted a loop in the strap of the water bag and fastened it around the pommel of Jessyl's horse's saddle. He looked long at Jessyl and then deeply into his son's eyes to add agreement to his wife's words.

Jessyl gently nudged his horse with his heels and Ennar, watching closely Jessyl's every movement, did likewise. The horses ambled obligingly in the direction Jessyl had hoped, lighter without their armor and thankful for the water. When the riders passed the last of the buildings and were surrounded by the scrublands and the dunes, Jessyl spurred his horse to a trot. The boys rode faster than they had ever moved. The waterbag, though secure, slopped precious water. A slight pull on the reins slowed Jessyl's horse to a walk. Ennar, following his friend's lead, tugged gently on his horse's reins.

"The horses are well trained!" he shouted with exuberance.

He looked long at his companion and friend.

"You look as though you have fought off death."

Jessyl did not reply.

"And Vorguld with an arrow in him?"

Jessyl's eyes flashed about, dark and glittering. His wound was swollen and discolored, and the eye below it was partly puffed shut. His cheek was swollen and bruised where early that morning Swike Direoll had pressed the visor of his headgear cruelly into it. A black half circle under each eye and skin as pale and yellowed as an old altar cloth completed the picture. Ennar reached out to touch Jessyl's shoulder, but Jessyl shrunk away from this gesture of comfort.

"I wonder more of our health after we meet the two who hold Gelt at our southern border. Our hope is in their message. They come in peace with no wish to war. The messenger told us that they have knowledge and gifts they wish to share. They wish to learn from us and to return with knowledge to their homeland. More accurately, to their Mothers' Houses."

"Strange. Wizards?" Ennar questioned.

"Our hope is that they come in peace, whatever sort they may be. I am tired. I have no strength. They have overcome two of the Rangers, and I doubt that I am able to lift that sword from its sheath."

Ennar passed Vorguld's sword in its scabbard along with the sword belt to Jessyl. Jessyl wrapped the belt twice around his waist. He pulled the sword a handswidth from the scabbard and with a sigh, let it fall back into place.

The horses had taken them past the last of the tumbled down buildings of Harnell and into the scrublands.

"I did not sleep last night, Ennar. At my mother's request I journeyed to the hills of the West to escort a healer to my father. That journey is a story I would like to tell. First, let us stop and rest and plan what to say, and what not to say, to these Wizards. Whatever happens, we must be at the southern border by sunset if we are to meet with these two—at least so they tell us through Ranger Dern. I will feel better meeting them at sunset with Great Sur warming our backs and blazing in their faces, troubling their sight. For now, let us make a fire and tea, and eat some of what your mother has packed. We will talk as we travel, but not of what has happened in my Father's Keep. That is too painful to speak of; let us talk instead of what may happen when we meet the wizards."

Jessyl spoke with less and less energy in his voice, as though he were a child's toy that was winding down.

"And of my trip to fetch the Sybil. That tale puzzles me most of all."

His words were barely a whisper.

"I must rest. I feel us if my life is being sucked out of me."

Chapter 10
Two Quivering Specks

With a slight pressure from Ennar's left knee his horse moved obediently off the road. Jessyl's horse followed. Ennar slid off his horse using the friction of his belly against the saddle to slow the drop to the earth, and then tied the horse's reins to a scrub. He tied the reins of Jessyl's horse and helped Jessyl, who was tentatively beginning a dismount, to the earth.

"You must rest."

Jessyl nodded in agreement as he unfastening the sword belt and laid the weapon aside. He tossed a rolled blanket against a scrub and stretched himself out, toes pointing to the sun, as though to soak up as much heat as possible. Ennar kindled a small fire into which he placed an egg-shaped stone his mother had packed. He rested while the stone heated, and he watched his friend, who lay with his eyes closed, breathing slowly and deeply through his nose, the palm of his hand covering the wound above his eye.

After a time Ennar fished the stone from the fire and placed it in a water filled leather cup, along with shreds of leaf. The water quickly boiled. He poured one third of the tea into a cup for himself and brought the first cup to Jessyl. Presently Jessyl opened his eyes.

"Tea", he said as though he had forgotten and was surprised. "Many thanks, Ennar."

Ennar passed him a packet of dried meat that his mother or sister had hammered soft and mixed with berries.

"Chandra's blessings to your mother."

Each boy ate and drank slowly, watching the gap between the sun and the earth diminish.

In the late afternoon light, a large russet and white eagle floated silently and unconcerned towards the west. The boys stared in awe.

"An omen of the best sort, Jessyl."

They watched as the bird hung motionless in the afternoon sunlight, slowly becoming smaller against the vast expanse of horizon.

"I need a great omen, Ennar. Today I have been a fool. The worst of fools."

He had pushed the sandy earth into a pile with his feet.

"My mother and grandmother bade me fetch a Sybil to my father. 'The Sybil will heal your father,' they said. I dashed off to do their bidding, as excited as a youth of six summers. They used me as a Yanna player uses a chip, Ennar."

He stared without speaking in the direction of the eagle with an intensity of concentration that made it appear as though he hoped to forget all else.

"Did I ask my father's counsel? Not a bit of it. I set off on my adventure sure that this would be his cure—and with what results? I am cut: my father tells me that the scar will remind me always to be wary of the interference of women. The Sybil's blood as well as mine stains the floor of the Hall of Justice."

He released a large breath that became a rasp of anguish.

"You see why I cringe to speak of this morning, Ennar. How stupid I have been. And to see the pain in Father's face—he had hoped that he could trust his son, Ennar. I am saddened beyond words to express it."

The two sat silent, the eagle no longer to be seen.

Ennar spoke cautiously, aware, to a small degree, of his friend's torment. "Had you told your father of the Sybil, then what? You know that answer as well as I. And had the Sybil healed him, your story would have a happy ending. And Vorguld stuck with an arrow. That is happy news."

"He charged, his sword raised, shrieking for blood. I shot him, Ennar. I aimed for his heart, but in my childish panic I hit him low. And when he dies, today, or after a long life, then another of the Lords will take his place. They will find a way to make me pay. I am marked. And after all this blood, my father looks far worse: drained and deathly beyond what he has been. He said to me, 'Are you your father's son?' It cut my heart to hear it, Ennar."

Ennar stared hard at his friend. Jessyl looked intensely for some minutes to the horizon where the eagle had been.

"As to the wizards," Jessyl mused quietly, almost to himself. "What to say and what not to say?" He turned and spoke to his friend: "What do we say to them, Ennar?"

Jessyl continued to speak as Ennar kicked the sandy soil onto the fire. "One thing is certain of these two men traveling alone in the wastelands: they must come in peace. How could two expect to pillage or war against us?"

Jessyl stretched and then placed his hand gingerly on his forehead over his wound. He rubbed a finger across the puffiness beneath each eye and turned to walk to the horses. The boys mounted and rode towards the southern border.

"The wizards...they could be spies or scouts. Though the Sybil chided me earlier today whon she said, 'Why would anyone be interested in this worthless Kingdom?' When we meet this pair, the less we say the better. That the Chief Lord lies suffering on the floor stones of the Hall of Justice; that the King is near death—yes, Ennar, unless I find help for him, he will soon be naught but bones and die—that the Lords and Swikes are blinded: all this we must keep to ourselves.

Though our wizards come in peace—would my father have sent us had he believed otherwise?—that could change quickly, no doubt. Who are we, you and I? Yes, who are we is yet another question to be answered."

Ennar added: "And why we are sent and not some powerful Lord with a following of well- armed Rangers?"

"We have many questions of them but few answers for them," Jessyl chuckled bitterly. "You are correct, Ennar. Why send two boys on horses too big for them, with swords they can barely lift?"

"Speak for yourself!" Ennar said laughing as he snatched his sword from its scabbard and swung it about his head in wide circles. "Being a blacksmith's son has some advantages," he whooped. And don't forget that one of the boys has seven stitches holding his head together. And he looks as if the Sybil had her way with him for most of last night."

Now both were laughing.

Ennar continued to wildly circle the sword above his head. "Come fell wizards and taste our steel!" he yelled out into the emptiness.

Jessyl's eyes ran with tears. "Stop, stop. I hurt from laughter. Enough. Quiet, my good friend," he pleaded as he laughed. "The tale of last night's journey is large in my mind."

Ennar brandished his sword about his head one more turn but then lowered it to his side though his eyes still gleamed wide and large.

"Spare me from more laughter; my wound aches," Jessyl pleaded. "Spare me, and I'll tell you the tale of last night."

"'A Night of Frolic,' by Jessyl Hadda Asybil," Ennar purred in a throaty voice.

Gelt had told the Windriders all he knew of the King-dom of Harnell. The source of water, the crops, animals, boundaries, defense, weather, the population and system of rule. If the Windriders fell, he would fall.

The sun was low in the sky: a quarter of the day remained at most.

Leason, who had been scanning the horizon, raised an arm and pointed towards two specks quivering and black in the late afternoon light as they moved across the crest of a distant rise. After a time the specks disappeared and then reappeared on a nearer crest.

"There, Gelt," he pointed. "We have two visitors."

Then to Jolar he said, "Strange only two."

Gelt strained his eyes. Not Vorguld and Direoll, he knew, for they would come with many.

The Windriders scanned the horizon, looking everywhere but the direction of the two riders.

"Gelt, would they send only two if they came to take us by force?"

Gelt was silent to Jolar's question.

Jolar continued laughingly: "Gelt, after what you have told us, you had best cast your lot with us."

Leason interrupted: "These are small men riding large horses."

Gelt stared at the riders. "Small men do not ride horses in Harnell."

The Windriders scanned the remainder of the horizon.

"And, so far, no one following them," Leason added. "They will be a while arriving. Before they do, I'll retire and watch you work your charm, Jolar."

Leason then motioned to Jolar to walk with him away from the Ranger.

"If what he tells us of this kingdom is true, it is as I first thought: there is naught here for us."

"Certainly no amount of water worth sending out settlers," Jolar replied.

"Whoever these riders turn out to be, let us take no risks. To leave these two riders and the Ranger for vulture food sounds far better than you and I in trouble. Agreed?"

"Agreed. We will take no risks," Jolar answered.

"They will be a while arriving. Before they do, I'll check the snares and see if we will have supper. I will return and watch them as you speak. If they try something foul, the desert will have their flesh and Yama can have their souls."

Chapter 11
The Evening Meal

The King rested, elbows on the table, chin on the palms of his hands, eyes closed, face ashen.

He whispered to no one in a voice he himself could scarcely hear: "There is little left."

His wife and her mother would dine with him as was usual, though tonight the Sybil would join them. A smile flickered across his pained face as he remembered Jessyl saying: 'She may be of some use yet.' The thought of his son's counsel filled the King with fleeting warmth.

Wise counsel, my dear son, but don't let anyone hear you say it.

Queen Elearim and her mother entered with the Sybil largely hidden behind them. The Queen took her seat across from the King; her mother took a seat to the right side of King Gemar. He motioned for the Sybil to sit at his left though it was the only unoccupied chair.

The Prime Healer, Kindeen, entered the dining chamber carrying a bottle sparkling deep purple and moist, and set it between the King and Sybil Kalla. The King offered the wine to his wife, who held out her glass, and then to the Queen mother who declined, and then to Kalla. Kalla's eyes widened slightly, but she too raised her hand in a gesture of decline.

"Very good," the King rasped.

"My son has brought you to me, and it is his counsel to keep you here until he may fulfill his pledge to return you to your sisters. Welcome to our table."

The four sat in silence. Finally Kalla spoke.

"Though my sisters chose me for this journey, they cautioned me many times. Avoid your weakness, they said repeatedly. Avoid it with all of your strength. My foolishness has been costly, King Gemar. In my long life I have seldom asked forgiveness: please forgive my weakness."

"Foolishness is a more apt description. The results—my son nearly slain—might have been far worse. I too might lie slain beside him."

He paused to allow the full meaning of his words to become clear.

"Nonetheless," he said, lifting his glass as if in a toast, "the past, it is certain, will not change from what it has been. The moment we once held so dearly is no longer ours except in memory. This moment, now—all we ever really have—is soon gone, a memory to haunt us or to fill us full with life and pride."

The Queen raised her glass and bowed to her husband. All drank as though a toast had been made: the Queen Mother and Kalla drank water.

Queen Elearim spoke into the silence. "And I have been remiss to invite a guest without seeking your counsel, King Gemar."

It was an exceedingly unusual event to hear the Queen apologize. Certainly in a large gathering she would be polite and if necessary, even demur. Afterwards, when she and her husband retired, more often than not, she would sift through what had been said to determine if they had missed some nuance of meaning spoken by one of the Barons. True, her mother, Elada, had been the wife of a Baron, the Baroness of West Drewmore. And the Baroness of West Drewmore had taught her daughter what was proper. And true also though her baronetcy was ages ago but a Baron and his Baroness were figures of importance. The Edicts had changed all that. In this age the baronies provided wives, fortunate women indeed, for the Kings of Harnell, but scarce little else.

The King savored a small amount of wine on his tongue as he nodded his agreement to his wife's words. Plates of food were being set on the table. He swallowed, but little of the liquid remained to wet his throat. He sipped not more than a few drops of water to help him swallow. The servers stepped away from the table and waited.

"Had you asked my counsel, Sybil Kalla would not be here," he said. "Sybils are not welcome in my Kingdom, nor were they welcome in any of the kingdoms of old. I can tell you what is said, and what has been said during the generations since the Edicts were established, but you know all that."

He turned from looking at his wife to focus his attention on the Sybil: "You know what was said of your role in the Long Wars before the Sweltering. Harsh words against you and yours have stood the test of time."

Elearim and her mother were still as statues. Kalla knew if she was to have any influence in the Kingdom of Harnell her words must be well chosen.

"King Gemar, I speak with only your well-being to prompt my words."

The King sipped more wine.

"Sir, you are afflicted—grievously afflicted. Your healers, with much respect to them, have, with their many skills, been unable to heal you. Little wonder. You are far beyond their help. You fare less well each week—each day. Not well is not accurate: you are not sick. Your life is being leeched from you."

Kalla watched his eyes intently, hoping to make contact.

"You need no Sybil to tell you that. You are in the prime of your life. What do you make of the creature you saw gazing above your shoulder this morning?"

Momentarily, the King opened his eyes. "What has been said of the Sybil is that you would rule men. That I am unwell is evident. You have shown me a vision that cannot be seen but through your showing of it. What do you want from me?"

Queen Elearim spoke.

"My Lord, this illness is not some summer sniffle. Yama licks his chops hungrily at our door. And who of yours can heal you? I have summoned Sybil Kalla. She has journeyed to us at great peril. She will heal you. That is her only mission."

Kalla spoke with faint jest in her voice.

"If, for comfort's sake, you require that I set a fee for my services, then that is easily done."

King Gemar, with both elbows on the table, rested his chin in the palms of his hands and stared at Kalla with a watery grin. The wine he had last sipped he now rolled through his teeth and across his tongue, and fondly swallowed. He closed his eyes.

"Please, Gemar, listen to what Sybil Kalla has to say."

All were silent, and Elearim nodded for Kalla to begin.

"King Gemar, I am, as you so clearly recognize, not a goddess invincible."

He nodded and smiled faintly.

"In answer to your question as to the wishes of The Sybil and my fee, let it be that you give us the babes left on the dunes. Require that they be left at our gate where we may safely retrieve them."

The King blinked awake.

"And what will I give the Lords in return for this?"

"That I cannot answer. Yet this is our fee."

The King, his forehead deeply wrinkled, returned to his former pose.

Elearim, though disturbed and angry at this unplanned request, nodded for Kalla to proceed.

"I have no control over the burden you carry. Of this demon that sucks away at your life...neither spells, nor potions, nor fire, nor steel will purge you of it. The only hope for cure is with you, the one who carries the burden."

The Sybil lifted her glass, sipped the water, and, startled, made an unpleasant face.

"The Wars of these last two-and-a-half millennia spawned great terrors and this, one of many, is yet with us. This Succumon was created by a necromancer, ordered by a king—a man, of course—designed to be cast against royalty, most likely an enemy king. The creature may be destroyed but only at the time it was created. That time is a time that is neither night nor day."

The King's eyes had opened at the Sybil's words, 'a man, of course.'

"Interesting. A time that is neither night nor day. What a long discussion we might have about that. A discussion where you might hope to twist and tie me into knots. That is not likely to happen, Sybil Kalla. Hearing the word 'time' does remind me of your earlier comments regarding a great opportunity. You had drunk quite a great deal of wine and were quite eloquent about Time. Is there something, other than the babies, that you wish for? Something to do with Time, by chance?"

He waited.

"Would you care for a glass of wine? Merlow, I believe."

Hearing the King's offer, the Sybil breathed deeply through her nose.

"There is much I want. Time gives each of us an opportunity. An opportunity for each..."

She stumbled in her thoughts and speech.

"For your Kingdom, for my children. You know the children of whom I speak. They are set as bait. You know the price we often pay to spare them death. Some of them are your daughters, no doubt."

She glared at the King and then at Queen Elearim before snatching the wine bottle by its slim neck and slopping wine into her glass.

Chapter 12
Sooner or Later

The two young men rode towards the south border of Harnell. Jessyl, still laughing at Ennar's humor, gingerly wiped tears from his eyes.

"Thank you, Ennar. I needed to laugh. Put away your sword and I will tell you this story you so much wish to hear. There are women in this story. One with large violet eyes and sun- browned shoulders."

Ennar slid his sword into its sheath.

"I do wish to hear the tale Jessyl—as much as you wish to tell it."

"To begin, then. My mother and grandmeer summoned me to them and begged and insisted that I journey west into the gullies of the mountains. To leave at the first light of morning, as I did, and to return before nightfall as I did not. I returned at first light this morning."

"You traveled at night?"

"I did, as we shall no doubt do again tonight. Did I tell my father of this plan? You know the answer to that question. Why do I ask it?"

"Easy on yourself, my friend. What has happened will not go away by pounding on your head or your heart."

Jessyl looked at Ennar and nodded as though in agreement, but the comment made no sense to him.

"Mother urged caution and haste, and insisted that once I entered the gullies, I would wear a red scarf given to me by Grandmeer.

"'Caution?' I asked. 'There will be no Rangers in the gullies.'

"'No,' Grandmeer replied. 'Be wary of The Sybil's children.'

"Whom she meant by 'The Sybil's children,' I had no idea.

"My message to The Sybil was to be this: 'Our King is grievously sick. The Queen sends her son Prince Jessyl and entreats The Sybil to travel to the King's court.

"'A healer, a great wise healer,' Grandmeer chanted many times as my mother instructed me in what to say.

"'They will know which of The Sybil to send,' my mother assured me.

"The entrance to the gullies I found easily. The directions were accurate. Once inside, the way wound around gentle mounds and often beside steep graveled slopes. As I traveled further the mounds became larger and appeared much the same, each striped with various colors of earth. Deep within this confusion the way led to a ravine with walls that reached to the clouds…a thousand times the height of you or me, even as we sit on these horses."

Ennar patted his horse's neck.

"From the dunes I had not seen any hint of the ravine. Curious, I thought. I had not heard of such a place."

"Nor I," Ennar quickly added. "My father and uncles in all their travel in search of metal have not mentioned such a place."

"What was more curious was to find myself sprawled on my back, a spear point pressing into my throat. And more curious still," Jessyl said as he turned and looked deeply into Ennar's eyes, "the spear was held by a tall sun-browned girl with eyes as large and clear as the night sky. A girl no older than ourselves. I pointed to the red scarf.

"'Any fool may wear a scarf,' she said.

"She was flanked by two companions. I remained silent.

"'Any ideas as to what to do with a boy with a red scarf and no tongue?' she said but with laughter in her voice.

"One said: 'We could stake him out and have him for our pleasure.'

"'Or' the other said, 'we could stake him out and warm his toes.'

"'Your underwear is always warm, Muley. And you, Lesha, always wanting to warm someone's toes.'"

"They said that?" Ennar shouted in disbelief.

"With much humor the tall girl continued to chastise her two aides. As she spoke, I lightly pressured the spear point to one side, but she held it firmly where she wanted and moved it a little closer to again touch my skin. She returned her look to me.

"'We could do both,' she said with a grim look, but she could not keep the laughter out of her eyes. Tell us, boy with the red scarf, what should we do with you?'"

"No!" Ennar exclaimed. "You tell this tale to make me the fool!"

"I responded, 'My mother, Queen Elearim, and her mother, Elada, have sent me to entreat The Sybil to send their best healer to my father, King Gemar.'

"I slowly moved aside the spearhead, which she grudgingly allowed me to do.

"'I am Prince Jessyl. I understand, at the sight of me, your need for pleasure. Surely that will await the import of my work. Take me to The Sybil.'"

"You said that?"

"Every word of it—except for the part about 'the sight of me' and 'the need for pleasure.'"

"But the rest of the tale…?"

"As it happened, I swear Ennar."

"The leader of the three introduced herself as Jesthya, daughter of Sybil Pura. Her two companions she introduced as Mula and Alesha. They look me to The Sybil. There are three women, Sybils each, I guessed, but they are very particular to be called The Sybil. I have no idea why."

At this point Jessyl began to speak mockingly of them, pretending to have the voice of an old woman.

"After much dillying and dallying, and mumbling and arguing, and shillying and shallying, it was agreed to send

Sybil Kalla to my father's court.' Great Sur, can women not make up their minds in less than half a day?' I thought. And after this endless discussion, I was told to wait with Sybil Kalla who surely is the most useless of the three. She dawdled insufferably and at this morning's first light, almost within the safety of my father's keep we were almost killed. Though later she blinded the Lords and Swikes. 'Useless' is not the word I seek to describe her. What is the opposite of careful and exacting? Help me, Ennar."

"You ask me for help with words?" Deeply puzzled Ennar looked at his friend. "Who are these Sybils and who are the children? Who are the fathers? Why have we not heard of them?"

"The children are certainly not daughters of these Sybils. No woman as shriveled as these could have children. And the children are not just young girls: there were women, and a gray hair waited upon The Sybil. I heard a baby cry." He looked at Ennar. "I promised you a curious tale, and you have heard a curious tale. I am left with many questions."

"And would you like to again meet the girl with the sun-browned shoulders?"

"We will see," Jessyl replied, evading his friend's question.

They rode on, Jessyl deep in thought and Ennar wondering not as much about the story, but about how his friend had changed from the friend he had known all his life.

As Jessyl was telling the story to Ennar, the Windriders tied Gelt's wrists and hobbled his ankles. A cord used like a horse's bit separated the Ranger's jaws to serve as a gag.

Leason jogged into the dunes to the east, away from the sun.

He shouted, "I'll check the snares and return in time to cover your back."

Jolar smiled at Leason's interest in supper and then turned towards Gelt.

"Gelt, you have done well today considering what might have happened. If you look towards Leason's concealment, he may put you to sleep again, and this time you may not awaken. A difficult task to not look where one must not look."

Leason laughed to hear Jolar's words. *Jolar, my dear partner. Always the teacher.*

Jolar rested, thinking: *Finally we have met others. Leason...I should call him back. Always wanting something to sink his teeth into. Agreed, they have no water: but what might they have? Yes, he and I are quite opposite but well matched—though I have agreed to err on the side of caution.*

He stood abruptly.

"Leason?" he shouted, as though questioning Leason's presence.

Gelt had been pondering as well. *Small men on horses. Not two Lords. Not anyone in the company of the Lords. Surely not two of the boys. Strange. A ruse, a distraction? If these Windriders are taken, I will roast along with them. How I would enjoy even the slightest chance to cut their throats.*

Jolar spoke: "Gelt, you are trussed up on the chance you will betray us. Don't think poorly of us. If one takes thousands of small chances over the course of one's life, then small odds become near certainty. Hence we have tied and gagged you."

Leason overheard Jolar's advice and chuckled as he reached the top of the dune to the west.

Always the philosopher, he thought. *Always the teacher.*

"Yes, Jolar!" he replied to Jolar's call.

When Leason saw Jolar jogging up the dune to him, he squatted, awaiting his friend's arrival.

"Leason, I agree that we should be cautious. You are correct: there is likely no water here. But what if there is something else that may be of great worth to us? Leave the firing of the first shot to me."

"It is beyond my imagination. What could be of value here?"

"Suppose they have plants that require less water and yet produce the same amount of food—or more—than our plants?"

"What a great imagination you have, my friend. You fire the first shot. But do not be lost in your imagination, or I will reclaim the honor."

Jolar nodded thanks to Leason and walked back towards the fire.

Gelt had been thinking as the two spoke: *If I could alert the Lords or aid them in any way or better yet, help subdue these two. That would pay for all.*

His mind scrambled for a solution. He cautiously tested the knot that held his wrists.

Jolar saw him working the knot with his teeth.

"A puzzle these two small riders, eh Gelt?" Jolar turned and looked out towards the riders. Since the last sighting, they had traveled more than half the distance to the Windriders' encampment.

"They are small, Gelt, and they ride poorly. Decoys, do you think?"

Gelt remained gagged and silent.

"If I were you, Gelt, I would think as you are thinking: 'How may I play both sides of the game and end up with the winners?' Or, at times you maybe think, 'How may I be of help to my masters?' Leason and I, much against Leason's wishes, gamble that we will be the winners. Otherwise, why would we stay? I have no idea at all as to what we will do with you, win or lose."

He looked pointedly at Gelt's wrists and said: "Could we ever trust you?"

He looked again in the direction of the approaching riders.

"If these two are a ruse to get us off our guard, our sails lie ready and the wind is good on the windward side of the dune. You will be left with your friends to convince them that you were coy with us and yet somehow came out of the afternoon unmarked."

He looked long at Gelt.

"Men in armor we will hear for a great distance. If they come without armor, which is unlikely from what you tell us, we will stop many, likely, all of them. We wish for peace and trade and learning: that is our intent. We do as best we may: after that, what follows may not be of our choosing. We hope for a congenial talk with two small men."

"Sooner or later," Gelt mumbled through his gag, "there will be more than two."

Jolar bade Gelt to sit by the fire, and then he jogged to the top of the dune and waved to the riders.

Chapter 13
Kalla's Rant

The sight of Kalla about to again drink wine filled Queen Elearim with fear bordering on terror. She rose from her seat and shouted at the Sybil, "Kalla! Give that glass to Elada. Mother, take it from her."

Elada stood with her hand outstretched to receive the glass. Kalla raised her palm in a gesture of decline and unconsciously rotated her body to set herself between the wine and the Queen mother.

"Today I will be moderate," Kalla whispered. "Merlow," she said as she took a small sip and closed her eyes. "I will be moderate," she murmured, the other members at the dinner now forgotten. After a few moments her eyes snapped open, as though she had just awoken and suddenly remembered she had business with the King.

"Yes, King Gemar," she said as she focused all her attention on him, "my interest is in the various turnings of Time, and particularly in the progress Time will support in the years to come. 'To all things a season,' the lore of old tells us. And you are correct that I would rule men. Only then will the folly and destruction come to an end. The nonsense, the bickering, you men strutting around like so many young bulls, the inevitable slaughter: all of it I would end. But I know from my long life, and from our long history, that for men to be ruled by The Sybil is not likely in this age."

"What do I want?" She sipped her wine and closed her eyes.

"What do I not want? I do not want you to die. I do not want your fifteen-year-old son at the mercy of your Lords. The situation, as now set out by the Edicts, is far preferable to these Lords, your thugs, unbridled ruling Harnell. Your Edicts were not written by fools. They have kept your manly ways somewhat under control," she laughed. "Nonetheless, if I had my way I would scour the Earth clean of your so-called Lords."

She drank deeply.

"Believe me, when I prophesize a fruitful world, I do not desire to see those fruits gobbled by the monsters who rule alongside you. Be certain of that."

"As to your being healed that you must do yourself. Do you understand?" she shouted as though talking to a child. "You are not sick in the least."

She looked closely at the King, measuring his reaction to her last remark.

"When you destroy this demon, your strength will begin to return immediately. You will be at your full strength in matter of a week. Even after a day you will feel a great difference."

She sipped wine. "You like the sound of that? To again have your full strength and vigor? To have your life...and your pleasures returned to you?"

She sipped more wine and said, "All that, you will have—with my training." She swallowed the last of the wine from her glass.

"Healers, bring a near steaming kettle and a brazier of coals to boil it. Quickly!" She turned to the King. "King Gemar, I will show you how to be rid of this curse."

The Queen had been pensively focused on Kalla.

"Kalla, put away the wine," she warned. "It is poison to you."

Elada nodded in agreement and held out her hand for the glass.

"What will your sisters say?" the Queen chastised, holding her hand outstretched to take the glass. "Give me the glass!"

Kalla moved the glass protectively away from the Queen and her mother.

"Answer me this," Queen Elearim commanded. "Why are you chosen for the healing and not one of your sisters? Pura, many times my guest, could more easily have undertaken this task. Why is it you who are chosen?"

"I have been chosen. Leave me to my work, Queen Elearim. You rule a kingdom: is that not enough?" She refilled her glass and sipped deeply of the wine, chanting quietly to herself, "I will be moderate; I will be moderate."

Kindeen reentered the room with a kettle of hot water and a brazier of glowing coals.

"Set the kettle on the coals. Hurry," Kalla said impatiently.

"Blow on the coals. Blow," she urged. "The King is to be healed." She elbowed Kindeen away from the brazier and fanned the fire with her hands.

"Now silence, all. Listen, dear King, listen."

She blew on the coals, making them glow red.

"Listen carefully! There will be a precise time when the water is no longer water—when the water is neither water nor steam. Listen! Listen."

After a long wait she continued.

"What will be when we have neither water nor steam?" She let silence reign. "Only silence. What is this glorious silent hum? No, the word hum cannot describe the delicacy of it. What do we hear—hear is not right either," she laughed. "What do we hear in this time between water and steam?"

The room was hushed but for the hissing of the coals. Kalla sipped wine.

She whispered, "The air in this room has the same feeling as the air before a summer storm. Do you sense that feeling?" With her eyes wide she looked encouragingly at the King. "Feel it! I will teach you to find the silence between one thing and another. The silence between breathing in and breathing out. Between wakefulness and dreaming. Between dreaming and sleeping. Between day and night. Between water and steam. It is in such a gap as this that your burden was created King Gemar. Only there may your burden be dissolved."

The room was filled with a most pleasant but entirely faint humming sound of water about to boil.

The King had been sitting waxen-faced, his eyes closed and his hands supporting his chin. He opened his eyes.

"It appears that our Sybil has kindly heated water for our afternoon tea. Some tea, Kindeen?"

Kindeen's eyes sparkled, and his face lit up in a wry smile.

Kalla, shaken out of concentration, looked at the King in shock.

"Damn your feeble soul!" she shrieked. She kicked away a chair and with a swipe of her hand toppled the boiling kettle and the brazier of coals to the floor. Steam filled the room. She gulped the remaining wine from her glass and shrieked again.

"Damn your stupidity! Damn your manly arrogance!"

She slammed her empty glass on the table.

The Queen and her mother stood between Kalla and the King.

"Damn men! Always the same: hunt and whore and plot and fight. Too stupid to see the value of the greatest of gifts. I offer you the most precious secret of life, and you laugh."

"I am too wise to take a gift from a Sybil," the king rasped. "Take your witchery, and yes, the bottle, if that will get you gone, and leave."

"Always the same!" she raged. "The same stupidity for the last eight generations; the same stupidity during the Long War. And the most poisonous lie in your entire monstrous fable is that the Long War, the twenty-four hundred years of slaughter, was the work of The Sybil. That war, that abomination, was caused precisely by what you have done today. Knowledge, precious knowledge...knowledge from the Great Mother, offered and left through your ignorance, unheeded."

Before the Dawn

The King was laughing with all his strength. Kindeen was attempting to hold back his laughter, but was shaking with the effort.

"The monstrosity of the torture and slaughter of the Sybils," she gasped, catching her breath. "Millions slaughtered. You men destroyed your own salvation. And I remain. And I you ridicule. You and your servant dare to mock me, Sybil Kalla."

She snatched up the glass and the bottle of Merlow. "You no longer have the protection of The Sybil."

"She takes the bottle Kindeen, and we no longer have her protection. Imagine! The horror of it all. What will become of us?"

"How your slop heap of a kingdom will survive without The Sybil, I cannot imagine. One more thing I will tell you: my children and I will deal with your partners, the Lords. My children? You know of whom I speak. Babies left as bait to trap my daughters: babies, all girls of course, your flesh and blood among them, left on the dunes to die.

The King became silent, as did Kindeen.

"Rot and venom be upon you!" she shrieked. "Rot and venom upon your slop heap kingdom!"

She threw open the door and was gone.

Chapter 14
A Prophesy from the South

Ennar pointed to a figure slowly waving from a dune to the south and a bit to the east.

"Just one?" Jessyl shouted, squinting into the distance at the figure. "Stay between him and the sun."

The boys rode to the dune top where minutes before a man had stood waving. Behind them the sun was setting in a blaze of scarlet. Whoever they had seen had now disappeared. With the warmth of the sun on their backs, casting long shadows to the east, they sat on the horses peering into the dusk at a flicker of light. The figure they had seen was now standing by a small fire at the base of the dune with his arms outstretched in a bow of welcome. A second figure, obviously uncomfortable, sat on the sand, his hands tied in front of him.

"Join us! My partner hunts supper." And, after a moment of silence, "Are you followed?"

"We are just two," Jessyl replied.

"Welcome. Come to our fire."

As they cautiously urged the horses down the dune, Jolar moved towards them with his hands outstretched, palms facing them, fingers pointing towards the earth.

"I am Jolar of the House of Geldof. My companion will join us shortly."

"I am Jessyl, Prince of Harnell. My brother Prince Ennar."

"Join us by the fire. You recognize your countryman Gelt?"

As the youths moved the horses down the dune and out of the glare of the sun, Jolar could see them clearly. In contrast, he and Leason, though not much older than these two, were men, fit and sinewy, and well trained in the craft of combat. These two were yet boys: the one who remained silent was more muscled than the other, but they were boys nonetheless.

"Are you at war?" Jolar asked upon seeing the gash that had been earlier hidden by Jessyl's hood and the glare of the sun.

"A slip at practice," Jessyl lied.

Jolar's voice became stern.

"Those swords you carry are too heavy for you, and your riding tells me that you are not the owners of the horses. Leason!" he shouted, "Leason, join us. All is somewhat well."

Leason appeared behind them on the dune where the youths had sat on the horses with the sun at their backs. He carried a forked branch in each hand, and upon each branch dangled two rabbits.

"Roast rabbit for supper—again!" he shouted as he loped down the dune. "Come, lads, off your horses. Jolar, loose our friend Gelt. Gelt, skin and skewer these rabbits. What have you brought to eat, lads? Come, off your horses. We have been living on rabbits these last twenty-three days. Blessed with rabbits, one might say."

As he spoke he had given the rabbits to Gelt, along with a short knife, though he looked at Gelt with an exaggerated smile of unconcern. Gelt bowed a slight nod to the Prince and walked away from the camp to prepare the supper meat.

Leason jogged to stand beside Jessyl's horse and extended his hand in greeting.

"Prince Jessyl?" Leason reached up, taking the boy's hand in his. "Leason of the House of Sarandon."

Leason held Jessyl's hand and looked long into his eyes as the boy began to climb down from the horse. Then he turned to Ennar, who had quickly dismounted, and extended his hand, introducing himself and also testing this boy's grip and firmness of eye.

"A calloused hand, young prince?" he questioned.

Jolar's voice, which had earlier become stern, remained so.

"Gelt, I noticed, bowed only to you, Prince Jessyl?"

He stood looking at Jessyl for a moment and continued. "Fortunately for you, the wound on your forehead was not made by a sword. A thrown knife more likely: the hilt has left a bruise."

Leason added, "The hands of your 'brother' are calloused."

Turning to Ennar he said, "You have the hardy looks and smell of a blacksmith."

Jolar added tiredly, "How can there be gain for we four on the basis of such stories?"

Jessyl threw back his hood.

"Certainly, as perceptive as you are, you understand our caution. Particularly so, with Leason away hunting rabbits."

Jolar smiled and relaxed somewhat.

"Sometimes a fresh beginning is possible. We are just four: let us make a fresh beginning."

Gelt returned, carrying the expertly cut strips and joints of meat on a rabbit skin. There was no skewer as Leason had hoped, so Gelt set the skin on the earth and placed the meat on stones that had been heating in the coals. He had cleaned the knife, and he now returned it to Leason. Gelt knew that by being allowed to handle the knife he was clearly marked as an ally of his captors.

Jessyl replied to Jolar, "What I will tell you — so that we are at ease during our meal and our talk—is that the chance of interruption is exceedingly slim. The Lords who would, on a usual day, have met you are unavailable...blinded. Their sight will return, though I do not know when. Their Rangers are untouched. It is unlikely Rangers will be sent without the

Lords or their Swikes as you have easily subdued two of our weaker Rangers." He glanced disparagingly at Gelt.

Jolar and Leason exchanged glances.

Jolar broke the silence: "In addition, we would hear the horses and the armor."

Leason added, "Without armor, they should not march against us."

The foursome had moved to the fire. Gelt tended the meat. Ennar retrieved his pack from his horse and began to brew tea.

"Tell us of your travels," Jessyl requested as the four sat circled around the fire.

"Where to begin?" Jolar asked, glancing at Leason.

"We are from the south: a distance so far that our people will never meet," Jolar said pointedly. "Twenty-three days we have followed the winds north. We ride the winds up the side of the mountain wall to where the air is cold and thin—then glide north, and down to the desert again. Flight—a glorious gift. Each night in the few moments before sleep I wish for many more mornings of cool wind and sparkling sunlight."

He watched Gelt turn the meat. The Windrider appeared deep in thought of another time and place.

"I have a tale for you if you will hear it," he said.

Jessyl nodded in agreement; Ennar's eyes widened with anticipation.

"One clear morning, just after sunrise, we came upon hundreds of eagles their unmoving wings spread wide as they spiraled effortlessly higher. As we sailed closer to view this sight, two eagles, with only the slightest movement of their wings, floated effortlessly to us—one to Leason and one to me—each setting a wingtip nearly touching our sails. Such beautiful creatures. They floated dark and golden and silent beside us as though we were their brothers since ancient times and guided us to a spiral of warm air. Up, up we rose with our eagles seemingly bound to us—forever up—time left behind. Higher and higher. Higher than we had ever flown. At the top of the updraft the air froze our fingers; winds tossed us about. Neither we nor the eagles wanted to leave the golden silence of those gracious moments. What a great pull our hearts felt for those creatures…and they for us. It was as though the air, the cold, my fingers, my bones, Leason, the eagles—everything—was one."

Jolar savored the silence of the moment.

"One—all was one—if that makes sense."

He looked long into the fire.

"If eagles may feel sadness, we each suffered in parting."

Leason had nodded agreement often throughout the tale and did so again but said nothing.

"We floated away from the eagles as though we were made of something finer than the thin mountain air. We sailed till past sunset and to near darkness. That day is warmly stored in my heart. I am most thankful for it. Always I would fly with the eagles if they would have me."

Leason again nodded in agreement.

Gelt had been turning the meat and Ennar passed tea to each of the party. Jolar spoke: "Our Mothers tell us that Earth's people will grow again in number. That we will do well to find others, and learn, and share what we know. We visit your land to learn and trade and profit."

He looked at Jessyl. "You puzzle at the mention of our Mothers?"

"Yes, that also," Jessyl responded as if from shock, "but mostly from your statement 'Earth's people will grow in number.'"

"Our history tells us that mankind once crowded the Earth."

"As does ours," Jessyl replied. "Yet in my life I have heard it said only twice that man will increase and prosper. That is what you say, I believe? Both hearings I have heard this day."

Jolar's round black face widened as did his eyes.

"Tell us of that, if you may."

"The story of today must eventually be told. Ennar has not heard it fully. It is a tale to take us to the middle of the night." He sat silently, thinking of what he might say.

"Tell me, was the blinding done with blue dust?" Leason asked.

Jessyl and Ennar stared at each other, at a loss for words.

"Your looks speak yes."

Jolar rushed his words, "The person with the blue dust told you of the coming change in Time?" he asked.

Jessyl was looking into the fire, stalling for time to think. He nodded in agreement.

Leason motioned to the food. He passed meat to his three companions. Gelt served himself last.

After a moment of silent thanks, Jolar spoke as they began to eat: "In our land, Mothers care for history, and healing, and foreseeing, and counsel. Any of such arts are happily the domain of the Mothers. Many centuries ago, during The Everlasting War, our Mothers counseled the men to seek refuge behind the high mountain wall. There is a gap in the wall, 'too difficult to climb' many said, that led to a lake hidden in the mountains. Once our people transported what was left of our animals and possessions, we made the entryway impossible to pass without permission. Protected, we have enjoyed life, for the most part, during the last two centuries since the End Times."

Gelt looked at Jolar, astonished.

The black faced monkey lied to me, he thought in amazement.

"Our Mothers gave us these windsails which had been saved since the time of The Everlasting War. This year they bade us to again travel, this time north along the mountain wall to search for an opening that might lead to water and people."

Leason added quickly, "In our travels we have found only yourselves."

Jessyl spoke.

"The Sybil whom I brought to my father's Keep told us that 'Time presents us with a great opportunity.' An opportunity to build a new world. Yes, it was she who blinded the Lords and Swikes. I left her on the floor stones of my father's Keep, one of our healers sewing up a gash across the side of her head. My father banished her never to be seen in our kingdom again, though I counseled that she may be of help with...I speak more than I should."

Leason broke the silence: "You would have been standing beside her—on the side where she was wounded—with your head turned, looking almost behind you. Your head being turned was good fortune, if I have it right."

Jessyl nodded in agreement, his head aching miserably.

"A Sybil," Jolar shook his head in disbelief. "Our mothers' foremothers were trained by the Sybils of the Great Light, and that training passed on from generation to generation. We doubted that any Sybils were yet alive."

"This one claims not to know the Sybils of the Great Light, though she said this while under the spell of my father's wine."

"Under the spell of your father's wine!" Jolar exclaimed. He held a leg of rabbit, entirely forgotten, close to his lips.

Leason continued, "We have surveyed this wall since the last full moon. In places it is lower than others but always immeasurably high. Wherever we have searched, it is at first sloped and then continues nearly straight up to peaks where there is scarcely air to breathe. Do you know of an opening in the wall? Where people may live? Gelt tells us there is no such place."

"Gelt knows that there are other people - women. I traveled to such a place to fetch Sybil Kalla: of the three she was chosen by her sisters to return with me to my father's Keep."

"Three!" Jolar exclaimed. "Three Sybils?"

Leason questioned, "Is there water and a kingdom?"

"There is water, but hardly a kingdom. Poor folks with nothing to trade. But let us not interrupt your story...continue please."

Jolar laughed: "Leason, he gives us nothing and teases us with tales of a valley with water, and we babble on like fools."

The meat had been eaten. From Ennar's stores bread had been provided to sop the grease off the hot stones. Bitter tea was being drunk.

Jolar continued: "Our Mothers tell us that two hundred years have passed since what came to be known as The Everlasting War ended. After twenty-four hundred years of darkness and these last two hundred years of dark twilight, humankind will again increase and prosper. By how much and how quickly is a concern for our Mothers.

"Our people, and no doubt yours, expect that the way we now live is the way life will be. And the history of the dark ages tells us that the life we now live is the order of things. For twenty-four times one hundred years our people fought murderous war after murderous war. As did your people. Your people for two hundred years have struggled and scratched in the dust. Any sensible person would ask: Why would there be a change? Only a fool would expect a change. But there was a change—an immense and unexpected change—in the history of your people, as well as ours. A breath of sanity filled the air. Sur's Great Clarity we call that time. Two hundred years ago in a time of great darkness, peace, of a sort, blanketed our land and yours."

He paused to soak up the drippings of roasted rabbit from a stone.

"Those who survived found a way to quit spilling each other's blood. And in our case, our people fought their way to a lake. Protected by the mountain wall, we survived. Your people also found a way out of the bloodlust. Our history tells us that before the peace descended, men, women, and children fought until the last person died. And our travels show us the signs of it. Lands burned of all life, wells filled with bones, civilization destroyed. Yet amidst all the horror, these startling changes I speak of took place. A startling leap forward from what had been. The fighting stopped. And our Mothers tell us that the change before us now will be far, far greater than the progress since Sur's Great Clarity."

All were silent and staring at the fire. Even Gelt was lost in thought.

"Time, our Mothers tell us, calls on us for a great step forward. Far greater than the peace of two hundred years ago. Should we embrace this opportunity, life will flourish. Should Time have to drag us kicking and screaming like frightened children, then progress will falter, possibly never to recover."

The meal was finished, the tea was drunk, and the men rested.

Leason spoke from a near slumber.

"I wonder greatly what you mean by, 'This day has been the strangest in all our Kingdom's history'?"

Though Jessyl might have thought these words, he could not remember saying them aloud. Though on the surface it was seemingly enjoyable being with these two men they somehow tired him. Nevertheless he said to Ennar for all to hear: "Ennar, my thought is to tell all that has happened today. My thought is to travel with Jolar and Leason to meet The Sybil."

Chapter 15
Rawlings' Dream

Outside the fortress Dern had painstakingly led the Lords each to their horse. Once all were mounted, he walked leading the long column of horses and riders. The riders had been ordered by rank and Dern held the reins and guided the foremost horse in the procession, that of Lord Rawlings. As the horses were hot, thirsty, and unaccustomed to being out in the heat of midday, they hurried to reach the shade and water of their masters' Keep. Each pressed the animal in front of it; Rawlings' horse often nudged its snout into Dern's back. Dern shouted respectfully over his shoulder to the column of riders, "Keep your horses in check, my Lords. We will reach the Keep in good order and all the sooner."

Occasionally Rawlings bellowed loudly in the hope that anyone brave enough to view the scene would hear his words and be terrified.

"You sluds who dare cast your eyes upon us, hear me: I will return and take your eyes."

After much complaining from the Lords and Swikes regarding the heat, dust, and the slowness of the pace, Dern, dripping with sweat, his tongue dried and rough as preserved meat, led the riders through the North Gate of their Keep.

As they entered, each Lord and Swike began shouting and soon all were screaming for their Rangers and boys to come to their aid. Horses circled and reared, iron-shod hooves slashed at the air. In the dust and confusion, two riders fell from horses to the hard earth. One of the fallen men shrieked long and painfully as a horse, wild and out of control, stepped on his thigh: the bone snapped like a twig of dry scrub. The other fallen rider had charged in blindness and rebounded awkwardly off the gate. He lay huddled in the dust, both hands holding his bloodied face, while all around him horses continued to career about, often crashing into each other, their riders cursing and fighting to stay in their saddles.

Rawlings, his neck arteries bulging and his face contorted in fury, shouted for silence. "Control your horses!" he roared. "Silence all!"

As the melee began to subside, he shouted to Dern: "Dern of Rawlings, the next man to make a sound, scar his cheek."

"Silence all!" Rawlings bellowed.

The horse of one of the Swikes continued bucking and twisting in tight circles, completely out of control. The rider, who had dropped the horse's reins, loudly cursed the horse, while struggling to stay in the saddle.

"Scar that noisemaker's cheek!" Rawlings roared. "It need not be pretty."

Dern pushed his way through the horses and danced alongside the crazed horse. He snatched hold of the reins and drawing the rider's dagger, sliced him on the cheek as neatly and gently as possible. Blood flowed and the man screamed in rage, but his scream quickly ceased and he became silent, fearing another scarring.

"Lords, Swikes, all of you, hear me," Rawlings spoke at first loudly but then in a soothing tone.

Riders became quiet; some of them stroked their horses' forelocks; the cut and bleeding Swike held his hand to his wound but remained silent.

"If there was ever a time for clear heads, now is that time. Hear me, your Lord Rawlings, that we may prepare a defense for our Keep. Hear me, that we may soon retire to our quarters and regain our eyesight."

The horses and the men but for the two men that lay quietly groaning in the dust, were now settled and silent.

"This blindness must pass from each of us as it passed from Swike Direoll.

"By now you men with your sight no doubt understand, we Lords have been blinded. Blinded by a blue-skinned hag. Aye, someone must have boiled her blue to mark her... they should have finished the job. If you see her, throw your daggers without hesitation. Whether she be alive or dead, bring her to me. But enough of her for now.

"On this strangest of days we must set a watch throughout the nights and days to come. For the present, one Ranger and two boys guard each gate. When we are settled, the Lords and I will meet, and I will set a plan. For now, you sighted fellows lead the blind to their quarters. Tend to the horses. Be ready if the guard of the gates calls you to action. Aye, the witch with the dust that blinds may have more disturbances fermenting in her wicked mind.

"Dinar!" he shouted. "You notice that your Lord and his Swike are not with us? Lord Vorguld lies on the floor of the Hall of Justice, an arrow stuck in his vitals."

Dinar emerged from the crowd and bowed to Rawlings even though the Lord was blind.

"Swike Direoll lies beside him, victim of a different fate. Take eight of the lads and rig up two stretchers. Retrieve your Lord and Swike."

Dinar again bowed to the Lord. He moved through the crowd, slapping his hand on the shoulder of one boy after another until he had chosen eight of the fiercest. As he chose the first two, he bade them each to fetch a stretcher. Rawlings spoke again.

"Carry swords as well as your throwing daggers."

Dinar nodded to the third and fourth boy to fetch swords for all.

"If you see a bundle of rags the color of sand with a blue face glaring out at you, do not hesitate for a snap: throw a knife into her. The lad that downs her will be well regarded by all. To have her alive would be even better."

He laughed and was joined by several of the listeners.

"If you dally to chit chat, she will blind you, or worse. Go quickly. Carry Lord Vorguld and the Swike Direoll to us with great care. We will cure them."

To the gathered he continued: "This blindness will pass. Dinar and his lads will return to strengthen our force. Vorguld and Direoll will be hale again. The blue witch has disturbed the peace of our kingdom. We shall recover our sight and plan a means to repay her for her treachery. For now let us retire to our quarters and await the passing of this blindness. To the watch I say be vigilant. The witch is fey but crafty. We will relieve you presently."

Four Rangers chose two boys each. They drew lots for which gate they would guard. The North, being near, was the choice of the winner. The other Rangers and boys led Lords and Swikes to quarters. Dern led his Lord and Swike to their compound.

Once inside Rawlings said hurriedly, "Bar the door. Open it for no one until I have my sight. Find butter. Boil it ever so lightly till it slightly darkens. Careful not to burn it. Strain it through a cloth and bring it to me."

Rawlings stumbled about and found a chair, as did his Swike, Misrup. Dern clattered about a cluttered pantry looking for butter.

"Quite a day, Swike Misrup. And quite a day for you, Ranger Dern."

The formality of his speech indicated that a meeting was underway.

"What are we up against at the border? Keep about your work with the butter."

"These intruders have weapons we have not seen before, my Lord. We faced them and demanded that they come with us for questioning. The conversation grew heated. Next, I plucked a small dart from my neck and fell in darkness to the earth. When I awoke I found myself tied to my horse. Gelt lay tied in a bundle, his face pointed towards the sun. They would not be a challenge to you, my Lord, and Swike Misrup. Though they fire their darts in a blink of an eye."

"Have they other weapons?" Misrup questioned.

"I did not see other weapons, Swike Misrup," Dern said, stopping his work momentarily. "They travel by air, my Lords. They float through the air carried by large sheets of cloth."

Rawlings and Misrup momentarily looked puzzled.

"The air carries them? They must be naught but skin and bones," Rawlings mused. "As that may be, their weapons must be light. And certainly they carry no armor. No swords? No bows? No spears?"

Dern nodded agreement. "Yes my Lord."

Rawlings continued, "In the blink of an eye they dropped you both?" he sighed. "We will come back to them. What of Vorguld and his idiot? Will they live?"

"My Lord, the arrow has pierced Lord Vorguld below the belt, the point full through, sticking out of his back."

"Ha!" Rawlings exclaimed. "It sounds like a painful death," but became more serious as he said, "though Vorguld may be so overly gruesome that even hell may not want him."

His two underlings laughed at Rawlings' joke.

"If Yama takes him, the Edicts dictate that I will be Chief Lord. Will Gelt be alive when we find this pair of intruders?"

"I wager him to be alive, though one of the pair seemed ready for sport, my Lord. Though the second of them seemed like water to the first man's fire."

"Gelt will not talk?"

"Gelt will not talk, my Lord. Though he did something that I must report at our meeting this moon."

"Tell it now instead," Rawlings offered.

Dern hesitated, pretending that he was reluctant to speak.

"We are directed by the Protocol for Outsiders to follow intruders, to see what they may do, and to catch them unawares. As this pair passed by us, Gelt blew his horn."

"Eyeball to eyeball with them, and you blinked and were dropped? And now I hear that Gelt blew his horn against the rules of the Protocol? That my Rangers are slow and daft is not something I wish to have bandied about at a general meeting with the Lords. Keep this talk to yourself." He sighed his weariness becoming clear to him.

"Let us rest, the sooner to bring back our sight. We will find our way to our rooms. Do not disturb me. Prepare the butter as I have instructed. I will join you when I am ready and not before. Do not disturb me. And do not unbar the door: it is not only I who wishes to become the Chief Lord of Harnell.

Rawlings found his way to his bed chamber. He laid back, his hands behind his head.

Vorguld will not live, he thought. *An arrow stuck through his innards. Ha! My dreams are a step closer to reality. What a pleasure to have time to think...twice now on the same day? I have not had such leisure during this entire last moon...nor the one before, and now that I come to think of it—not during the last year. How odd! I can't remember such a day!* He chuckled quietly.

No matter. Vorguld is dying, and I will be Chief Lord. How pleasant and very unusual to have time to lie back and enjoy such a pleasant thought. Vorguld dead and I Chief Lord. I have held this wish locked within my heart for all these years. But what is the use of being Chief Lord? Oh yes, it has its advantages. Two Swikes instead of one, first choice of women, and so forth. But all that amounts to a pittance. To be Chief Lord is but a step up for me. He chuckled again. *A step to what will be. And what will be? Land, green land, as far as the eye can see,* he sighed with pleasure. *And I see far. I see far because I stand on the highest watchtower, of the highest turret of my fortress. Yes, my fortress. The fortress of the King of Harnell.*

And when will I reveal this vision? When I can strike safely against the King, and against the Edicts. Then I will cloud the minds of the foolish with promises of what they desire. Each of them to have a woman, or as many women as they merit. And each with land. Ah, green land as far as the eye can see. And strong sons. Many strong sons. Sons for my army. And strong, healthy daughters to bear more strong sons. Of course, I needn't tell anyone of my army.

And I will have women. That wide hipped Queen being one of them. She bears her King one puny son! As the Edicts allow: only one son, and no daughters. Daughters are sent to the weak and useless Barons. And sons? Maybe they go to the Barons also. But I suspect they are sent to Yama. The large-eyed Queen? I have seen her look at her shoes when I am about. I will grind away at her willing hips day and night. She will give me a dozen sons.

Of course, with the Edicts gone, the men will be ever at each others' throats to get what they want. And their women will fiercely goad them on, as in days of old. But that is the way of life. Struggle. Two rats fight for a crust of bread while the bitch rat waits, hoping for more bread than her bitch neighbor. The writers of the Edicts tried, and almost squeezed the life out of living. And but for me they may have succeeded. "But you have failed, whoever you were," he laughed out loud. I will rid the world of the sickly King and his scrawny son, and their sickly Edicts. There will be grain and livestock and horses. And women and hunting, and the borders of my kingdom will extend far beyond the borders of this paltry kingdom. As far as the water will allow me. I will have the King's water. And—as he should have done long ago were he even half a man—I will sweat the jiggle off his woman.

Rawlings fell into a peaceful sleep.

He slept deeply for several hours before being awakened by the racket and clamor of horses and the sound of splintering wood.

Chapter 16
Kalla and the Horses

Sybil Kalla walked as though she tip-toed along a tightrope, the bottle in one hand and the glass in the other. She moved westward towards the land where she had lived since before the end of the Great War.

In a whisper she slurred, "If I had a cork, I'd cork this glorious juice and save it for my sisters."

"Merlow, Merlow," she sang, "when will I see you again?"

To the south and west stood the Keep and holdings of the Lords. A stacked stone wall, clearly the work of the present age quarried from the ruins of the old city, stood no higher than a tall man. The huge expanse of land that the Lords controlled was far larger than the remainder of the city. Living quarters, stables, fields, and most important, the Lords' water. It was the Lords who parceled out water from their well in return for labor or anything else the Kingdom had to offer.

Kalla rested, leaning against the last of the buildings that stood before the desolation surrounding the Lords' Keep.

"I wonder—they would still be blind," she mused.

She poured most of the contents of the bottle into her glass. The wine, nearly black in the moonlight, hovered higher than the rim of the glass as though by magic.

She laughed: "A favorite sport: who could fill their glass to its fullest and ferry the wine to their lips unspilled?"

Her hand steady, she gracefully raised the glass to her lips and drank without a drop wasted. She sipped an additional sip to reward herself.

"Out of practice but as good as ever! Many times I laughed as my sisters tried to match me, the wine running down their arms. If I had but a small portion of what we slopped…"

As she talked and laughed quietly to herself, she had walked a few paces closer to the Keep.

"I need a horse."

She drank greedily, finishing the wine.

"Surely the Lords will lend me a horse."

She smashed the glass on the wall that she had earlier rested against.

"Damn them!" she snarled. "One horse? I'll have all their horses!"

Kalla scampered across the desolate landscape and presently stood outside the North Gate. She stood pondering, swaying slightly and dimly aware that the desolate surroundings offered no protection for a distance much farther than she could run.

Nonetheless, she began to chant: "Horses. Oh, horses. I can feel you. Come to me." She closed her eyes and whispered: "Come to me. Come to Sybil Kalla."

At first there was only silence. She also remained silent—eyes closed, her body swaying slightly. And then faintly from within the Keep, a horse whinnied. Kalla remained still. Then an excited clamor of horses neighing and crashing about disturbed the stillness she had somehow created. The North gate splintered outward. A large horse staggered through the opening. Other horses charged by the stumbling horse directly towards Kalla. She spread her arms wide and the horses veered and scattered to the east and west of her. They stopped and milled about, looking at her quizzically.

Kalla pointed at a small, younger horse. The horse immediately trotted to her.

She pawed the horse's muzzle and gushed, "A beautiful night for a wondrous ride. Come with me, beautiful horse. We will ride to my wondrous sisters."

Shouting came from within the gates. With her left hand Kalla grabbed the horse's mane and, pressing the horse's withers towards the earth with the bottle still clutched in her other hand, she swung herself onto its back.

After riding a few paces towards two young boys who had stepped outside the gate, she sat for a moment and stared at them.

"Some blue dust?" she chuckled malevolently. "You have heard of the blue dust? And the terrible witch who dispenses it?"

"Sybil Kalla of the Destructive Light speaks to you!" she thundered. "Tell this to your masters: Sybil Kalla will decorate her garden gate posts with their ugly heads."

She sucked deeply on the bottle for the last of the drink it had to offer.

"Awww, dregs," she spat, and squealed painfully. Quick as a snake she threw the bottle at the boy on her left, hitting him squarely in the middle of his forehead. He dropped like a stone. She shrieked gleefully: "Tell the lords of the turkey turds that we are at war!"

With that said she whistled sharply and rode to the west in a spray of dust and stones. The horses followed.

Chapter 17
Vorguld's Gamble

Vorguld, when conscious, suffered painfully throughout the afternoon. The healers watched as he crawled to Direoll, clutched the fabric of his Swike's tunic and turning from the man threatened the healers should they hinder him. Then he passed out after whispering into Direoll's ear.

Direoll was as cold as a stone at midnight in midwinter.

Dinar and eight youths arrived with stretchers late in the afternoon to fetch the injured pair.

Kindeen reported all of this to the Queen as Dinar and his company awaited permission to retrieve the fallen men. The Queen ordered that the two men be carried away, and she instructed Kindeen to have the outside doors to the Hall secured with both bar and bolt. She told Kindeen to say that the King had decreed that there would be no morning meeting with the Lords and that those carrying the stricken were to convey this message to the Lords.

Queen Elearim doubted that by morning the King would have enough strength to talk. She could set him in his throne, his crossbow readied, but whether he could aim and fire was doubtful. Whether he would remain sitting without falling to the floorstones was also doubtful. Now it was late into the night and Jessyl, who was all that stood between her becoming the bedmate of one of the many repulsive Lords—particularly the one that often stared at her wantonly—had not returned.

For the King and the Lords not to meet was a contravention of the Founding Edicts.

Well so be it, she thought. *Damn the Edicts! I would burn them if I could.*

◦❦◦

Vorguld awoke with a flash of pain.

"Curse you all," he rasped, his mind confused by agony. "Who is with me? Dinar? Ah, good, Dinar."

He shivered and clutched an arm across his throbbing chest.

"Water, Dinar. Water," his voice trailed off into silence.

Vorguld slowly sipped the water, but he did so greedily, his eyes large at the taste of it. "I see you cart our blind Swike?

"Where are we? We must not go to the Keep. Oh no. That would not be wise. No, not to the Keep." In his fear he spoke quickly his pain forgotten. "Take the north road and then on to the bent tree. You know it? Good, and then through the boulders...to the left. There appears to be no path, but there is. Take us to the safety of that place. A place well prepared for such a day as this."

As he closed his eyes, his forehead crumpled as though in deep thought, but it was mostly a consequence of the pain.

"Dinar, you are now First Swike of Lord Vorguld."

He paused as he had paused many times during his talk, breathing sharply between his teeth, his eyes squinted shut from the pain.

"Direoll?" he rasped. "Anything from him?"

"He moans, my Lord. Mostly he rubs his hands together as though cold, and moans."

"Good...he returns to life. We will need his sword, Dinar. Direoll has his strengths, though in these last hours he has failed us miserably. There are eleven of us, Dinar. Are the lads loyal? Are they ready for blood?"

"I chose the best, my Lord. They seek advancement. Many of the Rangers are wary of them. "

"Good. We will take them to our armory. Yes, Dinar, our armory. Well fortified. Stocked with food and water. We will train the boys in the art of the crossbow."

He looked unflinchingly at his Swike. Dinar returned the look with eyes that glowed like coals.

"Now what you must do, Dinar...the next time I faint. More water..."

He forced himself to drink slowly.

"Next time I pass out strip the feathers off the arrow. Smooth the shaft and smear it with this."

He handed a packet to Dinar.

"Do not break the arrow off close to the wound. Paint the entire shaft with a poultice of this powder mixed with water. Make it thick. Then slowly push the arrow through and pull it slowly out the other side."

He closed his eyes and breathed heavily.

"If Yama will have me, Dinar, then Yama will have me. For certain, if we do not ease this arrow out of my guts, He will have me soon."

He forced a laugh of unconcern.

"If I die, you will not get my Lordship—even if Direoll were to pass on with me."

Dinar understood his meaning.

Vorguld clutched the Swike's sleeve. "It is good that these eight seek advancement. If I live, you will be, in time, a Lord."

Dinard nodded in agreement, though he wondered if his Lord was losing his mind as death approached.

"Out of the greatness of my heart, I have a secret for you."

Vorguld laughed a tight, choking laugh but pain again consumed him.

"I will tell you this secret on the slim chance that Yama will call for me." He looked intently at his Swike. "I have allowed the blacksmith to make a change to the armor—the breast plate. Not the armor that we have stowed. No, our armor will stop an arrow. You understand me?"

"I do, my Lord."

"What do you understand?"

"That, my Lord, an arrow that strikes high may find flesh?

"And...?"

"Eleven of us will overcome the others."

"Precisely," Vorguld hissed as he passed out.

Chapter 18
The Horses Are Gone

Lord Rawlings jolted awake to the noise of splintering wood and rampaging horses. As he vaulted out of bed, he noticed the familiar shapes of the room appeared to be mere shadows and he remembered that he had been blind.

He shouted as he strapped on weapons, "The butter. Quickly, Dern!"

As he reached the south door of his quarters, he could discern men and boys running towards the North Gate. Dern appeared with the skillet of amber colored butter and held it close to the Lord's face for inspection. Rawlings dug his fingers into it and slathered it into his eyes. Blinking, he wiped his hands on the thighs and hips of his pants and moved through the doorway towards the commotion with as much haste as he dared.

A cloud of dust outside the north boundary of the Keep reflected the moonlight. He saw the glow only faintly and at the same time heard a distant cackle of the same laughter he had first heard early that morning in the Hall of Justice. The laughter subsided and the sound of galloping horses filled his ears. A small shape appeared. One of the boys scurrying through the gate to join men gathered around a fallen form which appeared as a smudge in the Lord's vision.

Rawlings reached the men to find a Ranger sprawled crookedly in the dust, trampled dead by horses. Short of breath from his hurried walk, Rawlings rasped at the boy who now stood staring dumbly at the dead Ranger. "Speak, boy!"

Lords and Swikes and Rangers continued to gather from more distant sections of the Keep.

The boy's eyes were large with fright, and he was clearly stunned by what he had seen and heard.

"Speak, boy. Has the witch got your tongue in her pocket?"

The boy haltingly began: "Sh-She says to tell the L-Lords that the blood...of your heads will p-paint her g-g-gate posts...," he hesitated, "...red. And to tell you that we are at war. T-That she will have our heads."

"Curse that venomous, man-hating hag. Curse her!" Rawlings growled under his breath, pretending to be in deep thought though he was stunned by the boy's message.

There were various murmurs of assent to his cursing of the witch.

The stunned boy who had delivered the Sybil's message spoke again: "She has stolen the horses."

Each knew this to be true, and all were silent at the message.

Rawlings barked, "Where is Vorguld? Dinar and the eight boys? They are here, returned?"

"No, my Lord," the Ranger who had guarded the East Gate reported. "I sent one of my boys to the Fortress. He was able to look between the doors of the Hall of Justice and could spot neither Vorguld nor his Swike. Upon reporting this news to me, I sent him back, this time to the East Gate, to ask the healers what had become of our Chief Lord. He reported that Dinar and his boys carried our comrades away before sunset."

"Sur preserve us. That hag could not have had her way with Dinar and eight of our lads."

Although he appeared to scrutinize those in the assembly, and though the salve of butter had improved his vision, he could not see to whom he was speaking.

"Are we all here? Who now guards our other gates?"

There was no answer, as those guarding the gates had left their posts and hurried to the disturbance at the North Gate.

"Quick, a Swike and two Rangers to each gate! Repair this North Gate. This Sybil witch—she must be taken alive. The six Lords and I will meet and plan our defense. The remainder of you prepare for war. Prepare for war, lads. Prepare for war."

⚓

Earlier that afternoon when the Chief Lord Vorguld and his Swike had been carried to their hideout, and after the boys had sworn allegiance to him and had been given duties for the coming night, Vorguld, through pain and exhaustion, lost consciousness. Dinar prepared the poultice as he had been instructed, and slathered it thickly on the shaft of the arrow. After a deep breath and a watery grin, he slowly pushed the arrow through, and as far as possible into Vorguld's belly. He then slowly pulled the arrow from Vorguld's back.

If Vorguld died, Dinar would be alone with eight boys and Swike Direoll, who, though awake, slurred his speech and had staggered to his left in his one attempt to walk. Even if Vorguld survived, which could only be a miracle, the prospect of he and the boys facing the Lords, even with crossbows, would be taking on odds of the most ridiculous proportions. And the penalty for failure would be most hideous.

With or without Dinar's help, if Vorguld were to die in the night, the Swike would have the opportunity to return to the Lords and report that he had, through gulle, uncovered Vorguld's plot and hideout. After mid morning he would not be able to explain why he had waited. He bandaged Vorguld's wound both front and back but remained deep in thought about what glory—or disaster—might result, and what course of action he might dare to take.

Chapter 19
To Heal and To Travel

Jolar and Leason expectantly awaited Jessyl's decision. Their inability to bend him to their will as they had the Ranger was a surprise though not all was in vain: they had learned of a lake.

Jolar spoke: "You need rest and healing, Prince Jessyl. Leason let me propose this to you as well as to our friends. We ride tonight to the lands of the Sybils. You ride with me, Jessyl. A week's rest I promise in this one night. I will sing songs of healing and describe for you our homeland. In the early morning, before dawn, we will ride to your Father's Keep. It may be that from the Sybils we will find what weakens him. A cure is not too much to be hoped for. Guide us to the Sybils."

Jessyl looked at Ennar who, after a time, spoke. "You are weakened. More than you know. If a week's rest may be had on a horse, it may be had here, by the fire. What good will come if you are worn away to nothing?"

Jessyl considered Ennar's words.

"A hope is strong within me that The Sybil has the means to bring my father back to health. I ask myself often, why would they send Kalla unless there was hope?"

He turned to Jolar: "I will hold you to your promise of 'A week's rest'."

"I'll have you as full of life as a young ram in spring. Come, I'll treat your wound."

Jessyl looked at Ennar, Leason, and, lastly, Jolar, and said with firmness, "We must be at my Father's Keep shortly after dawn for the morning meeting with the Lords."

Each nodded in agreement. Jolar spoke: "All are agreed. Gelt, build up the fire. Boil water. Quick, men. Move. Be about your business."

Leason walked towards the west dune where Jolar had first waved to Jessyl and Ennar.

"I'll see to the sails," he said.

Ennar had been watering the horses frequently but sparingly, as his father, in what now seemed ages ago, had instructed. When he finished, he looked toward the two sitting by the fire and saw that Jolar was washing Jessyl's wound. Gelt sat in the light of the fire with his eyes closed. Ennar hurriedly followed Leason's path up the dune. Leason stood scanning the western horizon.

Leason saw the young man and called to him. "Stand with your back to mine. Scan half the horizon and a bit more." They looked for some minutes. "There is much you need to know, Ennar. If you saw riders approaching, you would tell me. But we would continue our scan. Why?"

"The riders we know of are less a worry than the ones we have yet to see?" Ennar answered.

"Yes," Leason replied.

He turned, and Ennar turned to face him. "When you first arrived, Jolar led you to the top of this dune. It was wise of you to stand where the sun would be in his eyes. He expected you to do so. But I was behind you, though I made no shadow for you to see. Had I been you, I would have watched the west, your partner scanning the east as he spoke with Jolar. "'Where is the second man?' would have been my question."

He waited and watched Ennar. "One mistake and this lifetime could be over in a snap. You need to learn—and quickly, from what I piece together."

Ennar nodded in agreement. "Yes," he said looking into Leason's eyes as though he had met a friend from a long forgotten life.

"When Jessyl spoke with Jolar, your horse was too close to his. Even if you knew how to use your sword, to draw it would have disturbed the horses. We knew you to be ill-trained and relatively harmless. You are a young man who wants to learn. Do not waste time feeling bad about what you don't know. Watch and learn."

They had been scanning the dunes as Leason spoke. "Do you see any movement?"

"None," Ennar replied.

"Nor do I. The meal was good. Nearly a moon has passed since we tasted bread."

They looked down to see Jolar gently slathering a paste on Jessyl's wound. He was humming a soothing chant. Gelt was asleep on the sand.

"Your friend will be much improved when we reach the Sybils. And even more improved by morning. Let us gather what water has collected on the undersides of the sails and pack them for the journey.

Chapter 20
Kalla's Return

Kalla rode with abandon across the moonlit countryside fiercely clutching the mane of her horse the newly christened Merlieo. With a wild grin on her blue face and her slanted eyes nearly shut against the rushing wind, she rode holding her left arm outstretched parallel to the earth, her hand cutting through the night air much like a bird's wing.

"Time, Time, Time!" she shrieked. To a macabre tune, she sang: "Time to rid the world of the ugly slugs, the ugly thugs of Harnell."

When she reached the entry of the ravine, she reined the horse to a halt and shouted: "Watchers! It is I, Sybil Kalla the Magnificent, riding Merlieo the Magnificent. Merlieo has been recently liberated from the Lords of Harnell. We are at war with them. Allow us to pass."

"Forward, Merly."

She nudged the horse ahead with pressure from both her heels.

"No rocks will rattle down on our heads..."

Once through the ravine, she again rode recklessly, shouting: "Awake, awake all; all awake. We are at war!"

The frothing herd of horses thundered after her.

She pulled Merly to a halt at the doorstep of her home. The horses milled about at the side of the building; the Sybil placed her horse between them and the gathering crowd. She sat stroking her horse's neck, waiting for her sisters to appear.

Ursha stepped out of the house and stood on the stoop, holding a smoking pipe with the long stem clenched between her yellowed teeth. She, and Pura who stood beside her, looked up at their sister.

"None of this looks good," Ursha half whispered.

Pura whispered in response, "Hardly what we had in mind when we sent her off with the boy one night ago."

Women and girls of all ages and descriptions continued to gather. All wore the same type of sand-colored blanket and swaddle as Kalla. Young girls of three or four summers stood sucking their chapped thumbs, often holding the hand of an older woman. Older girls and young women, their hair braided or tied in outlandish tails, gathered in groups of their own. The older women wore a uniform hairstyle: parted down the middle and hanging long at the sides and back.

Kalla, eyes sparkling in the moonlight, looked disdainfully from the height of her horse at her sisters and continued to stroke Merly's neck.

"Wondrous Time!" she shouted as she waited for the crowd to quiet. "Wondrous Time affords us a great opportunity. The Lords and their Swikes are blinded. Their horses have followed me home. The 'lards' are afoot, larded down with lard and armor."

She laughed riotously.

"Who among you would like to ride a horse? Mother Kalla will teach you. Gather closer. Come, hurry and hear me, you stragglers."

She glanced disdainfully at her sisters.

Ursha shook her head from side to side.

"She has found wine," Pura said.

"An opportunity. A great opportunity," Kalla continued in her exuberance. "An opportunity is presented to us. A 'present,' one might say."

She giggled, and then sobered and returned to her theme: "Two hundred years after the end of the Long War, now, and at this very moment, Mother Time takes us by the hand and promises us a rich green and golden world. Will we dig our heels deep into the dust and rubble of the past to be dragged forward sniveling and stubbing our toes? Or will our duty and our valor pull us forward, in step with Mother Time's wishes?"

All the gathering remained silent trying to understand what she had said.

"I have come from the Fortress of Gemar of Harnell. A king...of men."

She spat in the dust behind her.

"He is weak and soon to die. I, Kalla, Sybil of Light, offered The Teaching of The Sybil...yes to him, a man. And with what result? He laughed at my gift. Can you imagine? He, in his dying days, laughed at my gift. How like a man. They are foolish all."

"And the Lords: the monsters who ordered you as babes to be left in the scrub to die; monsters who will use a suffering baby as bait to trap you for their sport; these monsters who may have been your fathers: what of them?"

She stared piercingly at the crowd.

"I blinded them," she cackled heinously. "Oh they will see again. But they may be blinded again as I choose. And I took this horse, Merly, from them...Merly named after a fond friend of mine...but I digress."

She licked her lips and began again. "Vorguld: you know of him. He lies groaning on the floor of the King's Keep, a crossbow arrow stuck in his gut. It could have stuck him lower—and to the center if you ken my meaning."

The crowd chuckled for the first time as they understood what she meant.

"He lies as I left him, dying or mayhap dead by now. He will not live. The putrid juices of his gut seep into his vitals.

"Since when has there been such a day? Need I tell you what all this means?" She looked about the crowd.

"Ripe!" she shouted. "They are ripe for the pricking of our arrows."

Some in the crowd hooted and crowed.

"Have you heard the story of their armor? Of course not! For I discovered it and have not told you of it as of yet.

Well, guess and be amazed. The idiots have made some changes to their armor. An arrow from one of you—you, young lady," she pointed to a young girl. "Are you deft with the bow? An arrow from the bow of this girl of eight summers will send them to the fires of Yama."

Many in the crowd murmured approval.

"You women gathered before me, Mother Time is with us. In a short time, well before Sur's first light, I will ride bathed in Chandra's Moonlight. I will ride to be with the Lords at dawn: to wake them and to then put them to sleep...forever. Where are the best of the archers? Who of you will ride a horse?"

Ursha scoffed. "At dawn the wine that fires your blood will be cooled. You will hold you head and groan and wretch."

Pura spoke: "What a great risk you propose, Kalla. The Lords do not bother us here in our keep. And your head is held together with stitches! "

Kalla spit back vehemently: "Not bothered us since nearly one hundred years ago when we stoned them as they tried to enter. Two of their heads we set on pikes at the entrance. They have not paid us a visit since, nor will they. But if they are able to trap us outside our ravine, what then?"

Many in the gathering groaned a sound showed rage was soon to follow.

"And what of the women of Harnell? In the dark of night they are taken; many of you are children sprung from such nights. And many of you have been taken as you sought to rescue a dying, innocent babe."

Many of the women shouted hatred into the night air.

Expending more of her strength, Kalla focused her violent energy on the crowd: "Women of the Lake, Mother Time cast this day's turnings ages ago. She demands we act. I will ride before dawn. We will rid the earth of these lards.

The crowd cheered.

"Drink a full sack of water and you will awake on time to ride with me."

She laughed and the crowd cheered and hooted in response to her humor.

"Meet here when the moon reaches the mountain-tops in the west. Bring your bows and as many arrows as you have. I promise you we will use the Lord's fat rumps as footstools while we feast at their rich tables tomorrow midday."

Pura spoke: "And if you could slaughter every one of them, would their corpses be the building blocks of a new world?"

Ursha spoke: "You speak as warring men spoke prior to the Founding Edicts. This insanity you speak is no way to build a new world."

Ursha continued the barrage: "You are besotted, Kalla. You wish for The Sybil to rule the Earth. Those days are gone for now. You know your wish to be a foolish hope."

Pura continued without room for a response: "There is no more wine, Kalla. Now you are again on your own. You will be on your own for a long time. Come, rest."

Kalla jeered at them: "Damn the wine! And yes to your damned question. The Sybil shall rule. This time the Sybil and our daughters shall again rule Mother Earth. I will have my way!" she shrieked.

In a low hiss, she continued, though a tiredness had crept into her voice. "This time I will have my way. You will not sway me as you two, together, have so often done throughout the past. At dawn I will ride against the Lords. I will have my way."

Ursha blew warm smoke across her dry lips and stared at Kalla with large, unwavering eyes.

"Come, dear Kalla. Talk with your sisters. Talk and tea. And rest. Come, dear Kalla."

Pura spoke also in a cajoling voice as though soothing a child: "What have you done, foolish sister? Drunk, you have offered our teaching to a man? A man who would not beg to be blessed? What have you done? Come, talk with your sisters."

Ursha spoke kindly also: "Come, dear Kalla. Tea and talk and rest. Come with your loving sisters."

As Ursha continued to comfort Kalla, Pura ordered that the horses to be walked but not given water until they had cooled from their run.

Beset by exhaustion and aching in every bone Kalla slumped forward her eyes dull with fatigue. Ursha reached up and took her sister's hand to keep her from falling. The spent Sybil slid off Merly and stumbled along between her sisters towards their house.

Chapter 21
Dreams and Darkness

As the five men rode towards the Valley of The Sybil, Jessyl fell into a deep sleep. He rode with his arms wrapped around Jolar, his entire body filled with the energy of healing. The skin around his wound was warm; his forehead and scalp tingled with life. Jolar's songs and chants conjured dreams as real as life itself.

Above the shores of a dark blue lake, stone houses, ornate with turrets and trim, carved from mountainsides that rose up to, and into, impossible billowing cloud gleaming brilliant in the sunlight. Among the buildings, gardens and greenery sparkled on this west side of the lake, appearing as though the scene had grown from, and belonged to, the earth. To the north of the lake a mountainside patterned with orchards and fields baked and glistened gold and green in the noon sun. All the land was crowded with livestock and grain fields and orchards.

A wave of doubt flooded through Jessyl's mind. *Only a dream*, he thought, but then with a wave of pleasure he returned to this shining land of his dreams.

Gaily painted sculls the color of silver slid across the surface of the dark blue lake. Paddlers straining, their sweating bodies gleaming in the sun, propelled long, slim boats, each with a portrait of a gleefully smiling animal painted along its sides. Spectators cheered from balconies and rooftops and shoreline.

Winter flashed through Jessyl's dreams.

Ice sleighs, their colored sails filled with cold wind, hissed across slate blue ice. The force of the wind tipped the lead sleigh onto one runner. A crewman—a woman, to Jessyl's amazement—leaped onto the raised runner and stood bobbing her weight up and down. Her hands were stretched tight above her head, her chest and shoulders straining on a line attached to the mast top. Shards of ice sparkling like jewels flew from the straining running blades as the sleigh was forced back into balance.

Dreams of celebration and carnival festivities filled Jessyl with delight.

A clown, face painted scarlet, swathed in a costume of white and gold, waved and peered at him, pointing with a scarlet finger, the tip adorned with a tiny devil's face that, as Jessyl focused on it, became as large as the moon. From one of the stone balconies a woman with rouged cheeks and a moist grin rolled her hips at Jessyl as her distracted husband shouted cheers to the revelers.

Jessyl awoke. Immediately, he missed the dreams. "Was that your homeland, Jolar? The lake and the stone houses?"

"Yes, that is the homeland our people have built during the last two hundred years. From the sound of your voice, you have had a good rest. You are somewhat healed?"

"I feel as though fresh life courses through my body. My wound is warm. What wonderful dreams. They are better than life. Thank you, Jolar."

"You are most welcome, Jessyl," Jolar replied and then asked, "In your youth, what did you study?"

"Study?" Jessyl asked, jarred awake by the question.

"Yes. But excuse me: it must sound an odd question, you having just come from your dreams. Let me ask it another time."

"No. I will talk with you of my youth. We have some hours ahead of us." Jessyl rubbed a finger gently beneath each eye. "The Healer Kindeen has taught me something of his arts: the stars, and herb lore, and healing. But of much more use to me, I have sat by my father all the years since I have been able to sit. I have followed his speech and judgments with great care. And as the Edicts require, I have mastered the crossbow. How to repair the bow and how to use the bow with great accuracy. And, too, I have learned how to construct a bow and the arrows it requires."

Jolar replied, "It doesn't surprise me that you have sat and listened to your father's judgments all these years. I knew at our first meeting that you are facile and considered in speech. Tell me, though, of your education. Is there mention of The Seven Pillars of Self? Means of Governing? Strategies for Negotiation and Consensus?"

Jessyl's voice hardened, though he did not wish to show it.

"What you speak of I have learned, no doubt, at the side of my father. As he learned from his father. Both ruled our land well. I will rule as they have."

"Forgive me, Jessyl. Leason chides me for being too much the teacher. He is correct: it pours out of me whether the listener wants to hear it or not."

Jessyl relaxed again.

"I believe you will be a great king. Your father has taught you well, no doubt, though you may face different challenges than those faced by your father or his father."

Jessyl began to speak, but Jolar interrupted.

"I was foolish to speak of such things at this time. Tonight, your rest and your health are important. Rest and I will sing."

"The peace of the dreams calls strongly to me, Jolar."

The mountains ahead were warmly blanketed with moonlight and Jessyl pointed to them. "The mountains appear small. They will look much larger before we reach them." He shook his head in disgust at his mistake. "Though, of course, you know this."

Jessyl shook his head and silently berated himself for his stupidity, and then thought it best to resume the conversation with Jolar. "Let us speak for a while regarding your question."

Jolar nodded. "As you wish."

"I will tell you what life has pounded into my thick head again and again. A king, though surrounded by many, is alone. I am alone, Jolar, and for me to expect help is weakness. That is what I have been taught, and in more way than just words. I am alone. It is a lesson writ large in the story of my life."

"Teaching pours from me, and kingship pours from you. It is difficult for the leopard, whatever that was, to change its spots. If you wish, when you are healed and rested, and leisure allows, ask me and I will recite for you The Seven Pillars of Self. I believe you will find much of that recitation will speak to this idea that you are alone. But for tonight, let us leave this discussion. I promised you rest and healing. Return to your dreams, Prince Jessyl, and heal. That is what is important, not my need to be the wise teacher."

Jolar began to hum. Jessyl closed his eyes and waited for the dreams to begin.

Dogs bayed from deep in the high mountain scrub. Crashing rattles the bushes. Jessyl holds a spear, his fingers sweating.

"Hold...hold...hold," his father says.

The brush parts. A deer, full antlered, proud eyes flashing, is in mid stride, his front legs extended to accept impact with the earth. As his hooves are about to touch, Jessyl's father shouts, "Now!"

The boy hesitates for the briefest of moments as the stag's front hooves bite into the earth. With an effortless change of direction, the deer floats to the right, and Jessyl's spear floats through the empty space where the stag had been. A wave of sadness floods boy's heart.

The scene disappears and another begins.

His mother is with him. He is young. Five or six summers old. There is water, cool and contained in a pool lined with dark stones. Queen Elearim, glorious and loving, speaks to him. What does she say?

"You must remember what you have found today."
Remember what?

"No matter what happens, remember what you have found. What you have found is the greatest of all treasures."

A terrifying darkness rapidly filled the Prince's mind and swallowed his consciousness. At first Darkness and then not even the awareness of darkness engulfed him.

Chapter 22
Late Night Guests

"We will rid the Earth of them," Kalla muttered.

Ursha and Pura entered their home Kalla's arms draped over their shoulders, her body relying on them for support. Directing her towards a chair, they released her with a gentle push. As she staggered across the room, she held an unsteady hand in front of her, as though performing a balancing act. When she reached the chair, she grabbed the arm of it and slumped thankfully into her seat. Ursha, pipe in hand, had walked behind Kalla to catch her if she fell and seated herself, her hand touching Kalla's arm. Pura prepared tea.

"Their armor, oh, the fools. A hit at the top...and the arrow...into the meat...of the neck—ha! Their horses have followed me here. Did I tell you that? Fat men without horses—ha!"

She cackled weakly and then her head drooped to one side. She stared blankly at the floor.

Pura retrieved a smooth oval stone from the coals of the hearth and dropped it into the leather teapot. "Yes, you told us about the horses. They are now being walked to cool them down. What insanity possessed you to run them so hard in the cool of the night? You might have killed them all. And what will we feed them? Have you thought of that? You were not thinking about the well-being of those horses, Sybil Kalla."

Ursha took up the assault, speaking as though Kalla was not present.

"It is true that Kalla, of the three of us, was most in need of this assignment...the least likely to succeed, but the most in need. She has failed miserably."

Pura whispered to her sister: "Look at her. She will not stay awake for tea."

Kalla's head had slumped forward; her eyes were closed.

"Let us be gentle, dear Ursha. She is asleep now."

"Gentle! What has she done? Drunk and offering The Teaching! Only to be refused. What an affront to The Great Mother!"

"The Great Mother will somehow survive. She has seen far worse."

"What a time we live in—Divine Mother is nearly as frail as she has ever been—and now another slap in the face."

"Life's grace increases this night, tomorrow, and for years to come. All will change."

"Let us hope. And what has Kalla said to the Lords?"

Ursha placed the tea flask and two cups on the table. "Let us drag Sybil Wineskin off to her bed—not for the first time and probably not the last."

Briefly Kalla resisted, but soon, with the help of her sisters, she shuffled along to her room.

"At least we have her here with us where she may do little harm," Pura whispered as they lay her on her bed.

"She looks grim. Look at her face: it is as though she is already in a land of black dreams," Ursha chuckled quietly.

The sisters returned to their tea.

"A stranger day I have not seen," Pura said as she sipped tea. "The horses, when released, will return to their masters. The Lords will not attack us fortified as we are."

Ursha replied, "The horses will return to their food is more likely what you mean. I am sure they would be happy to be far from the Lords. And yes, the Lords would be fools to attack us. They would not survive the tons of rocks guarding our ravine."

Pura remained silent, thoughtfully sipping her tea.

"Kalla must have been mad with wine, no doubt about that. Nonetheless, the Lords without horses are a novel twist in the order of things."

Ursha knew that each sister could have insights that at first might seem outlandish to the other two. Over their two centuries together, they had learned to listen respectfully to one another's counsel.

After a time, she questioned, "Surely we have no feed for horses?"

"No, not for any great length of time. But for some time, yes. We might keep them long enough to cause the Lords discomfort."

"But we have no food for them, Pura."

"We could water them. Their coats are glossy; they are well fed. They could be taken outside the ravine to graze on the scrub, though we could not feed them long. I wonder what might unfold from this?"

Ursha, after some thought, replied, "What would become of the Lords without horses? How comic to picture them waddling about, sweat rolling off them by the bucket, shouting orders to anyone they were lucky enough to be able to catch up to."

She laughed quietly and was then lost in thought for a moment. "But to risk the wrath of the Lords without our thorough consideration would not be wise."

Pura replied, "Let us take rest. An answer will come during sleep."

"And we get to drag our besotted sister out of bed before first light," Ursha chortled somewhat gleefully and yet somewhat ruefully.

⚜

Jessyl awoke to hear Ennar calling his name.

"We are at the entrance to the Ravine."

Vaguely they heard Jolar laugh from a distance: "This coming night of tea and blather will likely be tough on bladders."

Ennar continued: "As you advised us, the ravine was not difficult to find. Jolar and Leason and Gelt are watering the scrub."

Jessyl shouted with vigor, "Guards of the Ravine! Prince Jessyl and four companions seek safe passage to speak with The Sybil."

"We announced ourselves, a while ago, as you slept," Ennar, with reservation, informed his friend.

Jessyl spat with disgust, "What an idiot. What is wrong with me?"

"How could you know?" Ennar replied.

"I could have asked!" Jessyl snapped.

The three others returned.

"Come with me, Jessyl. Let us choose a most fortunate shrub and give it a royal watering...more water than it gets in a year.

Jessyl and Ennar jogged off into the scrub.

As the women swallowed the last of their tea and rose for bed, three quiet raps were heard at the door.

"Don't break the door down!" Ursha snapped. "Enter."

Mula entered and stammered, "Jesthya sent me."

"Speak up," Ursha interrupted.

"Five men on three horses ask for an audience with The Sybil."

"Fifteen men?" Ursha snapped. "More than enough even for you, Mula."

"Three men. I mean five men. Prince Jessyl is one of them."

"And the others?" Pura asked.

"A Ranger sits tied to his horse. And tall, black-skinned men ride with Jessyl and his companion."

"Tall, are they?" Ursha mocked with a glint in her eye. "Two black-skinned men riding on one horse, or one black-skinned man riding Jessyl; the other riding who knows who? Is this the best you can do, Mula?"

Pura interjected: "Please, Ursha. Mula, tell them they have safe passage."

"The Ranger is securely tied?" Ursha questioned.

"Yes, well tied, Mother Ursha."

"Blindfold him. Make him walk. Check that he is tightly bound."

"Yes, Mother Ursha. One of the black men asks that someone guide them through the ravine. 'To keep an eye for falling stones,' he said."

"And arrows too, I suppose," Ursha ridiculed. "Tell him I walked through the ravine this morning. It is safe."

Pura intervened again.

"I will walk with them and guarantee their safe passage. Go, tell them. I will not keep them waiting long. Go."

Mula left in haste, though there was no reason to hurry other than to avoid Ursha's sharp tongue.

Ursha looked at her sister. "Tell the guard to keep their bows ready. Black men, the beanstalk prince and a companion, and a Ranger trussed, I bet, like a venison roast. Yes, my sister, most interesting are the events during this turning of the Earth. No doubt the next hours will be equally interesting. Leave the Ranger under Mula's guard. Have Jesthya and one of her strongest be with us. Four on four if trouble begins."

"More tea, dear Ursha, and they will be hungry."

Pura, too, left hastily for the ravine.

❧

When Jessyl and Ennar returned, a guard of the ravine stood holding a bow. It was Muley, her hand held in a peaceful gesture.

"Sybil Pura will walk through the ravine with you. She will meet you shortly."

Jesthya stepped out of the shadows, her bow in one hand, the other held in a gesture of peace.

"There is no need to wait for Sybil Pura. I am Jesthya, leader of the guard. I will walk with you."

She had looked at each of them fleetingly but piercingly as she spoke. Lastly, she focused intently on Gelt, looking first at his face and long thick hair, and then deep into his eyes.

"No Ranger has visited us willingly. You will remain se-curely tied. Mula, check his bindings and watch over him."

She looked at Jessyl.

"And you, Prince Jessyl, was your desire to see us so strong that you had to fight your way here?"

Jessyl replied, "Jesthya, daughter of Sybil Pura, your kind words and this gracious welcome is much preferred over your last greeting of me. Sybil Kalla is with my father. I must report on her. And my companions," he motioned to the Windriders, "Jolar of the House of Geldof, and Leason of the House of Sarandon, wish to speak with The Sybil. For my part, I would be with my father."

"You would be safe with your father," she mocked. "Sybil Kalla is with her sisters. She returned full of wine, rid-ing a horse stolen from the Lords, a gash on the side of her head bristling with stitches...similar to those you sport. Come, The Sybil wishes to speak with you. No rocks will fall on your heads. You and your companions will have safe passage through the ravine. Beyond the ravine I hold little sway over what happens in this land."

They rode in silence. Jessyl puzzled over his last dreams and the blackness.

He spoke to Jolar.

"Very different were the dreams I had during the last part of our journey, and then a blackness—nothing."

Leason interrupted: "Be alert."

They continued to ride in silence, the rock walls tower-ing above them, shutting out all but a little moonlight.

Once through, Jesthya instructed them to follow the path. "The moon lights the path to the House of The Sybil. Sybil Pura will meet you as she has agreed."

She stepped back quickly out of the moonlight and into the shadow of the wall.

They were left alone in silence but for the sound of the horses' hooves clip clopping on the stones. From time to time the riders caught glimpses of moonlight rippling wildly on the water of a dark lake.

"Eh, Gelt, we shall mind our manners with archers like her in the shadows," Leason cautioned as he quietly slipped off his horse. "Look up, Gelt. A brace is loosened, and we have a cart load of rocks in our laps. A good thing for you to know, should you ever get out of this valley alive."

"Little wonder they are secure these last two hundred years," Jolar added.

"Welcome to the Land of the Lake," they heard from a figure dimmed to the darkness of a shadow. "Thank you, Jesthya, for guiding our guests through the ravine. You and Mula and the Ranger please join us. Though caution your guards to be on watch and not chattering and giggling like excited girls."

"My watch does not chatter and giggle, Mother Pura. Have you been followed, Prince Jessyl?"

"I doubt we are followed."

He looked at Leason and Jolar.

Jolar spoke. "If your watch does not chatter or giggle, and a general with a well-trained army will not enter unless invited, then why chatter on about us being followed?"

Jesthya did not respond.

"Good," Pura spoke as Jesthya quickly stepped into the shadows. "Again, I wish you welcome to our land. It is not often we have guests. Seldom have men visited us willingly during these last two hundred years. My one sister and I are anxious to speak with you. Our other sister is fast asleep, worn out from a recent journey. Follow me: Ursha is brewing tea and preparing food."

"Though we are awake much later than usual, we are most keen to speak with you," she said. She turned and walked forward along the moonlit path.

Chapter 23
Ursha's Rant

Sybil Ursha, a pipe stem clenched between her teeth, the orange glow of an ember in the pipe's bowl illuminating her face, greeted the travelers with piercing looks and a wide smile. Jessyl had met her briefly the night before, but now he studied her shrunken face.

She looks not at all like Kalla, he thought. *Widely spaced eyes, sunken cheeks. Pray she is not mad like her sister. She looks ill.*

"A warm welcome to you, Prince Jessyl, and welcome to your friends."

Jessyl introduced the Windriders and then his companion Ennar.

"Come, down from your horses. Jesthya and Mula will protect the Ranger as we talk. He will do well to make himself unnoticed and to stay quiet. He has no friends among us. Come in, come in. We are pleased to have you four as our guests."

Pura entered the home and Ursha, holding the door open, bade them follow. They were directed to a table set for six. A women with shining gray hair and the warmth of silence about her, poured tea.

"We have long wished to meet souls from other lands," Ursha said as she motioned for the gray-haired woman to serve tea to those outside.

Jessyl, who had squirmed throughout the formalities, arose at this opportunity and spoke.

"Once we begin our questions and tales, I am certain we will talk until the first light of morning. Sybil Kalla has returned safely, without my assistance. I asked my father to permit her to stay until I might travel with her. I hoped also that in the time she spent with my father, she might be of some use...in regards to my father's health. I doubt that her return bodes well."

Pura replied quickly, "Kalla left your Father's Keep of her free will, and she has returned safely."

"Safely returned by her own devices," Ursha added. "Let us be frank, Pura."

She turned to Jessyl, "Kalla, as you may have heard, Prince Jessyl, has declared war on the Lords. She has returned with their horses."

"Though this news is of great interest to me, first we must speak of the well-being of my father," Jessyl interrupted. "My mother sent me to you, hoping that The Sybil would cure his illness."

Again Pura responded quickly before her sister could speak: "The cure your father requires would be a challenge were he in the prime of health. Even when first afflicted, great health and great focus are required to rid oneself of such a burden as he carries."

Ursha added: "We knew of his demon before we sent Kalla to your father. There is only one means to destroy this creature."

"You knew of this demon before Kalla came to us? How can this be taken well? Kalla was of no use to us. She drank herself to drunkenness and blathered on about time."

Ursha sat silently controlling her anger while Pura, without waiting for Jessyl to finish, responded, "We suspected from your mother's messages that your father's illness was not usual. We could give you half truths, Prince Jessyl, but you will see your father soon and know the whole truth. Do not think ill of us. Though Kalla fell to her weakness, what she has done is as it is."

"My mother asked for your aid. My father is dying. I risked my life more than once for your sister, and you tell me that 'what is done is as it is'? Father and Grandfather warned me of Sybils."

Ursha stood and glared across the table at Jessyl.

"Our sister offered a cure. The only cure. Your father laughed in her face. If he lies yet stricken, how is this anything to do with us?"

She pointed one of her long finger across the table at the Prince.

"You need to understand the history of the world, young Prince. And you are in my house, and you will listen! The tragedy of the last three thousand years may be summed up in one word: men. Men refused our teachings. Worse yet, they bent the little they understood of it to their uses. You will listen. The wars began because a few fragments of our teaching were misused and the remainder ignored."

Ursha looked at her sister's worried face and then began her assault anew.

"'First we must speak of the well being of my father...,'" she mimicked. "I will decide what will be discussed under my roof."

She turned to her sister.

"The time to speak the truth is now, Pura. The Sybil is blamed for the Long War. Nonsense!" she thundered. "I see you chafe at my words, young Prince. Your companions may know the truth, having grown up in a place other than Harnell. Listen and I will tell you how the wars began.

"First, I will tell you what is more important than any tale you will ever hear from your father. If you are able to understand this lesson, you could cure him. Listen and learn how to cure your father.

She closed her eyes to gather her thoughts.

"Listen and hear the story of life.

"On a sunny day in early summer you come upon the first of the ripe berries. You crush a berry on your tongue. Your mouth is flooded with taste—sweet, tart, or bitter—no matter. Taste overwhelms you." she laughed. "What an odd expression."

"In that moment nothing but that taste exists. Then it evaporates: the taste gone. What remains? The answer to this question, if you catch the ken of it, will cure your Father. Do you understand?"

Jessyl stared at her blankly, his lungs about to burst from the wrath building up within him.

"Then listen again. One feels joy, or pain, or sorrow, or any of the inestimable number of feelings we humans are blessed to feel. First we feel: we are overwhelmed. Then the feeling, as we say, 'goes away'. What remains?"

She waited momentarily and then spoke each word with force. "What remains will cure your father: what remains will heal the Earth. Do you understand?

Jessyl was breathing normally again and had somehow relaxed. Interested in any chance to heal his father he had listened intently but none of what the Sybil said made any sense to him.

Ursha continued unconcerned with her audience. "I will tell you what men did with our teachings in the centuries before the wars." She spoke rapidly and as though by rote. "Some men vaguely understood what I have said in regards to the emotions. And fear became their focus. Not any of the exalted emotions—oh no, of course not. Not joy, or happiness. Why focus on them when fear is so readily available? Stand on a cliff top high above water. Yes, there was water in those times—water enough to make our lake look a pittance. Stand on a cliff top and feel the fear. Then jump. And what happens to the fear? The fear evaporates. And what remains?

"The words, 'No Fear,' came to be chanted throughout the kingdoms. It swept through the world of men and infected them like a plague. All other emotions were forgotten or at best became secondary to this rush and release of fear.

"All manner of sport was crafted in order to feel this most inferior of all the emotions. Competition to see who could perform the more terrifying stunt abounded. And what, let me ask, churns the guts of men more than a competition? What is the ultimate competition?"

She smiled, knowing that her question would not be answered.

"You know the answer, boy. What churns the guts most? It is the drums of battle. The drums of battle and battle itself. No Fear! No Fear!" Ursha shook her head from side to side in disgust.

"And as darkness overshadowed the brightness and bliss of Life, this was what was left of our knowledge in the world of men. Of our entire, precious knowledge all else was rejected and quickly forgotten. And though men were full of fear and trembled even as they slept, all that could shake them from their drink and whoring and beef fed stupor was their silly chant, 'No Fear'.

"Tell that story to your father and his Lords, young Prince."

She spat the word Prince.

"Tell him that the past wars are the wars of men, not the wars of The Sybil. Tell him that he is blessed with the affliction that he carries in order that he may choose to go within himself to heal. Let this be your history lesson. This is how the world has been since before the Everlasting War. Since the time when The Sybil ceased to rule Earth. You have not heard anything of this from your father or grandfather, I'm sure. Yes, Sybils ruled the world and there was peace until the darkness of Time began its reign. She looked at each of the four men. "The swords and anger and quick solutions of men will never be a salve for the complexities of Life."

She had wound down and Pura finally interceded: "Good Prince, you have heard a true history of the last ages: all else is false. I beg you to ask your father to speak with me. I will go to him. Do not blame us for his misfortune. Now, of all times, is not a time for rash decisions."

"And why were you not sent to him in the first place, Sybil Pura?" Jessyl said, looking hard at her. But she did not answer.

"This meeting, for my part, is over. Today I have heard all the talk I wish to hear about this opportunity given to us by your Mother Time, and the goodness of all Sybils. And I have heard of the theft of the Lord's horses. I tell you now, and clearly, that I prefer the world as it is, rather than to have you Sybils ruling. This oration I have had to suffer through, I have been warned of since I could speak. I care little for what you call the Opportunity of Time or your rant about men long vanished from the earth. My concern is with my father. I leave you now to go to him. If you attack the Lords, the King and I will stand with the Lords and against you."

With that said, he turned and stormed out of the home of the Sybils.

As he left the table, Ursha began shouting at him, but Pura moved quickly to her sister and begged her to be silent.

Ennar followed Jessyl. As they mounted their horses, Jolar and Leason joined them and spoke.

"We will be at your Father's Keep shortly after sunrise. There is much you may choose to do before you choose to fight."

Leason added to this as he spoke to Ennar: "The Sybils ask that you leave the Ranger. Do you trust him?"

"Not in the least," Ennar replied. "Nor them."

"Nor them," Jessyl echoed. "I will not leave the Ranger. What do I say to my father and the Lords?" He mimicked the voice of a young boy: "'I took the Ranger to them but they commanded me to return without him!'"

He spat in disgust.

"They must be fools to think that I would leave the Ranger. Tell them this, Jolar, or I will tell them."

Chapter 24
A Chalk Drawing of a Spiral Galaxy

Jolar and Leason returned to the house. The two Sybils waited for them at the door, Ursha pacing back and forth behind her sister.

"As you understand, Prince Jessyl must have the Ranger," Leason said.

Ursha grimaced and was about to speak, but Pura quickly interjected: "Yes, he must have the Ranger."

She turned and looked at her sister and said: "He is of no use to us."

Begrudgingly, Ursha shouted to Jesthya, "Jesthya, release the Ranger to the boys! Make certain he remains bound as long as he is within our valley."

As the four returned to the table, Leason angrily shuffled his chair before he sat. He spoke with disapproval in his voice and looked directly at Ursha. "So they are now referred to as 'the boys.'"

Jolar interrupted before Ursha could answer. "May the time we four have together be fruitful," he said.

Pura spoke directly to Jolar, leaving the other two out of the conversation: "It is most important that the time we have together be fruitful." As she said this, she looked first to Leason and then to her sister, whom she affixed with a steady stare.

Jolar now sat down and said with solemnity, "Our time together is not, of course, an accident—but an opportunity. Our Mothers have told us that Time is again with us.

That men—that is, humankind," he said looking at Ursha, "will greatly increase in numbers and prosper once again. Prince Jessyl tells us that your sister Kalla announced the same prophesy to the King. You Sybils, we surmise, also keep the history of time alive. We wish very much to hear what you foresee."

"We foresee many challenges," Ursha laughed, recognizing the importance of their meeting and hoping to relieve the tension in the room. "Prince Jessyl may be one of these challenges. I see some hope for him, though he is clearly a young man who has been brought up to be a king."

"From where I sat, you prodded him mercilessly," Leason replied in Jessyl's defense.

"I thought it necessary," Ursha snapped. "He, as anyone, must cool his blood if he is to speak with The Sybil. And he should know that much of our work is far more important than his dying father. And, too, he must learn that there is no other cure for his father than the one we have graciously offered."

Pura added immediately, "We wish for King Gemar to live."

Jolar continued to sway the conversation to the subject of the prophesy.

"We have helped these young men, but that is not the purpose of our travels. Our Mothers sent us with the hope that we would return with knowledge useful to our people— that we might awaken those we met from, let us say, their slumber. We have no wish to fight a war. We wish to speak of what may be accomplished for the good of all."

Pura spoke: "We believe that you are well intended. We too are curious about what you know. Tell us, as your Mothers have asked you to do, what you know of these coming times."

"What I know of Time makes for a small story," Jolar replied. "Passed down through generations by our Mothers, and their Mothers before them, is what remains of the teachings of the Sybils of the Great Light. We are told that after the end of the Everlasting War—and then after two hundred years—mankind would begin to again flourish. Mankind, it is said, given the history of the last centuries, will doubt that change—more accurately, that progress— is possible. It is essential that all of us who remain recognize what is happening and work with Time. If we drag our feet the world will be a sorry bit of what it might have been."

"It is amazing to me that your Mothers have kept this knowledge all through the centuries. Our warm congratulations to them," Pura said.

Leason, whose long silence had shown little indication that he was interested in the conversation, spoke.

"Of what I can gather you believe that men are puppets of Mother Time."

Jolar interrupted quickly: "Though our Mothers speak of cycles of time, more important is the thought that mankind— humankind, if you prefer, Sybil Ursha—has dominion over the earth. Were all to band together with a common purpose in mind, the vagaries of time would be meaningless."

Ursha quickly responded. "'The vagaries of time'? Your Mothers do not understand the power of Time. It is a hopeless idea that mankind is able to bend the will of Mother Time to its liking.

"Slower, please!" Leason interrupted. "I am not a philosopher. Please allow me to speak before you push on with more argument. Our Mothers say that the wars resulted from many wills wanting many things, few of them good."

"We will not agree on this. There were many wills because of Time," Ursha sighed, forcing her thin lips into a smile. "Though we are just three old Sybils, and not Sybils of the Great Light, nonetheless I have a tale that will widen the eyes of your Mothers."

Ursha began to speak as though to a classroom of recalcitrant children: "As the galaxy we are a part of rotates—you know of the galaxy? Pura, sketch us a likeness of our galaxy."

As Pura pulled a chalk piece from her shawl pocket and sketched a spiral galaxy on the stone table top, Ursha continued.

"We are here," she pointed. "I mean, of course, that our planet is here, much closer to the edge of the galaxy than the center. You know that we live on a globe that spins, through seeming emptiness, around our star, Sur?"

Jolar nodded affirmatively, though he and Leason knew little of this.

"In summer, when you lie on your back in the dark of night, you see a brightness: the stars almost forming a sheet of light. It is the center of the galaxy that you look at. It is thick with stars. In twenty-six thousand years—a bit less, but the round number will do—our galaxy rotates once. I say 'our galaxy'!" How humorous. I mean to say the galaxy of which our world is one tiny speck. As our galaxy slowly spins, our star, Great Sur, and our Mother Earth along with Sur, move with the flow of the galaxy."

Leason's eyes were nearly closed, whereas Jolar's were wide and intent, moving back and forth between Ursha's face and the chalk sketch as she spoke.

"As the Earth moves, the Character of Time changes." She laughed after saying this. "You, Jolar, will ask, why does the character of time change? And you, Leason, may likely ask, what does this mean 'the Character of Time?" Of that later. For now, I tell you that during the last many thousands of years the Character and Quality of Time sunk to its lowest ebb—to the darkest of the darkness. Twelve hundred years prior to that time there was war. Twelve hundred years after that time there was war. Two hundred years ago Earth came out, so to speak, of that twenty-four hundred years of darkness. The warring ceased. At the end of the wars, at the time we call Great Sur's Gift of Sanity, mankind," she said looking wryly at Leason, "was blessed with an opportunity for a small bit of progress—enough to stop warring. But now, and for the next twelve thousand years—yes, you have heard correctly, for the next twelve thousand years—mankind will be increasingly blessed with advancement, and progress, and peace, and good sense."

Ursha looked at each of the men intently.

"As a point of interest for you, Jolar, can you guess what will happen at the midpoint of the cycle, at the high water mark, in twelve thousand years?"

She chuckled, waiting.

"The people of that era, given their understanding of the history of their last thousands of years, will not believe a decline to be possible," she continued. "Much like those living today, much like our young Prince, most do not believe that progress is possible."

"And at the high point of the cycle, in twelve thousand years, some few will understand the workings of Time, as do we few today. They will no doubt leave records both in writing and in monuments of stone and the like, but all will be lost in the years of the descending darkness."

Ursha laughed again.

"Regardless of what is done, the memory of the wonders of life on earth for one hundred twenty periods of one hundred sets of the seasons will be lost to most of humankind. But of course we will not be around in twelve thousand years. That time plays small in our concerns. Our concern is for today."

Leason looked up from his apparent reverie: "'The Character of Time' means what, I wonder?"

"That in this new age, there will be more of the energy of Life, more strength available for mankind," Pura responded.

"Available to the evil among us as well us the good?" Leason questioned.

"Though not a philosopher, Leason, you are quite quick to ask a very insightful question," Pura laughed. "And, too, I would talk with you about your idea of evil another time," she answered. "But yes, in answer to your astute question: the rain waters all plants. The misuse of this energy, or, if you will allow, this misuse of the grace of the Divine Mother as her influence increases, will harm the user—much the reverse of the dark ages when the misuse rewarded the evildoer. In this new age those of ill intent will falter. Sooner, if those of good will stand and are heard."

Ursha added: "Ill intent, and the results of it, is possible, particularly in these coming days of flux. We Sybils have choices to make—as do all people everywhere."

"You understand that all this talk means little to me?" Leason continued. "Why would there be more of this 'strength' at one time than another?"

Pura answered: "All of creation is fabricated the same. We are born, we flower, we die. It is so with all creatures. It is same with the stones and mountains of the earth, as it is with the seasons and the birds of the air. It is the way of all Creation. Cycles of strength and weakness, expansion and contraction, activity and rest are everywhere, Leason."

Jolar interjected.

"Have you become a philosopher, Leason? Next you will want to know how it works."

"I will not ask how it works. In that I have no interest. Just that it is, or it is not. That this is either a challenge from Great Sur in order that we may shine in glory, or a tale conjured ages ago by crones wrapped in rags, huddled around a fire. Later they became the Sybils of the Great Light, or the True Light, or the Dark Light, as the case may be."

"Our Mothers believe the world is bound into these cycles."

"Yes," Leason replied to Jolar, "it is one thing for a plant to take seed, and grow, and die, and quite another for the quality of time to change as a galaxy rotates. And I do not say that our Mothers are always correct—as is the case with anyone."

"Well, suppose all said is nonsense. What else have you to do with your life?" Ushra laughed with a clear note of a taunt in her voice.

"A good question," Jolar laughed. "Suppose the idea is false? What is the worst that might happen?"

"I will think on that," Leason replied firmly.

"Think too on this," Pura added. "Your history and ours tells of a great step forward for both your people and ours. Both our people and yours, quite independent of each other, and at the same time, somehow gave up the folly of war. And if, Jolar and Leason, you were to find another land, I believe that you would hear the same story.

"Yes, possibly," Jolar said. "Though the expression 'two swallows does not make a Spring' comes to mind. Though I strongly share your hope, Sybil Pura."

"And it has been the strangest of all days in all memory," Ursha sighed with fatigue.

"What can you tell us of the King's illness?" Jolar asked.

"And of what should we be watchful of in the Kingdom of Harnell?" Leason added.

"Each of these questions will take the night in telling." Each of the four laughed and Pura signaled for more tea to be poured.

Chapter 25
A Proposal

Jessyl and Ennar mounted their horses, and with Gelt riding behind them, they moved towards the ravine hoping to escape from the Valley of The Sybil as soon as possible. Jesthya appeared from the shadows and walked beside Jessyl's horse.

"I will walk with you."

She waited for a reply.

"Will you ride like a lofty nobleman looking down on me with disdain? Come, Prince Jessyl, off your horse and walk with me. With this early departure you will be at your Father's well before sunrise."

Jessyl, who had been staring at her wide-eyed and with a feigned look of disinterest that he hope would suggest a reluctance to speak with her, slid slowly off his horse and handed the reins to Ennar. Ennar had dismounted and began to adjust one of his horse's stirrups, in order to allow the pair to walk a distance ahead of him and Gelt.

Jesthya turned and called curtly to Ennar. "Are you not worried that your Ranger will gallop off to alert his masters of your approach? Muley, lend your belt to cross-hobble the horse, but hang on to your pants."

Muley appeared from the shadows and unfastened a cord that was wrapped twice around her waist.

"Let Ennar brave the hooves: he is used to them. String the hobble from a front hoof on one side to the rear foot on the other blacksmith. Stroke the animal's nose, Muley. That will be our part, other than telling the boy how to do his work."

Abruptly, she snapped at Ennar, "Leave the cord long enough so that the horse may walk but not gallop."

"As you wish, my Lady Jesthya," Ennar spoke through a feigned grin and in a tone of mock reverence.

Jesthya quit speaking and Jessyl said nothing as they walked out of hearing of the others.

Finally she said, "I tell people what to do. I always have. I boss them, and if they don't do as I say, I make them. The Sybil charged me with ordering the Guard of the Ravine. It is not enough to satisfy, but it is the best this land has for me. At least, that is what I have come to believe."

She waited for Jessyl to speak but he did not, nor did he look at her.

"Did you notice the Ranger's eyes? He and I have the same violet eyes. Are we brother and sister? Am I the daughter of a Lord?"

Jessyl looked everywhere but at her. He steeled himself and turned towards her, and as he did so she stared brazenly into his eyes.

Presently she said, "Enough of that. Let us talk about the days ahead. Kalla…I wonder if her sisters will be able to quiet her—again. Usually they are able to calm her, though this time, even foolish with wine, she has spoken good sense and stirred many to fight. The Lords without horses makes many of us believe there may be an opportunity. And though I do not wish to see a rash war with a drunken old woman as our commander, many would ride with Kalla—if by some miracle she should stir at dawn. Considering the wine, she will more likely awake at noon blistering with rage. "Something gnaws deep within her heart."

She waited again for Jessyl to speak, but he did not.

"What do you think of this idea of an opportunity for our lands to prosper?"

Jessyl had dared to begin looking at her, listening as she rapidly dealt with the chance of Gelt escaping, Kalla, and war, and now, time. Finally he spoke.

"I think all the talk of The Sybil is designed for the benefit of the The Sybil. They want a different world. From the sounds of it, a world in which they rule. Opportunity, or no opportunity, it is difficult for me to believe that the world will be much changed from what it is now or ever has been. Why would it? A King makes sure that what we have is not lost to some dreamer's whimsy."

"What do these men from the South say? Why do they make such a perilous journey?"

"So you have heard of our conversation of last night?" he grinned.

He had been looking at the moonlight on her shoulders and on her lips. Catching himself in his distraction, he chastised himself and returned his focus to the conversation.

"Their Mothers tell the same story as The Sybil: Mankind will prosper," he said in a matter-of-fact tone.

"It seems they have made a long journey just to tell us that. Are they liars who speak whatever serves them? Or have their Mothers deluded them and sent them traveling, seeking something else?"

Jessyl did not answer.

"Prince Jessyl, I do not wish to spend my life living with a gaggle of women, guarding a ravine. I want to believe these men from the south—that the Earth will prosper, not just for men, but for all."

Again, Jessyl was without an answer he dared to speak.

"Are women happy being married to men? Is your mother pleased to be married to your father?"

Throughout his life Jessyl had not met anyone who could ask such a number and variety of disconcerting questions.

"Yes," he managed to reply. "I will say yes: my mother is happy with my father. Why do you ask?"

"I wonder if I would be happy, bound and subservient to another."

"I can't imagine you subservient to anyone!" Jessyl laughed nervously at his frankness.

"I like the look of you, Prince Jessyl. You will need a queen one day."

Jessyl choked, and his face turned red.

"Do you like the look of me?" she continued.

"I do," he sputtered like a small and embarrassed boy, and immediately wished he had remained silent.

"Good. Is this how it is settled in Harnell?" she persisted, laughing at his discomfort.

"No, not at all," he hurriedly answered. "Mothers talk for months. There are various considerations. Those to be married must say yes, or at least agree."

"Is it settled?"

"Shouldn't we talk further?" Jessyl said.

"No, no," she laughed. "I mean, is there someone set for you?"

"No!"

"Good. Unless you are dead you surely feel the pull between us."

As she said this she faintly brushed her shoulder nearest to Jessyl with a brief caress of her hand.

"You like my eyes? You like to look deep into them: that I know.

They had reached the outer end of the ravine. Jessyl would not have answered even if he had been able to think of something to say.

"Do you suppose that The Sybil has sent me to ensnare you to our will?"

As Jessyl looked at her, his face darkened and was enveloped in a look of bewilderment and anger, neither of which he was able to conceal.

"I had not thought of that."

"Yet," she quickly retorted. "The Ranger chides me that his father is also my father. I wish to know if Lord Rawlings is my Father. Look into his eyes and you will know." She had turned, and Jessyl turned with her as she spoke, so that his face was awash in moonlight. She held his gaze until he nodded in agreement.

"I wish you a safe passage to the Keep of your father—and mother. Long life and a safe journey to you, Prince Jessyl."

"I wish to live long," he replied with formality, though confused and tripping over his words. "And I wish, for you, a long life, Jesthya."

He mounted his horse, and with the conversation between them ended, he hesitatingly looked for a brief time into her eyes and then abruptly dug his heels into his horse, riding away as though fleeing.

Ennar mounted and rode quickly to be soon riding beside his friend. They slowed their horses to a walk. The moon cast the long shadows of the two young men and their horses up the side of a striated mound ahead of them. Ennar remained silent, waiting for Jessyl to speak.

"My mind is full of her. She distracts me."

Ennar continued riding in silence.

"Between here and my Father's Keep, I have much to think on other than her," he sighed in frustration and near exhaustion.

"Is this what Shukra does to us? How am I to concentrate on the work before me?"

"I know nothing of what you speak," Ennar replied. After a long silence he said, "You surprised me greatly at The Sybil's. We would stand with the Lords?"

"My father lies dying and those old women speak with nonchalance of Kalla's foolishness. Damn them, Ennar. And damn their blather about time and whatever else. My father is dying and they drivel on about what? Something that will no doubt serve them! And now I rail at them. How does such pointless talk help me do what I must do? What is it I must do?"

They rode in silence for a few minutes.

"My father must be cured. To seek help from those witches has turned out to be a great waste of my time—and my father's time. What a child I have been to dally away precious time, and why? To see this Jesthya? What a fool I am! At a great price I am learning the results of women, and particularly Sybils, being allowed to meddle in the affairs of men. I have been well warned of them many times. What does it take for me to learn a lesson, Ennar?"

Most perplexed by his friend's behavior, Ennar waited to hear what else Jessyl might say. Finally, he spoke with the thought to sway his friend to a happier topic.

"And what does this girl who orders me about as her servant boy have to do with all this?"

"She is never far from my thoughts, Ennar. At the end of our time together she asked me if I imagined that she has been sent by The Sybil to ensnare me to their will. How clever she is! It is likely that they have sent her exactly for that purpose. I put nothing past them. And how well suited to the task she is...not at all like the giggling daughters of the Barons. She is as clever and wily as any man on Earth. Though my head shrieks caution, I struggle in quicksand."

Ennar thought for a time and then asked, "Well then, here is something else for you to ponder: Did you notice Leason's interest in water?"

"Yes...No, I did not."

"More than once he interrupted Jolar to ask of our water."

"Can I not trust anyone, Ennar!" Jessyl shrieked in rage.

They continued to ride, both of them deep in thought: Ennar wondering about the stranger that rode beside him, Jessyl wondering what was happening, not to himself, but to everyone around him.

Gelt's horse kept pace but was far behind.

Chapter 26
Advice from Friends

The two Sybils and the two Windriders were deep in conversation. The Sybil's servant a serene, gray-haired woman filled their cups with steaming tea. She placed a plate of sweet bread and jam on the table and stood nearby waiting, her presence filling the room. Pura thanked her for her service at the lateness of the hour and bid her leave them and take rest. As the woman bowed and left, Pura immediately turned and spoke to Jolar.

"You asked about the King's debilitation. To understand it as an illness is not accurate. It is a living demon, and of the worst sort. Created ages ago, certainly, I pray, not in this age, by one of the many necromancers during the Great War. It leeches the King's life from him. It began slowly but at the end, it will become fired with gluttony. There is no means other than the will power of the King to loose himself of this creature. Only through The Teachings of the Will may he rid himself of it, and I suspect that it is far too late for that."

"And no small task!" Jolar exclaimed in amazement to Pura's words. "As children at the age of first talking, we begin elementary practice of the Teachings of the Will. For the King, at this time of his life, and sorely afflicted, the Teachings would be a difficult undertaking."

"You practice the Way of the Will? Both boys and girls?" Ursha asked.

"We do," Jolar responded. "It is different, and less rigorous for men, as one would expect."

Pura added laughingly, "The young Prince was correct that we would easily talk till dawn."

Ursha continued: "Our sister Kalla, of whom you have heard, offered our teaching to the King. In her haste, and no doubt because of drink, she rushed and was rejected. Nevertheless, he was a fool to refuse such a gift. In our tradition we have not taught the Way to a man, ever. And we require our students to ask for the knowledge. They must recognize its worth, if only to a small degree in the beginning, and ask for it—even to the point of begging, but preferably demanding it."

Pura bent the conversation back to the King.

"It is unlikely that the King will be cured. We have our fears as to where the demon may go once the King passes on. I see by your looks that you recognize these fears. Let us not speak them aloud."

"Nor think them," Leason added.

Pura smiled warmly at Leason: "You understand well the power of thought. Thank you. It seems to us that the death of the King would be a blow to progress; frankly, we do not understand how his passing could bring any good. Hence we sent Kalla to the King with a strong hope that he would accept our teaching."

"We will look at this demon when we meet the King," Leason offered. "We may see some means of helping, though our skills, which are mostly Jolar's, are for healing the wounds of combat."

"Yes," Jolar agreed. "And we will pass what we understand of this creature on to our Mothers. They may have counsel."

"As you wish," said Ursha. "If The Sybils have no cure for the demon, it is unlikely that the disciples of the long ago departed Sybils of the Great Light will know of a cure."

"As to the dangers of Harnell, there are many," Pura interrupted. "The Prince has told you that the Lords are not allowed the bow, nor the crossbow. It would surprise me if they do not have these weapons: lacking horses, they may bring these weapons forth. The Lords are eight in number, each with a sublord: Swikes they are called. The Chief Lord is allowed two. Each Swike commands four Rangers, and there is a band of ruthless youths who aspire to be Rangers. Under the laws of the Founding Edicts, these numbers are all that is allowed the Lords. And this is fortunate, as they number over one hundred and they and their horses gobble up far more resources than the rest of Harnell. Properly managed, Harnell's small wealth could provide for many times their population."

She looked at both Leason and Jolar to gauge their reaction to this last comment. They listened intently but with the same inquiring expressions exhibited in previous discussions.

Ursha, who had watched them carefully, now took up the narration: "The Lords are completely ruthless and somewhat clever, although these last eight generations has rendered them duller than in the past. Nonetheless, during the last two hundred years they have tortured mercy out of their numbers. Only the cruelest and strongest of the band of youths survive to become Rangers. To become a Swike, or a Lord, is reserved only for those who are completely evil."

"They will be angered about the theft of their horses," Leason offered.

"I have given that some thought. They cannot walk far. They must have their horses, or how will they rule? They will create any horror to ensure the return of them. We have agreed to give more thought to this idea of keeping the horses."

Pura continued, "The Lords are somehow under the control of the King. How, we do not know. They supply him, and his many healers and their apprentices, with food. As we understand the situation, he has only a crossbow, his healers, and the Edicts to protect him. Concerning the healers, one hundred would not be worth a Lord in battle. As for the Edicts, though everyone in the Kingdom of Harnell fears, or pretends to fear any contravention of them, the King must have some other means of control over the Company of Lords."

Ursha added to her sister's observations: "The Edicts are replete with various curses that have become interchangeable for the various transgressions. Over the last two centuries people thought to have disobeyed an Edict have fallen victim to a number of gruesome deaths and diseases. It is quite humorous to see weak minds bring such a thing as a plague of boils or even death upon themselves for a real, or imagined, transgression. And sickness has come to mean that the Edicts have been violated—or even that someone has had the intent to do so."

Leason added a terse comment: "Showing that even a weak mind may sometimes be powerful."

Pura laughed with pleasure at his insight.

"It is so good to talk with someone other than ourselves, someone who understands the workings of the Will. I believe you understand clearly how King Gemar may be healed. But to return to your questions before we talk the night away: the Lords have no interest in your knowledge. Your gifts they would take after they pick clean your bones. To them, the world is as it should be. No other world is possible or welcome. That others suffer to provide their needs is to them the natural order of things."

Ursha took up the conversation: "We see that you two are wary, and skilled in the arts of conflict and negotiation. You, Leason, are teaching Ennar, and Jolar teaches Jessyl. As men they will need the skills you teach. Give them all you have to give; these skills have long been lost to the Kingdom of Harnell. Also, I believe you understand well that to attempt negotiation with the Lords would be futile. Strike first when you meet them. To them, as Pura has said, you are a disturbance to the order of their world. They will think of you as lice to be squashed."

Pura offered a final piece of advice: "Kalla tells us that they have foolishly made a change in their armor. An arrow that hits high on their armor may likely slip beneath their neck mail."

"Yes," Ursha continued with a dark chuckle, "and the darts you carry at your wrists will likely do the same."

Jolar returned the laugh. "Thank you for that advice. This blue dust that blinded the Lords might be useful to us."

"Oh no," Pura replied. "It is concocted to seek the eyes of men; it would be a weapon that would turn upon you. If ever it is used against you, wedge the heels of your palms tightly to your eyes and press hard until the prickles on the back of your hands subside."

"We are very thankful for that advice also," Jolar said.

"Though who would use the blue dust against us?" Leason said

"Precisely," Ursha replied. "You are not our enemies."

Leason bowed his head slightly to Ursha at this offering of alliance, though in his view the Sybils required as much watching as anyone they would meet in Harnell.

"I feel the calm of morning approaching," he said.

"Yes, it is time to leave," Jolar agreed. Turning to the Sybils, he asked, "May we begin our flight from high in your lookout above the ravine?"

"You will fly? I wish to see this. Come, Ursha, we will escort them to the lower lookout."

She turned eagerly to the Windriders. "Will that be high enough? It is seven hundred steps above the ravine floor. We can climb to one of the higher lookouts if needed."

"We are able to fly from any height if there is wind. Seven hundred steps are a gift indeed."

Viewed from the lookout five hundred feet above the dunes, the three horses and their riders appeared as crumbs on a tabletop. Jolar and Leason had hurried ahead of the two Sybils. Now Jolar sat with his eyes closed, facing the east where the sun would soon rise. Leason assembled the wind sail frames.

Pura, breathing heavily in the cool morning air and wiping sweat from her forehead, arrived at the stone ledge that was the lookout.

Paul Colver

"This is the stuff of legends," she wheezed, though her eyes were sparkling. "In the days before The Great War, we were told, the sky was filled with sails."

She shouted down the steps to Ursha.

"Ursha, hurry. Put your pipe away."

She continued to speak expansively to Leason: "And balloons—great tear-shaped globes of warm air like up-side-down tear drops, if you follow me—carried ships and barges filled with travelers. Do you know of ships and barges?"

Staring at Leason, Pura became lost in thought. "I never thought I would see such a stirring sight again: a well-muscled young man, his skin glowing in the moonlight, and dressed in clothes the color of lilacs, assembling a fluttering red sail. May the picture glow often in my mind's eye."

Leason's gold chain had slipped out of his shirt collar. His white teeth shone in the faint moonlight before dawn, and he flashed an unusually wide grin at Pura.

"Kalla likes drink, and Ursha the pipe. What would be your pleasure Sybil Pura?" He laughed as he continued to grin at her: "Who would have thought a Sybil would have thoughts to make her blush?"

Ursha had reached the platform. She was breathing heavily.

"The last we saw of flying were...crafts used in the wars," she said as she gasped for breath. "To bomb."

The wind sails were ready. Jolar had risen from his morning communion with his Mother.

Pura entreated: "Stay. Wait, please. Until Great Sur flashes first light."

Jolar looked at Leason curiously, and then said to him: "I sensed my Mother's delight that we have found The Sybil. Though she is disturbed by the thoughts of the Succumon, and more so at my thoughts of the King's health. In that regard I sensed a feeling of hopelessness."

"Just now as you spoke," Ursha said, "I had a foreboding that the King will soon pass from the Earth. His son has promise—considering he was brought up to be a king. He may take guidance from you, Jolar. Though, even as now as I speak, my heart feels a doom awaits him also—and soon."

"As to Kalla," Pura spoke, "she will not ride against the Lords today. Of tomorrow we cannot say. We do not know what needs to be done regarding the Lords. She may be correct in her wish to destroy them, but her heart is filled with anger. You understand that her rage makes her ill-suited to the task."

Jolar and Leason had strapped themselves into the windsails' harnesses.

A ray of light flashed from the eastern horizon and a thin arc of the sun rippled shimmering gold against the red morning sky.

"Another great morning. Long lives to you both!" Jolar shouted.

With that said, he and Leason each took three strides and leaped into the wind. As Leason ran these steps, he turned his head and winked at Pura. The air caught and lifted the sails and the men circled in a wide arc, waving to the two tired and frail women below. As they circled a second time, they took a long look at the ravine, the valley, and, lastly, with great interest, the lake.

Pura stood smiling at the figures of the Windriders as their sails became smaller as they rapidly sailed towards the rising sun. Ursha lit her pipe and began coughing her sharp hacking cough. Jesthya had climbed to the platform and stood silently behind the two small women towering above them looking out at the Windriders.

"Kalla is awake," she said. "She wails and rants for war."

The two sisters looked at each other hurriedly and began their descent. Jesthya sat down at the edge of the platform, her legs dangling over the rock lip as though she was a child sitting on a chair too large for her. Both her hands shielded her eyes from the sun as she searched the horizon for the horsemen. They were long out of view.

Chapter 27
Jesthya Finds Her Voice

The two Sybils soon found Kalla. A greenish glow colored the woman's face as she raged with ill temper haranguing a small gathering of the younger women. Members of the group turned to look towards the approaching Sybils, and Kalla followed their eyes. Upon seeing her sisters, she turned her anger to them.

"The guests are gone? Am I not of The Sybil? Why was I not awakened to wish them well on their journey? I have the Lord's horses. You were to wake me." She coughed, her face quickly changing from sickly green to red.

"We ride against the Lords today." She coughed. "They await our arrows." She hacked fiercely, and spat.

"If they wear armor, all the better. We will dance circles around them. The fat slugs are stuck in their slime without the horses. How dare you not wake me!"

Pura spoke with unaccustomed vehemence: "Kalla, you carry on as though you are yet drunk. Do you remember your responsibility in this life?"

Ursha quickly added, "Remember how important your judgment is to all our lives. Do you remember anything? Do you remember the task with which we three are charged and the short time we have remaining to us? I call for a meeting in the Arbor of Resolution."

"No!" Kalla screamed. "I'll not have you team up on me as you have done in the past. I am taking the horses and as many riders as they will carry. Two or three of the best archers to a horse. We will make pincushions out of the Lords and their boys. Then we will build the world anew—as it should be."

"Kalla, has sense left you entirely? You must be yet filled with wine. Leave now and you will arrive at the Lords' for morning tea. Come with us to the Arbor. There the three of us may decide what must be done."

"No!" She folded her arms across her chest much like a petulant child. "My plans will not be twisted about as has happened in the past."

"Then we will speak here for everyone to hear," Pura shot back, barely containing the frustration she so strongly felt. "Kalla, you are governed by your anger. How will a slaughter of the Lords lead to anything good? And if by some small chance you succeed, you will lay the foundation for a world much like the world the men built." Pura shook her head.

Ursha continued with many of the same thoughts: "Kalla, none of us have any love for the Lords, but how will bloodshed help? Even if you were to succeed, the spilled blood, which will include the blood of our daughters, will just add to the misery that engulfs Harnell."

Kalla replied with sarcasm, "And what will you do with the Lords in this new age? Educate them? Teach them The Way?"

She laughed riotously.

"Oh, let us imagine, you will lead them to The Edge?"

She laughed again, ending with another fit of coughing. When she recovered somewhat, though with her eyes still watering, she said: "My dear Sisters, I am for practicality. Rid the earth of this scourge."

Nearly the entire population of the valley had gathered by now.

"Practicality?" a hesitant voice spoke. "Mother Kalla, where is the practicality in your ill-planned attack?"

A hush fell; it seemed as though everyone had stopped breathing. Kalla's eyes searched the crowd. Jesthya stepped forward.

"What if the Lords have a crossbow? Or a dozen cross-bows? Or one hundred crossbows?"

"Who are you to question me?" Kalla snapped.

"What if they have horses? Or other weapons? Or a plan where half, or all of them, lie hidden in ambush. You have told them that we will attack. Do you remember? Or have you forgotten? What of all that?"

Kalla began, "How dare y...," but her voice was not as loud as it had been, and Jesthya quickly interrupted her.

"Tell us your plan. Should you need to retreat, what is your plan for retreat? Tell us, Mother Kalla: if you have a plan, when did you plan it? Last night with your head full of wine?"

A few of the onlookers laughed.

"This is no thing to laugh at!" Jesthya shouted at the crowd. "It is our lives we speak of...and our future. Sybil Kal-la, join your sisters in the Arbor. Resolve this matter wisely, from your heart."

Kalla choked with rage: "Who are you to speak to me of the heart?" Her face was scarlet with anger as she bent and spat at Jesthya's feet. "Damn your disrespect. It is me who has stolen the horses. I found the weakness in the ar-mor. Hear me daughters: since ages past, we have been subject...."

As she began to speak, Ursha grabbed her hands. Pura had already wrapped an arm around Kalla's shoul-ders. "Yes, yes, dear Kalla. All that we know. Come with us," Pura soothed.

Kalla dropped low to her haunches as she had done when Direoll attacked her in the Hall of Justice, and sprang backwards. She turned and faced Jesthya.

"You! You foolish child," she hissed with venom, "know nothing of men: nothing of the misery they have inflicted on earth, not only in the last centuries, not only in the war, but for ages and ages and ages. And you don't know of the war. Lands burned, water polluted, entire cities tortured and slaughtered and raped. Yes, raped. Raped: that you know nothing of.

"Foolish, innocent girl: what do you know of men? You get a smell of them and you think it might be a treat to lie under a sweating body. Is that it? Birthing their children? Raising their brats, and as they wish? Smiling at their stupidity? Ordering their houses? Giggling as you listen to their nonsense? Is it one of these black men that have stirred your juices? O! Ho! I have it. It is the young scarecrow! The Prince has stirred you. You will be his queen and set the world aright. Many, far your betters, have tried that. The men with black skin, the Prince, they are all the same. I say we keep a few for breeding stock and for the rest, its snip, snip."

A small number of the women hooted and laughed and some growled angrily in agreement with Kalla's proposal.

Kalla smiled weakly in response to the cheers, but her torrent of speech had rapidly exhausted her. Jesthya, though shaken, resumed her attack.

"You have no plan, and so you rail against men. Your head is yet clouded with wine from last night's drunkenness. That and your hatred of men make you reckless. Listen to the counsel of your sisters. How can a new world be built on a foundation mortared with blood?

All of those gathered Jesthya knew well, and she looked to them for support. "How can a new world be built by a woman with a ruined heart? I will not follow her to battle: nor will any of you with any sense."

Kalla's face paled as though her breath had been knocked out of her. Exhaustion overcame her.

Pura spoke in a consoling tone. "Let us leave this heated talk, Kalla, and retire to the privacy of the Arbor."

Ursha put her arm around Kalla's shoulders and held her as Pura had previously. "Let us retire to the peace of the Arbor."

The Arbor was not an arbor of trees but a ringed circle of stones no higher than one of the Sybil's waists. In the center, a large stone slab resting on three stone supports created a tabletop set at chest height. The land around the Arbor was barren; offering no opportunity for outsiders to approach and hear what was said.

Once at the tabletop, Ursha and Pura took their place at the southwest and southeast supports. Kalla took her place at the north.

Pura began speaking immediately, "'Keep a few for breeding stock'? Has your heart died? Explain yourself."

Kalla began: "The rule of men cannot but end in misery. Who fought the war? Who let the world fall into such a condition as to allow such abomination to happen? Who slaughtered millions of Sybils? Millions of us!"

She groaned. "Both our sisters and those of the Great Light...gone! 'Abomination': the word hardly describes any of it. If men are kept in their place, war would be forgotten."

Kalla's face was gray with fatigue: "Our serving woman has told me most of what was said last night. Look to the Land of the Windriders that you spoke of. How does that society flourish without a worry, while we are in misery? They have leisure to send two strong youths exploring. And not just exploring, but to help: to give. 'Give! The word is hardly left in the vocabulary of the people of Harnell. They, and we as well, scramble and scratch to survive. Go on like this for another two hundred years and what kind of a monstrous world will remain?"

Life had crept back into her voice.

"But these Windriders are from a sensible land. Their Mothers order the way of life. And this seems perfectly natural to them. This is what I mean by 'breeding stock.' Weed out the thugs and we will eventually have a world of men who accept the wisdom of women. We will teach both women and our new men The Way. What a world we could build! The time for this is now."

With tears in her eyes, Kalla truly smiled for the first time in a long time.

Pura spoke.

"We would do well to revisit the plans given to us ages ago for the rebuilding the world. You have tears in your eyes, but most of what you think is what you wish for and not what Time decrees. You are thousands of years ahead of to-day, and I foresee that the world you would build would be much as the last world. What was known as prosperity and abundance filled their tables but not their hearts. Have you forgotten that it is our doom to create a world that will seek the Keys to the Kingdom? Continue on your present course and you will create another world of people dressed in silk and gold, feasting on roasts of pork and fattened goose livers but emptiness and want in their souls."

Ursha asked: "Kalla, tell us what you said to the Lords in your drunken rage. You threatened them: this we know?"

Kalla wiped tears from her eyes and looked about the arbor but not at her sisters.

Ursha broke the silence: "It seems to me that you remember what you said. I see that in your look. Your memory may save the lives of many of our daughters. What did you say?"

Pura continued harshly: "It is not just on this issue that truth is important. Everything you say is of importance. What have you allowed to happen to yourself, Kalla? We have suffered and waited two hundred years to do as we must, and now are you lost to us? Tell us," she sighed with resignation, "what did you say to the Lords?"

"I told one of the boys to tell their masters that we were at war. And that I would set their heads on pikes."

"Great Sur," Ursha intoned. "Wine fires your rage, and you act the fool. You must think the Lords stupid, or do you think at all? They are hardly schooled in the ways of combat as the generals of The Great War, but they are not dull children. After what you have said, do you think it likely that they may set an ambush?"

Kalla hung her head.

Pura continued. "You paint a pretty picture of a new world, as you paint a pretty picture of your attack. But you paint with broad brush strokes, Kalla. In the fine details I see much suffering. What do the stars tell us, Ursha?"

Ursha answered, "Though I believe it to be the blood of the Lords, the stars drip blood."

"Likely much of the blood will of ours." Pura said with finality.

Chapter 28
Welcome and Laughter at the Smithy

As the sun cast first light on the streets of Harnell Jessyl and Ennar reined their horses to a stop at the gate of the smithy. Ennar slipped off his horse, leaped the low stone fence, and slapped on the house door with the flat of his hand.

"Unbar the door, Father, and welcome Prince Jessyl and your son home from their travels."

The door opened inward and Rebecca, weeping and red-faced, rushed by her husband and grasped her son, hugging him tightly to her.

"Don't do this to your mother ever again!" she sobbed.

"He has escaped death. Don't crush his life from him," the blacksmith admonished. "Your mother hardly slept last night," he said, rolling his eyes to make light of their worry. "Nor did I."

As his wife eased her grip on their son, the blacksmith had turned to look at Jessyl.

"And look at you, Prince Jessyl. You have a bit of a shine about you. Wizards at the southern borders?"

"I am much improved from yesterday, thank you."

"Yes, but you don't tell us her name."

Jessyl pointed to the sky above the Lord's Keep.

Paul Colver

"Our companions have knowledge of healing."

Not so high above them, two red sails rapidly circled in a wide arc. As Jolar the previous evening had gestured for Jessyl and Ennar to join him at the fire, Jessyl bowed as though on stage, and motioned for the Windriders to land.

The blacksmith, with one hand at the back of his neck to support his head in its unaccustomed position, squinted upwards at the two red sails. Neighbors peered out from house doors, trying to see what made the blacksmith stare so long at the sky. Ennar's brothers and sisters, their mouths open in astonishment, pointed at the approaching sails. People ventured forth from nearby hovels. A smiling, animated crowd gathered, looking up at the approaching Windriders. Ennar's mother had released him from her arms but still clutched the cloth of his cloak with her strong fingers.

Soundlessly, the Windriders guided their sails softly to the earth. They ran for half a dozen paces to slow their speed to a stop. Once landed, they surveyed the crowd and the surroundings, all the while smiling full, broad smiles. As Jessyl moved towards them, they began to fold their sails; by the time he reached them, though they had not looked at their work, they were packing the sails and frames.

Ennar gently leaned against his father and motioned for him to move with him away from the others. As they walked, he whispered, "Kalla, the Sybil brought by Jessyl to his father, has found the change in the Lord's armor."

His father eyed him intently.

"She has returned to her valley with the Lord's horses. At least, some of the horses. Are there other horses, Father?"

"We don't know. Jack the Miller saw some of her performance. It was great performance by his telling of it. He said a huge stampede of horses followed her."

Ennar continued to ask his hurried questions: "Have the Lords weapons other than their throwing knives, swords, and spears?"

"None that I have made for them. What is to happen?"

"The Sybil, Kalla, has declared war on the Lords. Her sisters may not agree with her, but she got drunk on the King's wine and threatened to set the Lords' heads on fence posts. Jessyl walked out of our meeting with The Sybil saying he would stand with the Lords."

The blacksmith whistled a breath of astonishment.

The Windriders approached the house and Jessyl began introductions, leaving Ennar and his father as much time as possible to talk.

"Only our family makes weapons for them. Where would the Lords find weapons other than ours? They have no skill to make anything themselves," the blacksmith mused. "What worries me more is if one of them gets stuck with an arrow. There will questions, Ennar."

Jessyl turned to the father and son: "And this is my Uncle Klayton, Lord of Smithy in the Kingdom of Harnell."

Jessyl introduced the Windriders.

The blacksmith broke the formality of the moment by chiding his wife: "No doubt, gentlemen, breakfast would be appreciated. Unfortunately, the women of this house are an unruly lot, and you will have to go elsewhere."

Rebecca shrieked at her girls, "Quick, set the table for four! Boil water. Quick! Eggs."

Jessyl, smiling from ear to ear at his Uncle's humor, interrupted: "Another time and soon, I hope. Dear Aunt I wish to meet with my father. We will eat at his table."

Amid much protest, the two youths swung themselves handily onto their horses. Equally as smoothly, Jolar joined Jessyl, and Leason sprung onto Ennar's horse. Each Windrider smiled and waved as the horses started off for the King's Fortress.

The blacksmith hurried beside them.

"Will I get breakfast when I return?" he said as a parting comment to his wife.

"Have you ever gone without breakfast?" she scowled as she spoke. "The size of your belt answers that question."

The neighbors and children laughed uproariously.

The blacksmith jogged a few steps, pumping his arms vigorously as heavy, older men will often do to try to create the illusion that they are running. Jessyl slowed to a stop and gracefully slid off his horse to stand beside Klayton. They were out of hearing of the neighbors.

"What should I do, Prince Jessyl, today and during the days to come?"

"Ennar has told you that Kalla has taken the Lord's horses and threatened the Lords with war?"

The blacksmith nodded.

"I must speak with my father. Under the Edicts we are allied to the Lords against all aggressors, as they are so allied to us. Uncle, are you able to find out if the Lords have other horses and weapons? Should the Lords hear that we know of an attack and have not forewarned them…"

He left this thought unfinished, quite sure that he was understood.

"I do not trust the Sybil. They could do most anything— if it suited them. Find out if the Lords have horses and weapons we do not know of. I will speak with you before the day is done."

The blacksmith nodded in agreement. Jessyl hurriedly joined Jolar on the horse and nudged the horse forward. The blacksmith nodded another bow of agreement to the Prince and bowed to both the Windriders. As he turned and walked to his home and family, he gave his son a long look of grave concern.

As the four rode along with Gelt following, the Windriders spoke of their flight.

"The Keep of the Lords is green and prosperous. Cattle and pigs and chickens and sheep, grain and produce. They must have a good source of water. Otherwise what a dry and poor land this is," Leason said.

"They have water. And they have all the labor they want. They bargain for it with water. You noticed the green parcels outside their Keep? The Lords supply the water, and sharecroppers supply the labor. The twelve Barons live also on the backs of the Sluds, though they are not allowed nearly as much water as the Lords. Our family is well provided for. We earn our water through smithy and mining."

"That explains the number of children, and the health and size of them. Most of the people in this land look as though the wind could blow them away. Yours is the only family we saw with more than two children?" Jolar observed.

"And often both are boys," Leason added.

"The Sybil's daughters!" Ennar exploded as though he had solved a mystery. "Jessyl, the Sybil's daughters..."

He looked over at Jessyl but received no reply. Jessyl was slumped forward deep in thought.

"There are other families that are allowed more water than the Sluds. The millers, and carpenters, and stonemasons. Mostly tradesmen like my father. And, of course, the twelve Barons. The Lords tell us that there is little water. I doubt their word."

"Is it a well they have?"

"Yes, that is what they claim. Usually in the heat of summer, often for a quarter of a moon, there is no water. Everyone in Harnell stores as much water as possible for that time of year."

"Where the land is watered, it is fertile," Leason said. "More water, and fairly distributed, would make this a different land."

Jessyl was unlikely to have heard any of the conversation, but Ennar noted every word.

Chapter 29
Battle Plans

An assemblage of expectant women watched as the three Sybils shuffled towards the entrance to the Arbor. Jesthya looked at the sky and the clouds, and listened to the birds: she attended to anything but the group of women. Her heart still raced from her exchange with Kalla. She had been prepared to say harsh words—to each Sybil—if necessary. Now, she felt thankful. And though unable to put the reason for this feeling into words, she felt somehow released from a tightness in her heart that as long as she could remember had stifled her happiness. Now that she recognized what she must do, she felt as though spring air cooled her body.

She walked to the east side of the group and turned and faced them with an arm's length separating her from the nearest person.

"The Sybil is deciding whether we war against the Lords."

She waited for a moment, intent on controlling the pace of the conversation.

"War is likely.

"I, who have overcome each of you who would try me, will not fight this war."

Minutes passed as she looked into each face that would look back at her.

"I will not fight this foolish war. Who of you will stand with me? Come, stand here with me."

None left the group to join her.

"Will you ride off with the wild hope that the Lords will fall like rag dolls before your arrows? With no plan but the ramblings of Kalla?"

Aslesha shouted from the crowd: "They are without horses. Their armor will not protect them from our arrows. There is no need of a plan."

Hasta, always impatient waded into the talk. "And Mother Time is with us. Now the horses are fit. In a month they will be skin and bone. Tonight I will be at the gates of the Lords. Many will fall to my arrows. You are brave enough to command the lookout but not so brave to do what must be done. Who cares that you will not fight the Lords?"

There was a rumbling of assent.

Bharani growled, "You are afraid!"

"Yes I am afraid. Afraid, of how many of you will die," Jesthya said with concern. "These three who have spoken will follow Kalla and attack the Lords? Who else?"

Many met Jesthya's eyes as she surveyed the group. No one moved.

"There is no plan, and you will have Kalla lead you? By tomorrow morning many of you may lie dead."

She continued to look at as many as would return her look: few dropped their eyes and she now knew that there would be an attack.

"I too believe that Time is now on our side. What might we do with our lives other than this stupid and dangerous war? We might do what we could have been doing all these long years. Building terraces. Planting gardens and orchards and grain fields. I say let the horses loose. Let Mother Time deal with the Lords."

Bharani pushed her way forward.

"Lesha and Hasta and myself and six others have banded together. Come forward, my sisters!"

She called the names of the six others: "Ardra, Swati, Shadha, Bhisthat, Bhadra and Muley join us proudly as you have pledged."

Nine now stood in front of Jesthya.

Bharani's voice grew louder and louder as she spoke. "We have made a pact among ourselves. We will fight. We have the horses. Now is our time!"

Alesha continued: "We will not spend our lives trapped in this valley and ruled by old women, or ruled by you, Jesthya. We will ride free across the plains."

A sound of approval was heard from many in the crowd.

Hasta continued the speech. "Mother Kalla is right about more than you know. When we have the Lords' wealth, we will set the world right."

Another cheer went up from others in the crowd.

"I see you have made up your minds. You may find yourself knocking on the gates of the Lords tonight. They may have horses and weapons you do not know of."

"You nine come with me," she ordered suddenly. "Come with me to the ravine."

She turned from them as though they did not exist. "The remainder of you do not be idle. You will likely get this war you wish for. Arrows are needed. Food and water. Care for the horses and prepare for your foolish war."

She turned to walk away, saying abruptly to the nine who awaited her: "Follow me."

As she reached the ravine she glanced briefly over her shoulder to see that she was followed, and as she did this, she shouted to the watchers: "It is Jesthya and nine fierce warlords who walk below!"

She waited until an all-clear signal was heard from above.

"Let the others wait in anticipation. But let us walk through the ravine and sit on the land of the King and the Lords. You must become used to enjoying the land you will conquer," she laughed.

When they arrived outside the entrance, Jesthya directed them to sit in a circle. She picked up a smooth stone the size of a small bird's egg from the gravel.

"Here there are just the ten of us. Ten pairs of ears. There is no need to talk later about who said what. Just the ten of us need to know the words spoken here today. Let us agree on that." She waited for someone to speak, but no one did.

"Lives, your lives, not to mention your sisters' lives, depend upon your good sense. Rushing off fired up by the speeches of an old woman has the smell of blood all over it. Plans are needed. Well thought out plans."

She looked hard at them, tossed the smooth pebble above her and caught it as it fell.

"The holder of the stone speaks. There is much to say for my part, but what have you, the wise warriors, to say?"

Brarani held out her hand for the pebble, caught it, and spoke.

"Our best hope is if the Lords charge from the Keep. Should they charge on foot, with armor, swords, and spears, they are fools. Many of us will be on horses. Others will fire at them from the shadows."

The stone was passed to Aslesha.

"And a better situation still is to have them peep over the wall at us. The size of a lord's neck is an easy target even for our youngest archers."

Jesthya held her hand out for the stone.

"It is easy to speak of the best of situations. What of the worst? You need a plan—many plans."

She tossed the stone up high into the air and caught it, a grave look of frustration clouding her face.

"The Keep of the Lords I have seen. Think on this. Low, loose stone walls, no taller than myself, with four wooden gates: facing north, east, south, and west. The wood of these gates is dried from the sun and the heat of many years. Late at night, well before dawn, set fire to these gates. Tonight we have moonlight, but the light of the fire will help you more than it will help the Lords. Kalla says that your arrows will find their marks. I hope for your sake this is not some drunkard's dream."

The stone was passed. The discussion turned to less favorable outcomes. Many of the ideas that had occurred to Jesthya were introduced. What if the Lords had horses and once the gates fell to rubble, they leaped the flames and charged with spears? What if they had crossbows or other weapons and fired from behind the cover of the walls?

And Mula added hesitantly, "What if they ambush us?"

Jesthya chided them, "If I had not dragged you here to think and plan, when would you have thought of these things? In the thick of battle with a spear hanging from your guts? Do not let yourselves be aroused by some fiery speech of Sybil Wineskin. I will leave you now to your talk. My work is entirely something other than yours."

She stood and remembered that she had an additional caution. She didn't know how she knew it but she knew with surety.

"Lastly, I caution you that there may be times when there is no time to talk. But you must decide what is to be done. You must decide. If you have time, good. But you may not have the leisure to think. Moments wasted may be lives lost. Decide. Do not get caught up in thinking that you may make a mistake. Do not ask, 'What if?' To think 'What if?' is a mistake."

As she spoke she thought of a test.

"And there is one element of this attack you have not yet considered. There is likely one large chance for disaster. Who of you will find it? And you need to choose a leader from among you. Unfortunately for you that leader will not be me." Jesthya turned to leave them.

"There is still time to choose good sense, though you are too far excited by what you hope will be a grand adventure." She looked at each of them in the hope that she would see any hint that they might waver from their need for war. There was none.

Jesthya walked back to the entrance of the ravine and called for the watch to let her pass.

After Jesthya's treatment of them the nine Captains avoided looking at each other though they went on working on plans that seemed to satisfy every possibility.

The gates were to be set on fire. First the North Gate, where the majority of the troops would gather and raise a clamor. Then, when the party at the South Gate saw the flames, they would quietly set fire to that gate. And so on with the other two gates.

Shadha would take the South Gate. She and two of her company would set fire to the gate, seven others with bows would stand guard, and one would hold the horses and be hidden among the old city a distance from the attack. Bhistha would set fire to the East Gate, and Bharda, the West.

In case the Lords had horses and charged, half the archers were to fire one arrow each at the upper breast plate of the lead rider to fell him with an arrow in the neck. Then the archers would mount the horse behind their riders who awaited them. The second group of archers would fire one arrow each at the Lord who led the attack.

The first of the archers would have mounted the horse facing backwards in order to be able to more easily fire arrows at the pursuing men. Hasta directed that the signal for this maneuver was two short soundings of her horn.

Aslesha raised her hand, caught the stone, and quipped, "If we see fat men riding at us on horses, we will not need the sound of a horn to wake us."

The group laughed hard and long until tears ran from their eyes.

Finally, Ardra retrieved the stone.

"If the Lords have horses, then let us hope Kalla is right about their armor. The Lords charging about on horses with spears is an ill thought."

Aslesha signaled for the stone and spoke with more than her usual grimness: "If the Lords charge on horses, shoot the horses. Better the horses stuck with an arrow than us...."

Her voice trailed off into silence at the ugliness of what she had said.

If the men charged without horses, the plan was to retreat to the west, peppering them with arrows all the while.

An ambush would be signaled by three long blasts of Hasta's horn. At that signal, all would move west for the ravine and hope the Lords would follow and brave the rock falls. If west was not possible, then north and then west was the plan.

Hasta, who had gradually found ways to gain leadership during the discussion, spoke to the others.

"I will present our plan to The Sybil. In the time we have spent talking it is unlikely that they have decided whether and when we are to attack. If they have not agreed, which is as sure as sunrise, I say we take the horses and attack without the blessings of these old women. Stand and swear that you are in agreement with me."

Each of the young women leapt proudly to her feet and swore her agreement to ride with Hasta regardless of The Sybil's wishes.

"Swear too that Jesthya is no longer of our council."

They all cheered at this, shouting that they agreed.

As Jesthya walked back through the ravine, she thought of the lack of purpose, almost a lack of life, among the women living in the valley. *The terraces we started to build were given up on. That work we will complete. Crops will be planted. Enough of these day long trips to a mountain valley to fill a jug with berries. Enough of picking grain seeds where one found them. Enough of the hungry days in the cold of the year. The valley barely feeds us: with work, it will feed many.*

The Windriders may be useful in this regard, she thought. *But they are not needed to oversee the work. We women are capable of that. And capable of more than that. I have little urge to rule men, but I have no urge to be ruled by them.*

As she approached the House of The Sybil, she stopped to watch a sight she had never before seen. Nearly every person in the valley had gathered and was working together with vigor and purpose showing clearly in their movements. One group peeled bark from straight sapling shoots for arrow shafts. Two young girls watched as a group of older women dripped boiling water along the edges of thin triangles of flint. Another group stripped and cut feathers.

At the lake, women fished. Others cut the fish into strips and hung it above a fire to dry.

They are happy to work once they have a reason to do so, Jesthya thought. *We will find many good reasons other than war. We will fill this valley with grain and fruit and livestock.*

Still, it will still be a valley of women going gray and old. Somehow there must be men—men who do not treat us as dull servants. And children. Not only children found on the dunes but children who are wanted.

Kalla could rail all she liked about men but the crows, and wolves, and geese mated for life.

Chapter 30
Decisions, Decisions

Jesthya leaned against one of the large rocks that marked the entrance to the Arbor. She saw Hasta approaching and withheld any greeting, waiting for the older woman to speak.

"You wait for me?" Hasta said, glowering at her.

"I wait for your answer to my question."

"We nine spoke together regarding you. Who are you to question us? We will fight the Lords, and you will remain behind with the old women. We will not be trotted off to one of your meetings again."

"If you value the lives of those who follow you, you will continue to seek my counsel. You are arrogant, Hasta, but we will talk after you have seen blood, though even that may not sway you from your path. Power interests you, and the others, but particularly you. It interests you far beyond your concern for those who will die.

Hasta's jaw was rigid and her neck muscles tightened like cords.

"Grow as angry as you wish," Jesthya continued, relentlessly pushing Hasta. "What have you and your impetuous warlords overlooked?"

She waited for Hasta to answer.

"What you have overlooked are the horses. What if they charge into the Lord's Keep to get to the water and feed? How will they react to the screams of battle? Are they trained, on a signal, to throw their riders? Did you think of any of that?

"You are ill-prepared to lead, much like Sybil Kalla. My counsel is to wait until the moon is darkened. Train the horses. Train their riders."

"You stay with the old women...," Hasta hissed, spitting the words out between clenched teeth.

Jesthya interrupted her. "You speak much like Kalla when you have no answer. You understand—I know you do—that many will die, and that is of little concern to you. Thank Sur that you lack my strength and will." Jesthya stared at her, daring her to respond. "Let the blood of your war be on your head! Yours, and Sybil Kalla's," she exploded.

Hasta darted between the stones of the gateway and moved quickly into the depths of the Arbor.

Jesthya watched her flee.

Have I done all I could do? she thought. *If there is something else I can do to stop this madness, I will do it.*

For a few moments she watched as Hasta stood and awaited permission to join The Sybil.

Ursha could see Hasta waiting but deigned to acknowledge her presence. After a time her eyes strayed again to Hasta, and Pura followed the look. Seeing the young woman waiting, Pura motioned for her to join them.

"Join us, Hasta," Pura called to her.

Hasta walked to the stone table, her face rigid and still burning from her confrontation. She stood between Pura and Kalla, but closer to Kalla. Kalla moved away from her to the northeast corner of the table.

"Welcome," Pura said.

Ursha and Kalla nodded as a sign of welcome.

"We debate still," Pura announced. "We see some risks in the attack. We thought it best to hear your plan."

Hasta snapped in reply, "What has our plan got to do with your decision? Is it wise to attack or not wise? That is the question you must decide. Say your answer is no, and let us be done with the formalities."

Kalla was quick to speak and directed her question to Pura.

"Does the Sybil say that if Hasta presents a flawless plan, we may attack?"

"If you had thought this through as me and my captains have, you would see that what you ask for is unlikely. And there is one area over which we puzzle. That area I will deal with presently. I wonder if The Sybil has thought of it."

Ursha, who had been waiting, quickly spoke. "What times we live in. First a hotheaded boy to set straight, and now a hotheaded girl. You will mind your manners with The Sybil." Ursha waited to see what Hasta would say, but there was no response.

"You are quite masterful. If we discover something for which your plan does not account, you are able to say: 'Oh yes, that is the concern I mentioned when I first spoke.' How clever," Ursha chided.

Hasta turned to Pura.

"May I borrow your chalk, Sybil Pura?"

As Pura fished the chalk from a pocket, Hasta reached for and placed a flat rock on the table. She set the rock on edge to obscure what she drew and then set the rock face down on the table.

"My captains and I are quite thoughtful. We recognize the responsibility we bear for the well-being of our sisters." She looked hard at Ursha her eyes like flint. "We welcome what you may add to our plan."

"That is spoken more as it should be," Ursha said. "Tell us what you have planned."

Hasta began to explain the plan for battle.

At this same time Dern guided Rawlings on one arm and Misrup on the other to quarters. Though they could see fairly well, they accepted his support. He felt that the three linked together must look like three of the Baron's daughters standing at a dance. He thought sourly to himself: *would this day and all its degradation ever end?*

Rawlings's mind fluttered with thought. *Vorguld, Dinar, and the boys were not taken by the Sybil. This I know in my gut to be true. Savvy Vorguld knew his fate were he to return to the Lord's Keep. But where would he be safe?*

These thoughts distract me from what I am afraid to think. Why get stuck in a plan so many times rehearsed? Why wait to be the Chief Lord before I am the King? What better opportunity to be King than tonight? The same opportunity that Vorguld sought as he charged across the boundary lines earlier today. I am sure of it. The difference between him and myself? I will have Mishrup, and Dern, and some of the lads with me. And I will be wearing armor. Madam Hag, your Mother Time gives me a great opportunity. Thank you for those words, Madam Hag.

When the threesome reached quarters, Rawlings ordered Mishrup to remain with him outside. Dern knew he was not wanted and went into the building.

Rawlings faced his Swike. "I chose you years ago as the best of the lot. You are the best of the Swikes, Mishrup; you will be a Lord and more. Are you bold?"

Mishrup was at a loss for words at the compliment as well as the question.

"Are you bold, my Swike?"

"I am as bold as any man, my Lord, and more so than most."

"Two pairs of ears hear what we say."

Mishrup nodded in agreement to these words as he had many times over the years.

"The penalties for disregarding the Edicts are as brutal as man could contrive. How bold are you? How bold, my Swike?"

"I know you, my Lord," Mishrup said, feigning light-heartedness. "You would not talk this way for a bauble. You seek a great gem, and I know, whatever it is, you are determined."

"Vorguld hatched a plan this morning as he stood among us pretending to be blind. What was his plan?"

"To slay the witch, my Lord."

"Yes, to slay the witch, and what else?"

Mishrup looked long at his Lord: "No, my Lord, he would not...."

"You underestimate him. He would slay both the King and the boy—slowly, if he had the chance. My gut feels it, Mishrup. And, too, you underestimate me."

"My Lord, the Edicts...."

"Damn the Edicts! Damn the Edicts, each and every one of them. They have trapped us in an earthly hell. We rot, Mishrup."

As he spoke, Rawlings had edged closer to the Swike, any sense of restraint abandoned.

He breathed hot breath into the man's face. "Are you bold, Mishrup?"

"I am, my Lord. I am bold. Damn the Edicts," he stammered, terrified at what he had said. But he was infected by the avarice of his Lord, as he had been many times in the past. "I am with you," he rasped.

"You are a madman as am I," Rawlings laughed. "I propose one roll of the dice—one roll for everything. Listen to the ease of it!" he hissed. "We take a dozen of the best boys left to us. I wish we had the eight that are with Vorguld, but no matter. What I propose is play for children, easy work. Our Ranger Gelt is not with us: that too is a loss. I wish he were here.

"I meet with the Lords. I tell them that we will patrol the Kingdom on foot to seek out and capture the witch. We will search for her this night, I tell them, and search every night until she is brought to justice. Who will search tomorrow night? If no one steps forward, I will swear in a fit of false rage to patrol every night until she is found. And that is of little matter: for after tonight, we will not see much of the Lords unless they are bowing before us." He laughed the laugh of a madman.

"We will armor the boys. They will bristle with weapons."

"And then, my Lord?"

As to Dern and the other two Rangers, we ask them one by one if they are bold, much as I have asked you. If they do not convince us, then one by one we cut their throats.

"Then, my Swike and partner and soon to be Chief Lord of Harnell, we will march to the East Gate of the fortress."

Mishrup betrayed his thoughts with a whistling intake of breath.

"I know that the Edicts prohibit that we enter through the East Gate," Rawlings said. "I know the penalty. Drivel, Mishrup. All drivel. The Edicts are as good as dead."

"Listen—the boy sent earlier today to inquire of our missing Chief Lord—he will be one of the twelve. He will tap on the door of the King's Gate. Whoever answers will be soothed by him. On my life, I will get us through that gate.

"The boys, my Lord: we will not tell them of our plan?"

"No. They will hear of it once inside the gate. Those that fight for us will live."

"And our Rangers? There is much advancement if one were to expose us, my Lord."

"Wise of you to think of this, as have I. We will ask them one at a time, separated from the others. They must agree."

"And the Healers?"

"Scrawny fools with no more meat on them than on their spears. We find the King. We find the boy. We find the Queen. The Queen I will marry on the afternoon of the funerals. She is my claim to the Kingdom."

Mishrup stared at him wide-eyed and swallowed, at a loss for words.

"You are bold, Mishrup. You will be Chief Lord of all Harnell. And Harnell will be green and rich with anything you may desire for as far as can be seen."

"You will be King, my Lord," Mishrup whispered in awe, nearly breathless.

Hasta had fully presented her plan of attack.

Pura spoke first: "The Sybil is divided on the wisdom of waging war."

"It is as I said to my captains, your answer will be no," Hasta responded flatly.

"In addition," Ursha spoke, "we question your control of the horses. The daughters are unskilled with horses. What is to happen if the horses riot during battle? Say the Lords gain possession of them? Who of you would survive?"

"In addition," Pura continued, "it is one thing to burn the gates of the Lords, but quite another to get lured into their Keep. Though to bargain with the Lords as they huddle behind burned gates without horses is a picture that pleases me."

"And all that would be most easily accomplished on one of the darkest nights of the moon, not the near full moon that we have," Ursha carried on. "Even at the worst, if somehow the Lords recovered their horses on such a night, there would not be enough light to ride them. Even with torches for light it would be dangerous to charge about in the dark. And their torchlight would make them easy targets."

Pura again spoke: "Too, the respite would give us time to decide if an attack is right. As I speak, my heart tells me that it is not."

Hasta had been feverishly rubbing the back of her right hand with the palm of her left hand as she waited pensively.

"Our plan does not say that we will enter the Keep," Hasta responded, her complete frustration clear in her voice.

"Nor does it necessarily prevent you from doing so. Unless it is said beforehand, enthusiastic riders, led on by a false retreat, might charge headlong into the Keep. What then? And the lack of control over the horses! We need the time, this coming half a moon, to prepare. I say we wait."

"I say the same," Pura said.

"As always," Kalla scoffed. "I can control the horses, but what of that? Hesitant, doddering, old grandmothers. You will have other excuses as the moon darkens. The horses followed me at my command. You use the horses as an excuse. I can calm them if they begin to rile."

"You controlled them in the quiet of night: that does not mean that you can control them in the storm of battle."

"As always," Kalla groaned in frustration. "In the time you ask us to wait, the horses will have turned to skin and bone. Then you will worry that they will charge to the feed troughs."

After moments of silence she thundered: "Tonight! Tonight we attack! Are you with me, Hasta?" Her voice cracked. "If not, I will attack without you. I will go alone."

Everyone spoke at once, and over the din of protests, Hasta slapped the back of her right hand into her left palm making a sharp smack of a sound. The Sybil looked at her stunned.

"My captains and I predicted your answer. We have long listened to your caution that traps us behind these walls of rock. The horses are fit. We have agreed to attack. Kalla is right about you. At the dark of the moon you will fidget and hem and haw with any number of excuses, and Time will forget we exist. We will attack tonight. Kalla will join us. She will calm the horses and provide the wise counsel that comes with age." Hasta clasped her hands behind her back and turned and walked away from the Arbor.

Kalla followed her with haste.

Ursha called after them: "When you see your comrades groaning in pools of blood, do not return to us sodden with grief, begging forgiveness. You two will not find solace with us."

She then shouted, her voice rising, "The Land of the Lake is no longer home to you. This land is closed to you."

She walked to where Hasta had stood and turned the flat rock to reveal what Hasta had drawn. Pura joined her. Sketched in a childlike manner, a stick drawing of a horse was revealed.

"Thankfully there is someone with foresight among them," she huffed as she pointed at the picture.

"How will we protect Mother Earth without all three of us? There must be three of us." Pura wailed. "I have failed." Ursha reached out and took Pura in her arms.

Chapter 31
The Fortress of King Gemar

From the security of their windsails high in the cool morning air Jolar and Leason had surveyed the Fortress of Harnell during their dawn flight. Now they felt quite insignificant as they rode along the south wall of the massive edifice towards the East Gate looking up at the dizzying height of the towers and crenellated fortifications. Clearly the Fortress had been built before the Long War, a symbol of a great kingdom rich with crops and labor and organization. From the air it was evident that the fortress could be self-sufficient and withstand any attempt at besiegement. Gardens and greenery and fruit trees had been planted throughout. Fowl, pigs, and cows roamed the courtyards.

As they continued to ride along, they saw damage from ancient battle, as well as the dry decay of mortar turning to powder. Loose and missing stones showed that the will and the manpower to maintain such a fortification were not available in the current age.

The four riders rode past the South Gate, the Lord's Entrance, and turned much later at the southeast corner of the fortress to proceed to the East Gate known as the King's Entrance.

The morning sun reflected off the towering east wall, warming the riders and their horses. When they reached the entrance, Jessyl tugged twice on a frayed gilt cord hanging by a passage door set in one of the vast doors of the gate. The dim peal of a bell was heard. Presently one of the apprentice healers slid open a small wood panel to speak with them.

"Prince Jessyl!" a voice exclaimed with enthusiasm.

A door in the gate opened. Jessyl warmly greeted the bright-eyed favorite of the court: "Good day to you, Rillian. Your smile is as welcoming as Great Sur's first light."

The boy was at a loss for words at this unusual compliment and, saying nothing, stared at Jessyl with a wide, friendly grin and large, clear eyes.

The riders had dismounted as Jessyl had instructed them. The four companions, Gelt, and the three horses were led through the door; the horses bowing their heads to enter.

"Have Kindeen announce that myself and three companions have arrived from the southern border. Say that we seek an audience with the King!"

The boy began to leave.

"Also tell the cook that we require breakfast," Jessyl ordered.

Again, the boy moved to leave.

"Water these horses sparingly but often. Feed them sparingly and then not again until evening," Leason instructed.

Kindeen arrived.

"Go, Rillian," he said to the apprentice. "To the kitchen first and then to Queen Elearim. And take care around the horses."

Leason called to the boy, who turned to face him but, in his excitement, continued to walk backwards for a few paces before he caught himself and stopped respectfully to listen to Leason.

"Do not stand behind the horses." The look on the boy's face showed that he was puzzled. "And do not get between them, or between a horse and a wall. They could crush you in an instant," Leason explained, snapping his fingers.

The boy bowed in thanks for the advice.

Kindeen had turned to Prince Jessyl but waited patiently during this interchange.

"Your father has not arisen. Queen Elearim has canceled today's meeting with the Lords."

"My Father in bed at this hour...."

"He has failed badly since you saw him yesterday," Kindeen said, looking long at the Prince.

"I will advise the Queen that you wish to see your father. Have breakfast. Rest. My healers will ready your father."

"The four of us, together, seek an audience with him. Thank you, Kindeen. And Ranger Gelt has traveled with us. Find him comfortable and secure accommodation."

Gelt stood facing Jessyl, his mouth open, ready to speak but the Prince gave him no chance.

"Gelt, you will be returned to your Masters shortly, but you must remain with us for now. I know you are clever and able, but don't do something foolish or you may never be heard from again." Jessyl turned abruptly and as he led his companions to the kitchen, he said, "This is the first day my father is not about at this hour."

They walked through a dimly lit stone corridor which presently brought them through the thickness of the fortress wall and into a large courtyard. Pale blue smoke rose rapidly out of the chimney of the building that was the kitchen. The foursome walked through one of the gardens that surrounded the building and entered through an east door.

Jessyl nodded a greeting to the cook and motioned for his companions to sit. Leason and Ennar sat at the far end of the table, removed from Jolar and Jessyl. The smell of butter, toasted bread, fried green tomatoes, and eggs filled the room.

"Let us heed the healer's counsel," Jolar offered. "When your father is ready to meet, I will look for the creature he purportedly carries. I hope not to find one, but that would surprise me greatly. There may be a way to strengthen your father...though I do not wish to build false hope."

"You trust The Sybil, Jolar?" Jessyl asked.

Jolar was silent for a moment. The breakfast was hurriedly served.

"We are alone in a land strange to us," Jolar responded when the servants had returned to the inner kitchen. "We are wary of all we meet. Leason more so than myself, but I too. The Sybils are, first of all, for themselves and theirs. They will not be ruled by men. And though Kalla would destroy the Lords if she is allowed to do so, I trust, for the most part, that the good sense of Pura and Ursha will rule her."

"I have no trust in them at all," Jessyl said with force and bitterness in his voice. "They turned a fool loose when what my father needed was healing. Why would they do that? Pura now offers to speak with the King. Why not send Pura in the first place? I see no sense in their judgment."

Jolar was silent; Leason and Ennar who had begun eating stopped and listened.

"And Kalla has stolen the Lords' horses. Is she mad? The Lords will do anything for the return of their horses. Kalla must have been out of her mind to have stolen them, and her sisters must be mad if they allow her to keep them. They are foolish women: completely without sense, Jolar." He continued after a short pause in a morose voice: "And I have shot, and, Kindeen tells me, likely killed the Chief Lord of Harnell."

Ennar and Leason were listening intently to Jessyl.

Ennar set down his cutlery and interrupted Jessyl: "Vorguld charged, a sword raised, screaming for blood. Whose fault but Vorguld's that he lies with an arrow in his guts?"

With fury clouding his face, Jessyl flashed a look at Ennar. He turned again to Jolar, the wrath still etched on his face. "And what of this change in time they babble on about? Today looks black to me."

Jolar replied lightly, "Black is not always such a bad color. In our land we say things look pale," he laughed, but Jessyl did not join him. "Nonetheless, no decision presses upon you. There is no need to set a course difficult to be wavered from, though that may yet be what is required of you. I will see your father, and I will determine what may be done. For now, husband your strength: eat, refresh your spirit. After a time, I will sing."

"And Jessyl," he smiled with warmth and encouragement, "though I do not make light of these troubled time, the time to announce the dawn is not when the sun has risen but during the darkness."

Jessyl nodded a grudging acknowledgment of Jolar's words. "We shall not have to wait long to determine the truth, or the falsity, of the old women's prediction," he said.

Chapter 32
The Wait and What was Seen

After many days of eating whatever they were able to scrounge off the land, the Windriders appreciated the breakfast. With the meal now finished, Jolar and Jessyl lazed in the kitchen garden, their chairs tipped back against a sun-warmed wall, coats thrown open, enjoying the heat of the sunlight on their stomachs. Leason and Ennar, deep in conversation, sat apart from them.

All waited for a messenger who would announce that the King was prepared to see them.

Jolar groaned, "I ate too much and too fast. That is why I advise others...to remind myself."

Jessyl nodded in agreement.

Both he and Jolar closed their eyes and leaned their heads back on the stone wall, enjoying the warmth of the sun.

Jessyl breathed peacefully within the security of the Fortress.

Small birds picked their way through the garden eating whatever they found.

Queen Elearim looked out from her curtained window at her son and his companions. They seemed friends, though they sat in two pairs. *Odd*, she thought, *how men could become friends for life, or lifelong enemies, in the briefest of time.*

She knew that the King was as ready as he would ever be to meet with them. His strength had completely dissipated during the night. Instead of a passive interest in living, he now seemed to hold on to life with a ferociousness he had not the stamina to maintain. It seemed as though the force of death tried to pull him from his body, and he fought back with strength he did not have to spare. The struggle tired him further.

I have been fortunate to have Gemar in this wasteland of monsters. Fortunate doesn't begin to describe my life thus far. But if he goes, what then? If he goes! Has my mind become feeble with grief? Short of these black men being gods in disguise who work miracles I will be a widow. A Queen without a King has not transpired since the Edicts were written. Without a doubt, each of the Barons would put his wife in chains in a dungeon in order to take me and become King. I could rule much better without being encumbered with a husband. Me sitting on the throne holding the crossbow—that would be Sybil Kalla's dream coming true. I must find a way to keep the Barons far from me. Yes, I could rule. How that would come into being, I have no idea. But, given the chance, I could hold this kingdom together until Jessyl is ready to be king. Though there is nothing in the Edicts to allow such a thing. And there is much to point against it. I would gather the Edicts and burn them if I had my way. Yes a grand bonfire. The Edicts have us trapped in Hell. Gemar would have none of it but I will look for a way to rid the world of them. I will think on that. That and much else.

Let the youths sit in the sun. Let them breathe easily. Once Jessyl sees his father, the peace of his morning will evaporate as quickly as a skim of water under the noon sun.

The King breathed shallow breaths though he was reluctant to breathe at all. He craved air and the life in it, but he knew his remaining breaths were few in number.

The Succumon devoured the King's remaining life in a frenzy of gluttony. Any impulse to savor what he sucked from his victim was long forgotten. Though the beast bristled with vitality, a sharp lust for more, and more, and more pounded within it like a beating drum. *More! more! more!* thundered the pounding from deep within.

❧

A cloud dulled the light of the sun. Jessyl shivered and awoke.

Leason and Ennar sat bent towards each other, their heads close together; Leason was speaking quietly and Ennar was listening and nodding agreement.

Jolar opened his eyes and looked towards Jessyl. "Time to see your father, it seems."

Kindeen was walking rapidly towards them.

"Yes," Jessyl replied in a tone as flat as a voice from a grave.

❧

Kindeen ushered the four men into the room where the King lay covered with blankets to his chin. The Queen sat in a straight-backed chair beside her husband, holding his hand. Kindeen took a place between the two healers standing at the foot of the bed.

Jessyl face darkened when he saw his father. He looked to his mother and she nodded for him to speak.

"Father, I have returned with two men from a land far to the south of Harnell."

He looked for a sign that his father could hear him.

"I introduce to you Jolar of the House of Geldof, and Leason of the House of Sarandon."

After the two had bowed to both the King and to the Queen, he continued.

"They have been of great assistance to me and my companion Ennar, who, as you wisely instructed, has traveled with us."

Ennar bowed deeply to the King and then to the Queen.

Jessyl wondered if his father could hear what was said.

"Jolar is skilled in healing. He offers his healing skills."

The King raised a hand from beneath the coverlet and laid it beside his head on a pillow. He moved the hand feebly as he spoke, "Welcome. As you see, I am not myself." He smiled darkly, "Miracles are most welcome."

The Queen stood and bowed slightly to Jolar and Leason. "Welcome to the Kingdom of Harnell. My husband and I are thankful that you have journeyed to visit our kingdom. Whatever you may require speak without hesitation to me, my son, or our Chief Healer, Kindeen."

Kindeen bowed to the Windriders.

Jolar replied. "Thank you, Queen Elearim, for your gracious welcome. Our Mothers have sent us traveling with gifts should we be fortunate enough to meet a King and Queen."

He produced from a small silver case an ornate silver chain. The filigree held a perfectly formed pearl that radiated a white sheen in the candle and torch light of the room. He handed the gift to Prince Jessyl, so that Jessyl might fasten the necklace around the Queen's neck.

"From our Mothers to your Mother," he said to Jessyl. He bowed to the Queen and once the necklace had been fastened, she returned a deep and prolonged bow.

When the Prince finished his task, Leason removed a small wine red leather pouch from a pocket inside his cloak. He untied two fine, green leather drawstrings and slowly withdrew a gold necklace inlaid with a sparkling ruby, and reverently handed it to Jessyl.

"From our Mothers to your Father," he intoned with dignity.

Kindeen moved quickly to gently raise the King's head so that Jessyl could string the necklace around his Father's neck.

The King nodded a slight bow of thanks; a faint flash of light sparkled in his eyes.

Jolar broke the silence, "Regarding your health, King Gemar, I wish to see if there is such a thing as has been described to us."

"Does it exist?" the King whispered. "Is it a hoax?" he breathed deeply. "Thank you." Jolar bowed to the King. "I require the curtains closed and the light, but for one candle, extinguished."

As he waited, he took Jessyl's hand and held it. "Hold your Mother's hand," he said. "Let us have one, quick, close look,"

When the room had been darkened, Jolar bade Kindeen to hold the last burning candle at the head of the King's bed. To Jessyl he said: "Look to the left of your Father's head, above the shoulder. This is where you saw the thing last time?"

He breathed in an enormous breathe and, after a time, released most of it.

"When I signal," he said, raising his hand, "extinguish the light." He released what little air remained in his lungs.

Both Jessyl and Jolar stared intently at the King, as did everyone in the room. Jolar lowered his hand, and Kindeen extinguished the light. In a moment that seemed minutes for most and forever for Jessyl, all those watching saw the creature.

"Light!" Jolar snapped.

The same cloud that Jessyl had seen on the previous day now had two greedy eyes staring defiantly from a lumpy, misshapen head that was the color of rotten squash. In this vision, the King had all but disappeared, yet the Succumon was clearly visible. Most horrific were what appeared to be seven mustard-colored fangs extending from the creature and into the spine of the King. One was affixed at the base of the spine, and the five others were spaced along the length of the King's back at equal intervals. Each funneled a thin line of blue fluid, which, as it passed into the yellowed fangs, turned the color of green decay. The seventh fang touched the crown of the King's skull and had begun to penetrate the bone. The monster grinned with glee at the terror it aroused in the onlookers, but it did not cease draining the life from its victim.

In that one instant all present had seen the Succumon, Jolar and Jessyl more clearly than any.

"The Queen! Prince Jessyl, to your mother. Take her from the room. Quickly," Jolar snapped, "awake healers…"

Turning to Leason, Jolar said, "God bless the King…it is a dread creature."

Leason replied grimly, "And far advanced in its business. Any healing, even the power of the gems, may be consumed by this monster."

Jessyl returned to the room. He looked at Jolar and then at Leason, and by their faces he knew the truth.

"Comfort your mother, Prince Jessyl and then return and sit with the healers at the side of your Father," Leason instructed.

❦

The afternoon waned: evening would soon be upon them. Leason, restless, wondered what went on within the Kingdom. He excused himself and Ennar, whom he instructed to ride through the town to see what might be seen. Leason would fly.

"Keep in sight of me," he ordered.

Chapter 33
On the Move

Kalla shouted for all who could hear her.

"Gather together! Come close to me! Call the guards from the lookouts—we no longer need guards."

Hasta stood beside Kalla, with the captains behind her. Women, both young and old of various descriptions, gathered in front of them.

"Though we have the Lords of Harnell in our clutches, The Sybil has not come to agreement as to what to do with them," Kalla scoffed, as she surveyed the crowd and waited for those still approaching the group to join them.

"The Sybil has not come to agreement as to what to do with the Lords of Harnell," she repeated, waiting for all the women to join the assembly. The guards were seen approaching from the ravine, and several other women were walking hurriedly towards the meeting site.

"I, Sybil Kalla, foretell this to be a time of great opportunity. I foretell this to be a time for bold action. I will move against the Lords—alone, if need be, though as I admire your preparations, I think it unlikely that I alone will feast at the Lord's expense."

A cheer of approval sounded from the crowd, lead by Hasta and her followers.

"Hasta and her captains are with me. Hasta will lead. She and her captains have a flawless plan. I will keep the horses calm and sprinkle about a bit of blue dust—and employ a few other surprises that I have prepared for the Lards."

The crowd cheered and clapped.

"Tomorrow, after we have piled their carcasses along the south wall of their Keep—pardon me, our Keep—and after we have laid them out to rot in the sun, we will then retire to their kitchens and feast."

More laughter, cheering, and clapping followed.

Hasta strode forward, her captains marching behind her.

"Those of you, who will not join us, step back from among the ranks of the brave."

Jesthya immediately spoke: "I will not follow you in this foolishness. Nor will anyone with grain of good sense. A flawless plan? How can there be a flawless plan in war?"

Kalla and Hasta and the captains hissed at Jesthya.

"Stay with the old women!" Kalla shrieked. "Stay with my sisters who have so long kept us in this prison. Keep your precious valley and guard your ravine day after tedious day, year after tedious year, until your teeth fall out. We will have none of it."

The crowd cheered and hooted.

"We no longer need this valley!" Hasta shouted to the crowd and to her adversary she sneered. "And we do not need you, a frightened old man." Her captains and many in the crowd laughed.

Jesthya shouted back at her: "As you wish!"

She turned abruptly and spoke to the group: "I have warned you of the horses. Now I warn you of the greatest danger of all: beware of Sybil Kalla." A rumbling of discord began. "Hear me, each of you," Jesthya shouted above the din, "beware of Kalla. Once she finds the Lord's wine—once she is bloated and drunk—then be doubly wary of her."

Kalla bent and picked up a stone, as did Hasta and her captains.

"That's right. Back away," Kalla crowed. "And you others who will hide here with my confused sisters, back away with old man Jesthya.

Jesthya and the older women, often holding the hand of a young girl, and in some cases two, backed away from the taunting crowd.

"Now," Kalla exulted, "brave captains, choose your warriors from among the fearless."

The nine formed a circle around the group, and the women and girls began to beg anxiously to be chosen.

"Choose nine each. That will make ninety. I will ride Merly and we will make it a party of ninety- one. Thirty horses carry the sixty riders who will set fire to the North Gate and stand with me against the Lords. Thirty horses carry thirty riders, ten each for the remaining gates. Those who rail shrill against our planning do not understand our savvy. Our attack is without flaw," she cackled.

The light of day was dimmed to near darkness as Ennar waited in the shadow of the towering fortress for Leason return from his flight. Presently Leason silently dropped to the earth, his sail scarcely making a flutter. He removed his harness and folded the sail, and disassembled and packed the frame. Ennar squatted against one of the great stones of the wall, waiting.

When Leason was nearly finished, Ennar called to him from the shadows: "Join me Leason."

Leason, surprised by the firmness of the request, focused his entire attention on Ennar.

Ennar remained squatting against the wall of the fortress for a few moments as Leason stood before him. At last he rose and stood close to the Windrider.

"My friend," he said, "you ask often of our water."

He held Leason's eye, as Leason held his.

"Yes, the water...," Leason stalled for time, thinking of how to best answer this question. "As Jolar might say, how can there be profit for all unless there is honesty from both sides?" He paused momentarily, but he knew that Ennar must have an answer.

"Yes, I am interested in water, and to be clear with you Ennar, my people have sent me and Jolar to seek out a land abundant with water. Though Jolar speaks of trade and learning and the message of a new age, I and he also, are first of all interested in water."

As he spoke, he looked to both sides of them and then stared intently into Ennar's eyes, using them as mirrors to see if anyone was behind him. When he was satisfied they were alone, he carried on with his reply.

"In our land, by the time the winter snows arrive, we are thankful because most of our water for that year has been used up. With our abundance, and without war, our population has grown and continues to grow. We have spread outside of our valley and onto the drylands. We use, and reuse, every drop of water, and for the most part wisely. 'To grow and expand is the nature of life,' our Mothers tell us. We have multiplied to where there is no water for more of us. We must send our young, adventurous people to build new cities. We need water."

Ennar continued to look at Leason intently. "Would you take the Sybil's valley? Would you take our kingdom if it had water?"

"Step into my shoes, Ennar. See as my eyes see. If we were to find a valley such as ours, unoccupied, our people would somehow travel there and build. In all our travels, Jolar and I have not found such a place. Now we have come upon the Valley of the Sybils, and though it is occupied, it would suit us very well. That valley, properly tended, not wasted as it now is, could be a homeland for many."

He waited, knowing that Ennar would not have forgotten the second half of his question. "The Kingdom of Harnell has more water than you know. And Harnell is a wasteland of misery—a hell hole. Look at this kingdom through my eyes. Would it not be good, for all, your people as well as mine, to have it set right?"

After a time for thought, Ennar replied, "That is not for me to say."

"I know that you will not make that decision, nor will I," Leason replied.

Ennar looked long at Leason in silence, thinking all the while.

"There must be great pressures in your homeland for you to travel on such a dangerous quest."

"You are wise to understand that. The peace of my land totters on a knife edge. All people want children, and most want many. The more powerful and wealthy have, and want, more water. They exploit those who have none. The poor have less and less and, in these last few years, the poor work harder for less water. Some men have more than one wife, while two, three, or even four poorer men share a wife. The Mothers have foreseen that war will result from the unfairness and greed, and the false pride that fosters it. One dry year will be the end of us. We need more water, or our land will be drenched with blood.

"Do you propose to strip our land bare of us?"

"You have lived too long in the shadow of your Lords," Leason lightly chided. "Though I have little say in the matter, that would be at the very end of our list."

"But it would be on your list."

"Yes, it would be on our list, but would your people not embrace good sense long before it came to that. May we not talk of all the good things that might happen Ennar? Suppose the King—Jessyl will be king one day—agreed that we could settle here. He would know that very soon we would be dominant. Is it power he must have, or would he give up his crown for a prosperous land filled with healthy people. Could he not be subject to our rule? Would that be so bad? We need your water, Ennar, but no less than you need us to help you find a way out this hell you have created."

Ennar had been listening carefully to Leason, and from the time he began speaking he had been watching even his smallest movement. "For now, only you and I speak of this. I have told Prince Jessyl of your interest in our water, and at some time, he must know the full extent of the story. Better that you tell him. He will no doubt be interested in the water that you claim that we have."

Ennar waited for a response from Leason.

Paul Colver

"You are of great value to your Prince, Ennar. Think on this: your people, healthy and prosperous, ruled by my people instead of the Lords, must be a far better situation for all—excepting the Lords, of course. Think on that, Ennar, and discuss it with Jessyl when the time is right. As long as you have water and we have lack of it, the situation that you and I now understand will not go away. And you understand that Jolar and I must return home, or others will search for us."

Ennar's eyes twinkled with amusement as Leason spoke the latter part of his caution.

"I doubt Jessyl and I would think of killing you and Jolar. It occurs to me that you may be as ruthless as the Lords."

"We are not the Lords. But you now understand Ennar that our people are at each others' throats. Factions prepare for war. We need water. Or do we begin leaving our babies on the drylands to die?"

Ennar's eyes widened and he nodded in agreement. "I understand."

"It has bothered me since we met you that we have kept the most important reason for our travels to ourselves. You understand that it would be difficult for us to say to you that we come looking for water—that we covet what is yours. I am glad you had the courage to speak. Thank you, Ennar."

"And thank you, Leason, for your forthright answers."

Now Leason's eyes twinkled, "You stood close to me thinking that if we should fight, your best chance would be hand-to-hand?"

"Yes, that is what I thought."

"Very good. You were correct, though you would not have won."

"Possibly not...You continue to teach me, and we shall see."

Both men laughed happily and in relief.

The sun had set, and the night was cool.

"What did you see from the air? I saw nothing unusual," Ennar offered.

"Oh ho, I have a tale for you," Leason blurted out in a lively voice, as though he had forgotten to give Ennar a present.

"North and west of the fortress, when I left you for one last turn, I saw a flock of lads. The words 'A murder of crows,' popped into my mind when I saw them. Eight of them, I believe, practicing with crossbows.

"Crossbows! Each with a crossbow? What could this mean?"

"I have no idea," Leason replied as they entered the fortress.

Rawlings had ranted and cowed the Lords to his plan to patrol the kingdom in the hopes of capturing the Sybil. The boys had been outfitted with armor and weapons. Now he rested. At midnight he and his troop would leave the Keep, and just before dawn they would be inside the fortress. The King would die. The Prince would die. No fooling around: just quick, painless deaths. The Queen would agree to him as her King—one way or another. The healers would be cowed and become his servants, or they would be sent flying off a towertop to the earth below. The portcullis at each gate would be dropped and chained shut. And the flow of water to the Lord's Keep, and to the Barons, would be stanched. He would talk with the Lords through the safety of the portcullis—none of this nonsense of using the boundary lines in the Hull of Justice or the Edicts for protection.

All would be made clear. The Lords could dry up and blow away from lack of water. Or they could each have a large section of barren land, complete with ample water. He would have their weapons and armor but for their spears. They would give him half of their produce and livestock. They would have wives, but the Lords and whoever they could subdue to their will would be his laborers.

And the Barons—that laughable lot kept around for breeding stock for the King—they would have the same opportunity. Any of their daughters old enough to bear children would be married to him, and Mishrup, and the Rangers, and the lads. These girls would provide his kingdom with children as regularly as hogs produced litters. The weak and ugly would be cast off to the Lords—his farmers. Bodies were what he needed. Young, healthy, strong, well-fed bodies: some to till the fields, and many to serve in his army. On the chance that other kings would arrive and covet his lands, he would have a vast army ready to squash them and to force them under his rule. If another green land was found, he would take it into his kingdom, or if it was too far away to be of use, he would plunder all that was of value and wipe the earth clean of it. Women and slaves and plunder: the thought of it made his heart pump with joy. He would send scouts in the dear hope of finding such a place. Rawlings breathed peacefully. What a wonderful world it would be!

Chapter 34
Jessyl Slept as Though Dead

Jessyl held his father's hand. The King's ashen face shone yellow in the candlelight. Jessyl thought aghast at the sight of his father. *How could he yet struggle to live? There is so little left of him.*

Near midnight, Jessyl's mother entered the room. The healers bowed respectfully towards the King, then to the Queen, and then to Jessyl, and left the room.

The Queen set her hand on Jessyl's shoulder and smiled at him sadly.

"Early this morning I gave your father permission to leave us behind, Jessyl. To leave to his reward for a life well lived. He has suffered and fought death far too long. If he remains with us suffering for you then release him my son. I will leave you alone with him.

Tears filled her eyes. She turned and left the room. Jolar went with her holding the door open for her to pass out of the room.

Jessyl sat in silence holding his father's hand.

After a short time he began to speak: "Father, I am young, but do not remain, suffering for my sake. I have sat by you all these years of my life. I have learned much— enough—more than enough," he faltered in his grief. "And now there are no more years for us. Father, you have given me all that Time has allowed. Go peacefully. Great Yama awaits you, and Great Sur chafes in his waiting to shower you with the rewards for a good life. Do not suffer the pain of this Succumon for another night."

At the word 'Succumon', the King shuddered and instantly Jessyl knew he had spoken a most ill-chosen word. The King's eyes slowly opened. At first out of focus, they became moist and intent as they slowly widened. Much like sharply pointed darts, the pupils of the King's eyes frantically sought Jessyl's pupils, and he was drawn into these pools of horror as though nothing else existed. Immediately the King's strength began to dissipate and his eyes began to close. Through great effort he moved his eyes from side to side.

"Nooooo," cracked from deep within his lungs. "You are gravely..., gravely mistaken."

Shaken and cold even within his bones, Jessyl whispered, "Father, go in peace. Go tonight."

After Jessyl had sat by the King for what seemed an eternity, his mother entered the room and stood behind him, her hand on his shoulder. He stood up and, stepping away from his father, said to her in a whisper: "He will leave tonight. Tonight his suffering will end."

The Queen embraced her son: "Thank you, Jessyl. What you have done is wise. You are a great son—and you will be a great king."

"Yes, and I will be a great king," he said, but his voice trembled and belied him.

Kissing first his father on the forehead, and then his mother, Jessyl slumped into a chair.

Queen Elearim left her son alone in the room.

A wave of fatigue swept through Jessyl's body. Every beat of his heart pounded painfully throughout his head. He slumped forward into sleep, and the torture of a violent dream began.

At that moment, life was sucked out of the air of the room, and the King was torn from his spent body.

The Succumon, at first, was startled. She had been pleasantly at suck during all of this last expanse of time. Warm pleasant life had flowed into her and filled her with nearly unbearable pleasure. Though she felt sated to the point of ecstasy, the flow of warm life had suddenly ceased.

She puzzled without words, for she had no words, yet somehow she understood that her life and pleasure would diminish and finally end...unless...unless? She felt a presence, a royal presence, which she knew somehow knew was all that would suit her. A wave of joy swept through her. A delightfully suitable presence, though in great pain, waited close by, brimming over with precious, youthful life. How fortunate!

Jessyl slept as though dead.

Chapter 35
Kalla at the Keep; Rawlings in the Fortress

The desolation surrounding the Lord's Keep shone luminously under the light of the nearly full moon. Kalla built a fire far to the west of the North Gate. Clearly illuminated, she sat proudly on Merly, out of the range of spear throw, and waited.

On the defenders' side, the wall of the Keep was supported by an earth ramp rising to half the wall's height. When the guards saw the fire, they ran along this ramp towards Kalla, shouting and waving their weapons. Hasta, and Alesha and her troop, waited until the men were far from the gate.

A wheelbarrow had been seized from one of the local tradesman and loaded with dry scrub. The axles' hubs had been greased to silence with precious fat. Hasta gave the order. Aslesha ran the cart up against the gate, and Muley struck a spark. The cart burst into flame; soon the dry gate was also in flames.

When Kalla saw the beginning of the fire and the women had retreated out of sight, she pointed a long finger and glared dramatically at the fire to convey that her fey power was the cause of it.

"I will have your heads!" she snarled gleefully at the three astonished guards. "I will have your filthy, ugly heads.

Your skulls will soon be drums and flower pots," she laughed heinously.

Panicked, the guards hurried back towards the burning gate. Arrows rattled off their armor for the most part harmlessly, but then a shriek was heard as one of the men toppled off the wall and landed hard with the cracking sound of breaking bone. Kalla rode to him heedless of the two guards remaining on the wall.

"Aha!" she shouted to the archers. "Through the neck, as I foretold."

All that could be seen of the guards were their helmets as they huddled behind the wall to avoid a shower of arrows. As Kalla had returned to safety, Hasta commanded the archers to save their arrows.

From the other side of the wall an uproar of shouting and stamping of running feet was heard. Lord Necrous stood at the ramp and then on the top of the wall, his sword in one hand, a spear in the other, his eyes flashing and his face red from exertion. He leaped from the full height of the wall to the earth. As he landed his body shot forward, his knees driving hard into the earth, and then pulled forward by the weight of his armor, he sprawled flat on his chest, his face plowing into the sandy soil. His Swike, Rangers, and six boys also leaped off the wall, but with much less vigor.

The Lord staggered upright and lumbered towards the archers. Ten arrows flew at him. Two hit high on his armor piercing his neck. He fell with a scream that turned into a gurgle as he died.

Spears had been thrown by men on the wall top as well as weapons fired by the men standing beside their fallen Lord. One of the archers was struck in the heart and died with a slight gasp of air escaping her lungs; another was struck in the belly and screamed hideously as she writhed in the dust trying to remove the weapon. The crowd of men on the wall cheered and each man in turn threw a spear, trying to outdistance his comrades. At a run, Muley grabbed the woman who had been crying out and began dragging her to safety. When the she suddenly became silent and went limp, Muley quit dragging the lifeless body and scurried for safety. Hasta had ordered the archers to move back two paces and the spears thrown by the men on the wall top landed short of their intended marks.

Ten archers knelt and fired arrows at the men who remained standing from the first assault. Another ten archers fired arrows as those who knelt in front of them notched arrows to their bowstrings and prepared to fire again. During several volleys three arrows struck home and three men had fallen. Kalla came riding at the remaining swordsmen shrieking a bloodcurdling war whoop. The men turned and ran, inciting Kalla to pull Merly to a halt and point majestically, laughing, "We have just begun our evening with you sluggards! Look to the south."

A shout from one of the men on the wall top turned the attention of all to the South Gate. It burned brightly even in the moonlight. The guards of the South Gate, as well as the gates to the east and west, had left their watches to run toward the fire and the battle at the north wall.

Outside, the few remaining men had retreated across the desolation and now began clawing their way up the wall. Arrows clattered off their armor until all but one lay dead or groaning. The lone survivor was pulled headfirst over the wall to land with a scream face first on the ramp.

Kalla sat proudly on her horse and shouted to the men: "Yes, the South Gate burns! That is our plan: to burn the North and South Gates and then hunt you like rabbits."

She wrenched Merly's reins and pressed the horse's ribs with her heels to force the horse to walk backwards as she spoke words of praise to her followers.

"Easy work, my young ladies? Easy, as I promised," she laughed. "You stood your ground. The bravery you have shown puts these bully boys to shame. I am most proud of you.

"And as of yet I have not had to use the blue dust," she laughed at the men, "or anything else from my bag of tricks!" She had shouted all she said so that those on the wall might hear her taunting words.

"Who among your rabble of cowards will dare to speak with me? Come forward cowering goblins and hear your doom."

As she had just witnessed the first flicker of a fire in the east, which was far ahead of schedule, she pointed towards the East Gate. As the crestfallen men turned to look, Kalla sneered: "Is that enough, or shall I burn the last of the gates? Someone will have to repair this mess," she joked. "Surrender to our mercy, and we will spare your lives."

Lord Voluent stood atop the wall, flanked by his Swike, four Rangers, and four boys. Each held a shield that covered them from chin to waist.

"Please, we beg you, ill-smelling hag," he said as he held his nose momentarily and twisted his face into a grimace of disgust, "come into our Keep. Leap the horses over the fire and join us. Come, what holds you back? It is one thing to be lucky with arrows when we are without shields. Come into our Keep and we will give you a warm welcome." He gyrated his hips as he taunted the women.

Voluent had hurried to the armory and outfitted himself and his men with shields to protect their necks. He was not fooled into believing that Kalla had lit the fires through some witchery. He had also sent six men to the West Gate with haste. Now he wished to stall for time. He retreated to the bottom of the ramp and ran with all his force against the waist-high wall, hurling his spear with a great show of strength. The spear landed uncomfortably close to Merly's hooves. In return, a hail of arrows skipped harmlessly off the armor and shields of ten men standing atop the wall.

"Hold! Hold!" Hasta shouted to her archers.

"Hold! Hold!" Lord Voluent mimicked. "Are we at war or in bed?"

The men with him as well as those behind the wall laughed uproariously.

"Waste your arrows now or later. Not another of us will fall to your paltry weapons. And your wicked hag plays the buffoon and lies to you that she has magic tricks. Much as she bluffs that she started the fires. Come close, and cast your blue dust, blue hag. Be certain of one thing: my dagger is the only thing of mine that will ever find its way into you." Voluent staggered about holding his mouth as though he was about to vomit. Again the men and boys laughed wildly.

Though the Lord boasted and his men laughed, he knew his numbers were few and that the men were much shocked by the sight of the blood of their own. The Company of the Lords was ruthless with sluds and tradesmen, but none of them had ever had to worry about their own blood staining the earth. And wounded men groaned yet beneath the wall. Amid all this chaos, Voluent's mind raced: *Would that Rawlings would show! Where is he? Surely he must hear the tumult. And Vorguld—that would be a miracle to be remembered. Where is he and those with him?*

He calculated the numbers facing him. *Fifty or sixty archers. They are quick to move though they are without armor or shields. And possibly ten or more to a gate. There will be ten less at the West Gate if all goes well. In total, eighty, or ninety, or possibly one hundred of them. They will pay dearly if they enter the Keep,* he assured himself.

"We heard all your silly talk this morning," Voluent shouted above the groaning and cries for help from the wounded. "You can burn all the gates, but you are a long way from setting foot in our Keep. Boys, bring water to put out the fire so the ladies may join us for a late night frolic."

Kalla jested in return. "From the lack of laughter at your manly talk, you have no boys to spare." She periodically looked to the west with the intent to wave her hand in that direction at the first hint of flames.

Observing this, Lord Voluent laughed, "Have your magical powers of setting gates aflame left you?"

Hasta had been counting. The firing was long overdue. She signaled to Bhisthat, who furiously drove her heels into her horse and rode off to the west, her troop following in her dust.

"There is no need to hurry!" the Lord shouted after the riders. "We will bring you their heads presently."

He laughed a berserk laugh and pointed his finger at Kalla. "Will she burst into flame from the heat of her anger?"

All the ten men who stood on the top of the wall laughed and pointed at Kalla.

"Burst into flame, you ugly hag. Burst into flame!" they shouted over and over, stabbing at her with their index fingers to the rhythm of their chant.

⚘

Jolar and Leason walked along the south rampart of the King's Fortress deep in talk, the light of moon illuminating the rooftops below. Leason recounted Ennar's questions and the discussion between them. At the conclusion of his narration, he added: "This great fortress, self-sufficient and able to easily withstand a siege for years, was not constructed with its water well outside its walls. What a foolish thought! The water supply of a grand fortress supposedly set in a hayfield for an attacking army to drink dry. Unbelievable! Who would believe such nonsense?"

"And that water must flow from the Lake of Sybils. We must make a proposal to Jessyl," Jolar said with finality in his voice.

"The Sybil must agree and Jessyl must agree," Leason added as though there was no chance of anything else taking place.

"We need the water, and they need order."

"Very practical," Leason chided.

"I truly did not expect to find water, Leason. Glorious, glorious water! The thought of this treasure among these wastelands…there is water here for thousands and thousands and thousands of people."

It was then that Leason, who had been scanning the sea of buildings below, saw the first glow of fire from the

Lord's Keep. He pointed for Jolar to look and continued his scan. The two men spent only a brief time looking out at the moonlit town and the surrounding lands. Not seeing other fires, they jogged into the fortress.

Leason went to find Ennar, and Jolar hurried ahead to the King's chambers. At the door he found Kindeen slumped forward in sleep. He roughly woke him with a vigorous shake.

"Are Jessyl and the Queen within?" he demanded.

"Only Prince Jessyl," Kindeen replied, confused and still nearly asleep. "Queen Elearim retired at midnight."

Jolar silently opened the door to the chamber. Jessyl lay as he had fallen, curled on the floor beside his chair, his knees clutched to his chest. Jolar went to him and felt his neck for a pulse. Jessyl's skin was cold far beyond the coolness of the room, but had a strong slow pulse, though deep within it was noxious slithery quality. Jolar moved to the King, whose skin was frigid. There was no pulse.

Kindeen, now fully awake, joined Jolar. He also felt for the King's pulse. His face saddened, and his eyes became moist.

"Help me with the Prince," Jolar said. "Sit him up and hold the light behind his head."

Kindeen did as he was instructed.

Jolar dropped his hand as a signal to douse the light.

Queen Elearim stood outside the room looking through the doorway as Kindeen extinguished the candle.

The Queen's body shook with a great wave of grief. "Not my son!" she sobbed. "My husband...please, not my son!" she wailed.

Jolar walked to her and put his arm around her shoulders.

"The leech appears to sleep—likely shocked by its loss. For now it rests harmless. My counsel is to send your son to Sybil Pura as quickly as possible."

Elearim had walked to Jessyl and held her son's hands as Jolar spoke.

"He will be loath to leave his father. He will brim over with grief and anger," she said amid her tears.

"Wake him, Queen Elearim. He must go tonight. Moments are without price for him."

Leason and Ennar had arrived. Leason took Kindeen aside.

"The North Gate of the Lord's Keep lights up the night sky," he said his eyes for once wide with wonder.

Rawlings and his troop rested far to the east of the Lord's Keep, and south and east of the fortress. To each Ranger one at a time in a secluded place far from the troop, he and Mishrup revealed their intentions. They offered each of the Rangers women, power, and wealth. One by one the Rangers accepted: at first with suspicion but finally with enthusiasm. The boys would be told of the plan once they arrived at the King's Gate.

As Rawlings returned with his arm draped over the shoulder of the last of the Rangers, one of the boys pointed to the glow of light from the Lord's Keep. Rawlings knew instantly that he was far too deep into his crimes to retreat.

"It's as I have planned; the Lords are well able to deal with it. We must capture the witch," he replied to the boys as though unconcerned.

Jessyl awoke and shivered. His mother stood beside him, her wrap draped over his shoulders. He looked at his father and then at his mother.

"Hold your grief," she said. "I speak bluntly for a reason. Your father held on to his life for you. He understood that when he passed on, this burden you now carry was to be your inheritance."

As Jessyl looked at his mother his eyes widening with understanding.

"The beast you carry now sleeps. For how long we do not know. Jolar says that 'moments are without price for you.' You must seek the aid of Sybil Pura."

Jessyl continued to look at his mother with wide expressionless eyes. "And my father's funeral?"

"Jessyl, your father's body will lie in state until the moon is full. Go to The Sybil and learn what you must do."

"And leave my father?"

"Jessyl, your father is not here. What lies before us is his body. To speak with your father as you ride is as well as to speak with him here. Your thoughts will easily find him. Wake up, my son, wake up; he is not here. Return for his funeral after you have the counsel of Sybil Pura firmly in hand."

"I cannot leave my father."

"Do not be the foolish child!" she shrieked, rage clear in her voice.

She wiped away her tears and forced herself to be calm, "Jessyl, your father is not here. If you remain, you will join him, your life sucked out of you." She watched his face.

"My son, I have lost my husband. Do you know what that means? Do not double my grief." she said and took him by the arm. "Jolar waits with the horses. Ennar waits at the door. Arise. They will ride with you. Leason has flown ahead to tell The Sybil of your coming. Jessyl, this monstrous thing attached to you sleeps peacefully: act before it awakens, hungry for your life."

Ennar entered the room and put his arm around Jessyl's shoulders. Stunned, and as though in a deep sleep, Jessyl walked with him to the horses, mounted, and followed Ennar's lead towards the Valley of the Sybils.

◦✚◦

Shortly after Ennar, Jolar, and Jessyl thundered in a gallop around the northeast corner of the fortress, Rawlings and his troop arrived at the East Gate. The boy who had earlier in the day inquired about the whereabouts of Vorguld was instructed to knock on the door and again seek the Chief of the Lords.

After the first set of knocking, Rawlings grabbed the boy's wrist and instructed that the knocking had been too light for his liking. Rawlings' voice whispered in a ghoulish tone: "Louder, but not so hurried."

After a moment he released the boy's wrist, and the boy continued knocking as instructed.

The Lord, Swike, three Rangers, and twelve boys waited scarcely breathing. From behind the panel in the door a voice as clear as that of a spring sparrow asked, "Who knocks?"

"Mullen, of the Lords. My master sends me for news of Chief Vorguld."

The panel slid open. "Hello," said the friendly voice. "It is Rillian, we spoke earli…"

In mid sentence Rawlings brushed Mullen aside and thrust his arm into the opening, grabbing the young boy by the throat.

"Open the door. Open it," he barked, squeezing the boy's throat.

Rawlings slipped the blade of his sword slowly into the opening until the boy saw it and cried out in terror.

"Open the door, or I'll carve your face."

As the boy unbolted the door, Rawlings sliced the sword quickly and lightly across the young lad's throat.

"I have cut my hand," he remarked nonchalantly to no one in particular. "So, lads, do you see what we are up to?"

The three Rangers and Mishrup stood behind the boys.

"Who will be the first into the fortress?"

At first the boys stood stunned, their eyes wide with wonder. As they began to fully understand, their faces became a study in fear, and then terror.

"Shall we pile your bones beside this gate, or will you share in the glory?"

One of the boys stepped forward and then set his foot warily through the doorway. As he did so, Rawlings wiped blood from his cut hand across the boy's forehead.

"Come to me after this night's work, and you will be rewarded."

Mishrup followed the blood smeared boy, and the Rangers bullied the others through the opening.

Rawlings entered behind them. He shut and barred the door.

"Seek out the King and the Queen and their son," he ordered them. "Any who oppose us die, but not the Queen. Hear me, and be clear: the Queen must live."

As he said these words he had been pushing his way through the boys and was now in the lead, walking boldly beside his Swike. Presently a spear glanced harmlessly off his helmet. Mishrup charged ahead of his Lord. Four more spears flew down the dimly lit stairwell from above. The Swike charged ahead and slashed and thrust and hacked repeatedly with his sword. A healer's lifeless body made muffled thumps as it tumbled down the stairs though not a sound was heard from the other that died. Their two companions turned and ran.

"See how easy it is!" Mishrup shouted. "After them, boys."

"Find stairs up!" Rawlings shouted. "Upstairs is where they will be. The Queen must be spared. No accidents." He bellowed, "or by Yama, I will have the head of any fool who touches her."

Chapter 36
The Battle at the West Gate

Voluent had sent two of the fastest Rangers along with four boys to attack the assailants at the West Gate. These runners were the fiercest and most fit troops he had available. Laden with shields, spears, swords, and their daggers, they ran across fields, their blood raging with excitement at the thought of surprising and easily overcoming the few women who dared to assault their Keep. To attack the attackers before they might fire gate was the plan. To capture prisoners would win the night and shower these six warriors with glory of which they would reap the first rewards.

Two of the boys reached the gate far ahead of their comrades. They rested, leaning against a fence, and waited for the others. As they used the time to recover, they heard the sounds of movement from outside the gate. One of the boys looked to the four struggling runners slowly approaching, and then to his companion.

He whispered hoarsely, "We throw the gate bar aside and force the doors outward. Anyone within our reach we put to the spear. Shriek as though you are a dozen warriors." He pointed to the four men running towards them. "They will be with us soon. Follow me. Quietly."

"Yes, but Charles, what if the witch is on the other side?" the smaller of the pair protested.

Charles breathed deeply and steadily, his dark eyes ablaze with wrath.

"Shall I tell Lord Voluent?" he said with disgust dripping from his voice, and then he stared fiercely as he waited for an answer. "Or, will I tell them how you threw open the gate and skewered a fierce wench?" He waited, still staring at his companion with a piercing glower. Finally when he was sure he had cowed the boy to his will, he turned and walked stealthily to the gate.

Seeing that he was followed, Charles reached for the timber that barred the gate shut, and signaled for the boy to take hold of the other end of it. When the boy had done so, Charles mimed how they would raise the bar above their heads and drop it behind them. He made this motion rapidly, twice, so that he would be understood, and then slowly nodded his head once, twice, and three times. On the third bob of his head, the timber was quickly raised and flung to the earth behind the boys. Each of them put his full weight against a door and the gate slowly began to swing open.

Outside, a woman squatted, piling dry scrub to start a fire. One of her companions stood surveying the wall top for enemies, and Bharda held flint and steel ready to scratch sparks into the tinder. All three heard the lifting of the bar and stared at one another, momentarily stunned. As the gate doors began to swing open, the three women sprang to life: the two who were standing ran back into the desolation to avoid being hit by the doors; the one who was placing the scrub scrambled on her hands and knees in an attempt to be out of the way. She was nearly upright when the door that Charles was pushing caught one of her heels. She stumbled and fell. The two boys, screaming as loudly as possible, charged. Both saw the struggling woman: both drove their spear into her. All present froze: two pairs of enemies stared silently across the lifeless body at one another. Charles yanked a spear from the corpse and took a step towards the two women.

"Surrender or your lives end!" he shouted in a voice much too young to be that of a killer.

A nervous voice from behind the women shouted: "Move to the side, Bharda; you block our line of fire."

Charles threw his dagger at Bharda. Stricken and wide-eyed, she grabbed the handle of the weapon as if by wrenching it from her gut she would be whole again. She collapsed with no more sound than a gentle sigh.

From within the Keep the women heard shouts and war whoops of what sounded to be a large number of attackers. The two boys charged and threw their spears. The third woman who had been caught unawares at the gate fell instantly, writhing in the dust, shrieking piteously.

Two Rangers and two boys charged through the gate and heedless of the safety of their comrades threw their spears.

Arrows flew from the shadows. The boy with Charles clutched his neck and fell; one of the four near the gate screamed as an arrow grazed his neck. Charles rushed forward and pulled his dagger from his last victim. Arrows deflected off his shield as he knelt behind it for cover. The two Rangers and the other two boys hid behind their shields.

A young woman mounted on her horse charged from among the buildings firing arrows as she rode. One of the Rangers looked over the top of his shield and an arrow caught him in the eye. He fell without a sound. Charles threw his dagger at the rider, striking her in the heart and killing her instantly. The remaining Ranger and the two boys threw their daggers. Three women fell: one dead, the other two screaming in pain.

The remaining Ranger and three boys charged, squealing like pigs that had been wounded. Arrows ricocheted off their shields, but they had drawn their swords and were raging with bloodlust. Charles was the first to make contact. He rammed the foremost of the women heavily with his shield, knocking her to the ground. He let her lie stunned in the dust, and turned and chopped with his sword at the archer standing next to him. The sword cut through the girl's bow and slashed her forearm. She looked at the blood dripping off her fingers and fainted.

She and two other women were all that remained of the ten who had set out to fire the gate.

"Spare them! Spare them!" the Ranger shouted as he pushed Charles to the earth.

He stood between the three boys and the women. "Spare them! We need them for dancing!" he roared loudly and with laughter.

"Aye—the one with the sliced hand will do as well as the others. Bind her wrist and staunch the blood: I have something special in mind for her."

The women were crying. The men laughed.

Charles laughed hardest of all, and with great ridicule and disgust.

"Women!" he scoffed. "You are crying! What will your rabble do when we hurl your ugly heads into their midst? By morning light they will be begging for our mercy."

"We have won the entire night with this battle, my lads," the Ranger roared, laughing gleefully. "When these three are dancing atop the Keep wall, the Hag and her brood will lose their spirit and turn to begging and tears. Then the fun will begin. Good work, lads; good work, Charles," he said shaking the youth vigorously.

Suddenly, one of the women laughed. Her eyes were bloodshot, her face deeply etched with lines and streaked with tears and dust. The men looked, stunned at her laughter, more so as the laugh became a feverish cackle.

"Laugh all you want, you wanton slut!" the Ranger bellowed, his lips nearly touching her face as he yelled. "When we have had our way with you we will set your sorry head on a spear for all your friends to see."

It was then that he heard the horses.

The voice of the young woman who had laughed now shrieked: "My name is Ralana. Remember it as you die and enter the cruelest depths of Hell!" Her voice turned into a horrifying screech of feral joy.

The men, who minutes ago had been planning the torture of their victims, turned to face the charge of Bhisthat and her riders.

Within in no time the horses were upon them, the thunder of the hooves and hideous war whoops drowning out the shrieking howl of the deranged woman.

One boy fell immediately. The other boy raised his hands in submission but was stuck full of arrows and dropped squealing with pain until his life left him. Charles, at first sight of the riders, had darted through the West Gate. The Ranger ran south along the desolation, away from the riders. When he realized that was no escape, he began climbing the wall.

Bhisthat rode by one of the dead women and snatched a spear from the body. She turned her horse and charged, driving the weapon between the shoulder blades of the man who was frantically trying to scale the wall. As he fell, the weapon was wrenched out of her hand. The body landed heavily, the spear making a tearing sound as the earth drove it through his chest.

Bhisthat shouted to her troops.

"Awake, to the aid of our fallen sisters!"

She looked at the tear-streaked faces staring at her.

"We are at war. Awake!" she shouted as though to jar them into action.

"We have won this battle, and now we will win the night. Do you understand? We must defeat the Lords or what you see here is but a taste of what will be. "

She looked into the eyes of those still staring at her.

"Care for Melsan. Keep her warm. Give her water. I will send Kalla to heal her. And then we will take her to Pura."

"Make rags of the clothing of our fallen foes," she said, directing two of the youngest and most shaken girls to the task. "Clean our valiant sisters of their stains of battle. Move them to the far side of the desolation. You others, quickly, gather the arrows. We will need them. Pile the spears and weapons of the enemy around our fallen sisters."

Several of the women held spears, and others had re-trieved the daggers which they tucked into their belts.

"These dead enemies...who will drag them to Kalla and set them up as scarecrows to fire fear in the hearts of our enemy?"

Bhisthat appointed the two women who had survived the attack and three of her most unsteady warriors.

"Drag the dead behind your horses. Take them to Kal-la. She will know what to do with them."

"Who of you will ride with me though the Keep to at-tack the Lords from behind?"

All those gathered, even those most loyal to her, stared at her with fear chiseled deeply into their faces.

"Few men remain. We are on horses: we will win the night!" she said trying to wrest agreement from them. Bhist-hat knew that the shock of battle had sapped their will to fight. She dismounted, snatched a sword away from one of the women, and pointed with it at the dead men.

"I say we carry with us, into the Keep, the heads of these five. We will sit on our horses, jeering at the Lords, a great fire burning behind us. After a time we will lob a head at our enemies...and after a time, as it suits us, another. We will laugh and cackle watching the weaklings go pale with fear."

She chopped three times at the neck of the Rang-er. One of her warriors turned away, sickened at the sight. Bhisthat lifted the head by the hair and set it on a spear. She held the spear high, and as far from herself, as possible.

"Who will ride along side of me to hurl one of these dainties at the Lords?"

All those watching, even the fiercest looked at her with revulsion writ large in their eyes.

Bhisthat mounted and prodded her horse towards the West Gate. Four of the women had set about the grisly work that she required of them.

"When the clamor among our enemy is at its height after seeing their five headless friends dragged before them, we will set a fire in their Keep. Tell Kalla, so that she may point her finger at the flames and fill the weaklings full of terror at her fey powers," she laughed. "Then, with a huge fire burning brightly behind us, casting long shadows towards the doomed, we will show them our trophies."

Wild-eyed and crazed, she shrieked a laugh of hideous glee as she entered the Lords' Keep.

Ralana, who had cursed the men in their dying moments, severed the heads from the bodies and handed one head after another to the first riders who would take them. She saved the head of the Ranger for herself to carry.

The bodies of the five men were each tied to a horse and dragged with as much haste as possible towards the main battle.

The girl who had thrown up at the sight of Bhisthat chopping at the first of the heads sat with another girl on the far side of the desolation guarding the bodies of their fallen comrades and comforting Metson as best she could. The faces of the dead had been wiped clean and their hands folded across their hearts. Those guarding them used a stone that they had pried loose from the rubble of a toppled building to drive the shields into the earth to form a barricade against a possible attack. There were no remaining swords and spears, as the warriors who had ridden into the Keep with Bhisthat had taken them.

The two girls sat on each side of Metson, each with an arm around her. One of them said to her companion: "I doubt we will be attacked."

The wounded girl groaned and shivered violently, her face identical in color to the face of a corpse lying next to her.

Charles was hiding behind a currant bush. He had no weapons. At best, he could pretend he was one of a troop of several and startle the riders at an opportune time. *Was it possible that the Keep would fall to these mad women? Where would he go? Without the Lords to protect him, re-*

turning to the village where he grew up would be foolhardy. After the riders passed by his hiding place, he crept low behind bushes following them from a safe distance.

Bhisthat spoke to the women who rode with her: "Toughen your spirits. Now is the time for thoughts of blood. The Lords will be our servants, or we will be theirs. Do you understand? There is no place for them to hide. There is no place for us to hide. Be firm. The Lords will fall. Think of their terror when Kalla shows them the five headless scarecrows. Shortly after, we will show them the heads!" she laughed riotously though she quickly checked herself and pinched off the laugh deep within her throat.

"Now we must be silent," she whispered. "Call up courage in your blood. Tonight we will rid the world of these vermin."

They rode in silence which Bhisthat again interrupted.

"Be wary. One has escaped. He may lie in ambush, or he may alert the others. Be wary. Be wary, all."

Kalla and the women had retired to the far edge of the desolation. The horses were being sparingly watered; the women ate and drank and rested.

"The sun will soon rise," Kalla intoned in a tired voice. Her lips were dry and cracked, and she worried them ceaselessly with her tongue. She sat resting her aching back against the rubble of a once grand mansion that had collapsed long ago. Her leaders and their troops had gathered around her.

"There are few of them left. The night has not gone at all well for them. They have bullied the Sluds these last hundreds of years, but it is a shock for them to face weapons. It is a shock for them to smell their own blood and to smell the death of their own."

She had eyed each of her leaders in turn as she spoke.

"All that said we may be in for a long siege: them baking in the sun as they defend their walls and burnt gates; we taking their lives one by one as opportunity allows.

"We will need food and water," Alesha spoke.

"The youngest and most silly know that!" Kalla snapped. "At the end of the day a troop must return to our land and beg my sisters for food and water. And who know but that the locals may help us in that regard."

Alesha began to speak against the folly of this idea but was interrupted by a shout. Horses were approaching and their riders were waving and shouting.

"Ride to them," Kalla ordered after looking long at them. "See what slows them."

Two riders mounted and galloped towards their slowly approaching comrades. When they were part way, one rider stopped and shouted back to Kalla: "Mother Kalla, come quickly!"

Kalla mounted Merly and rode rapidly, peering intently into the faint light. A smile lit up her worn face and she reined Merly cruelly to a stop.

She shouted to the women she had left moments before, "who of you can guess the precious load our warriors are dragging?"

"Wake up, boys!" she shouted to the men on the wall top. "Wake up! See the gifts we bear...gifts that will make you curse the morning sun."

She pointed, laughing with glee at the approaching horses.

"So you will have our heads!" Kalla continued with her taunting. "It seems that some of your boys have lost theirs. And this day, by noon meal, your heads will be lined up along the wall top. The West Gate is lost to you. Our riders are now behind you."

Paul Colver

The women understood what Kalla was saying. They mounted their horses and rode within a spear's shot of the wall, shouting and laughing and hissing. Muley dismounted, bent over, and flashed her behind at the stunned men. The women hooted with laughter at Muley's antics.

Kalla, though her sides hurt from laughing, pointed her finger at a faint glow of flames from within the Keep. The men turned and saw the bright flames of a rapidly growing fire illuminating five women bristling with weapons and mounted on horses holding severed heads high in the air at the ends of spears.

Kalla guessed what Bhisthat had done and she shrieked at the men, "Have you found your missing heads?"

The women with Kalla laughed hysterically, tears of shock running down their cheeks at the gruesome sight.

"Poor boys: you stand with your backs to our riders within the Keep, no shields to protect your necks. Turn to face them, and you are exposed to our arrows. Feeble and weakened old grandfathers that you are, throw down you weapons. We have no wish to take your lives. We require breeding stock and men to work the land. Not such a bad life. Much better than a tryst with Yama, I should think."

The remaining men shuffled about, some cursing the women, others looking worriedly for a place to flee or hide.

Kalla nodded to Hasta, who signaled for the archers to begin firing. As the men turned to protect themselves with their shields, the women in the Keep began firing arrows at their backs.

A boy shrieked and fell from the wall. A Lord died instantly, an arrow through his neck.

Voluent turned, shaking a fist at Kalla, when an arrow caught him above his shield and spun him around toppling him off the wall into the pile of embers that had once been the North Gate. He attempted to rise from the coals but collapsed howling piteously, his armor scorching hot, his clothing on fire.

Before the Dawn

Some of the remaining men ran along the wall to the east, others to the west. Riders followed them, firing arrows and mocking them as they fell wounded or dead.

"We will have your heads; we will have your heads!" became the chant of the women.

Three pairs of men stood back to back one man against another in order that their shields would protect them from both sides. All the men had heard Voluent's hideous screams, and smelled the stench of his burning flesh.

Kalla rode up and down the desolation shouting to her warriors.

"Leave them to live, my sisters. Leave them to live."

She rode to each of the captains. "Calm them. We need men to till our fields. Calm your troops."

She shouted to the men on the wall top: "You men—come down. Drop your weapons. Gather around me: I will protect you."

"Spare their lives, my sisters. Let them live!" she shouted. "Who will till our land? Let them live! Let them live!" she shouted again and again.

The men were herded into a gaggle by the wild-eyed, hooting riders. Bhisthat and her troop charged through the Keep gate and leaped their horses over the embers and the charred corpse of Voluent. Two of the horses collided. One of the riders fell to lie crumpled on the sandy desolation.

Kalla motioned for the captains to gather around her.

"Guard the captured," she shouted to the others. "Separate out any remaining Lords and Swlkos into a preferred group. Tell them they are to be in the preferred group!"

She led the captains out of hearing distance from the well-guarded prisoners and their guards. To those surrounding her, she said: "The Lords must die." She looked each of the captains fiercely. "They must die. Alesha, gather the most blood crazed among us. Dispatch these remaining Lords quickly—silently—one arrow for each is all it takes.

As you do this, assure the Swikes that they and the others will live. Do not hesitate. Deal with the Lords now while our blood is on fire! Go!"

Alesha rode off and selected the archers she needed.

Kalla continued speaking to the remaining captains: "The Swikes must never father another child. Cut them, but not so that their will to live is gone. But be certain to remove both their precious jewels. Do it now, not later when you are women again," she laughed hideously.

"Bharani, you and Muley go to Alesha and help her with the Lords. A quick arrow each and the chore is done. Then go to work on the Swikes. There are but a few of them left—a pittance in the whole scheme of things.

"We shall look the Rangers over on a man-by-man basis. Those that stood in pairs, back to back on the wall, to protect each other...mark them for breeding. Better those with brains fathering the children than those that ran like frightened geese. And have no doubt that the manners of the Rangers and the boys will be much improved after they hear what the Swikes have to say about their alterations."

The two who had guarded the dead by the West Gate had left their post to bring the wounded girl, Metson, to Sybil Kalla. She sat shivering violently in the cool dawn air; the rider on whose horse she rode wrapped her arms tenderly about the suffering girl.

Ralana, who had ridden with Bhisthat through the Keep, saw the three patiently waiting for Kalla. She moved her horse to Kalla and stopped though roughly jostling Kalla's mount.

"We are the remains of Bhadra's troop," Ralana snarled at Kalla. "Seven of us lie dead at the West Gate."

"Yes, yes," Kalla replied, shaken by the jostling of her horse but now staring at Ralana with a wry smile. "What did you expect as you rode off to war? A day of fun in the fields? I expected the toll to be much higher. All in all, your seven and these few strewn about is a small price to pay for what we have accomplished this night."

Kalla licked her lips after she said this and turned to one of the riders. "Fetch the blacksmith. Hurry him along. We will need shackles."

She turned to Ralana, "Still here? Take the girl to Pura. Be gone!"

Ralana drew her sword and held it, her arm stiff, setting the point close to Kalla's face.

"So, old woman, this is the way it is to be?"

Quick as a snake, Kalla nudged Merly a step back and with a flip of her wrist sent a star-shaped blade deep into the girl's throat. As Ralana's corpse fell soundlessly from her horse, Kalla turned, her attention drawn by a blood-curdling scream from one of the Swikes.

✦

Rawlings, after much stumbling about in the hallways of the fortress and with only one torch for light, heard a shout that the stairs were found.

"A wide set of stairs fit for a King and Queen," he chuckled as he followed the shouting to find himself at the foot of a grand staircase. When he had bounded halfway up, a hail of spears greeted him, clattering off his shield and armor. He charged forward continuing to take three stairs at a time.

"You scarecrows!" he bellowed. "Down on your knees before your King."

The cowering healers and their apprentices backed away from him, terrified at his words and his wrathful look. Few of them any longer held spears.

He held up his hand to signal his men to stay back. "I'll care for this rabble," he snorted as he continued to glare at the healers.

"I am King of Harnell!" he thundered. "Kneel before me." His sword hissed as he sliced a nearly complete circle through the air.

"Kneel!" he roared.

"Enough of this...," Queen Elearim commanded as she strode forward from the darkness. "Who are you to enter here?"

"I am Rawlings, Chief Lord of Harnell. I will enter whenever I choose." He glared at her wantonly to see if she would drop her eyes as she had so many times to his brazen looks. She did not. "I seek a brief audience with your husband, and also your son," he continued roughly, though he dropped his eyes momentarily in response to her glare.

"I wish I could take you to my husband as he once was. He would gladly have dealt with you, but that is not possible. Come, follow me. As to my son, he is safe in the Valley of The Sybil."

She turned, and the healers parted to allow the Queen and Rawlings to walk to the King's Chamber. Rawlings shouted back at his men, "Find out what we need to know Mishrup. Those who help us will live to serve us. Those that tell us naught, save them for later. We will see how well they fly from the highest of the towers."

"I'll have none of the healers harmed," the Queen said loudly for all to hear.

"You have heard that your Keep is aflame?" she continued, speaking now quietly to Rawlings, allowing no countermanding of her order.

Rawlings stopped and turned continuing to speak to Mishrup as though he had not heard the queen. "Gather all the copies of The Edicts. Tomorrow at sunset we gather the populace and have them dance around a bonfire.

"You will burn The Edicts Lord Rawlings?" the Queen demanded in a startled voice but with a glitter radiating from her tired eyes.

"Yes, and anyone who holds back a copy. We live in hell because of The Edicts. And in answer to your question about the fire in the Keep Queen Elearim I well know that the Lord's Keep is aflame—though it is of little concern to me. I will do what I wish to do from this fortress."

"And what is it you wish to do?"

"The land will be green," he stated as though repeating a well known fact. Then he leered at her with no regard for shame and said, "That is a tale that will take the rest of the night in the telling." The Queen returned his stare with a strained smile. As they entered the King's bedchamber she motioned with a sweep of her arm towards the body of the King. Rawlings strode to the body and felt for a pulse.

"The King is dead; the boy run away. You need a man."

Kindeen stepped out of the shadows, pointing an arrow readied in the crossbow at Rawlings' heart.

"Ah, my dear Kindeen..." the Queen said as she quickly moved to stand between Rawlings and the arrow point. "Don't be foolish. Loosen the arrow; give me the weapon. I prefer not to lose two men on one day." As she retrieved the crossbow, and smiling handed it to Rawlings, she continued speaking soothingly to the Healer, "Now, Kindeen, fetch a bottle of Merlow. After the exertions of this night our King is no doubt in a great heat."

The End of Book I

of the Satya Yuga Chronicles

Before the Dawn

About The Author

A former oilfield worker, shrimp boat deck hand, teacher, construction company owner, farmhand, management consultant, Paul Colver finished his first novel **Before the Dawn**, the first book of **The Satya Yuga Chronicles**, in the spring of 2006.

Currently living in the City of Parksville, Vancouver Island the author is writing **Gaga in Zanzibar**, the story of a 60 year old man who after completing a first novel travels in Africa for three months in order to get away from words, falls into a deep infatuation with a shining lass from Ireland, and lives out a long repressed Easy Rider fantasy by renting a motorcycle and exploring the island of Zanzibar. His infatuation prods the old man to puzzle out his relationship with himself, and the five wonderful women who at various times have graced his life.

Most happily Paul is blessed with two children, a granddaughter, Julie, and another grandchild due in February, 2010.

For work and amusement he dabbles in politics, affordable housing, Vedic architecture, and teaches the course **Aging Reversal: An Ayurvedic Approach** at Vancouver Island University keeping his time fully occupied as he awaits—completely terrified—enlightenment

Acknowledgements

Best wishes to the many people who supported and encouraged the writing of this novel. To the wise youth and the wise elders who read the early drafts, my thanks for your insightful comments—the book is a far better story because of your frank input.

To the wise elders Janet Walker, Dale Ferguson and Everett Marwood (*A Legacy Worth Leaving* www.marwood.info) many thanks for reading and commenting on the early and difficult to read drafts.

Thanks also to Dale and Pat Ferguson, Glenn and Jo Allen, Everett and Linda Marwood for your support and mentoring throughout the years. Particular thanks to Murry Furher (Extreme Esteem: The Four Factors www.extremeesteem.ca) for your encouragement and optimism and guidance concerning the dos and don'ts of writing and publishing. Many times I phoned Murray beginning the call with the words "Help! Murray I'm going nuts...." Thanks for being in my life Murray.

Many thanks to my son Ben. Thank you for your valuable contributions on just about everything from critique of characters, description, theme, pace, cover design etc, etc, etc. I am most thankful to have profited from your honors degree in Literature. Best wishes with your writing career.

Many thanks to my daughter Ellie. Your many contributions were invaluable to the novel, particularly your 'calling me' on the original Jesthya. I am most pleased to have had the benefit of your insight into human nature gained from your 10 years of working in various countries around the planet. Many thanks Ellie.

Thanks to the members of **Writers Ink** of central Alberta (www.writers-ink.net) for allowing me the opportunity to read passages of the book and to receive your frank and helpful feedback.

Thanks also to the **Sylvan Lake Book Club** and **Sylvan Lake Writers Club**. To Pam Snowden-Anderson: I appreciate your interest in the novel and your unflagging encouragement. Thanks Pam. Best wishes with your writing career.

To the wise youths who read the book in its early stages my deepest thanks to each of you. Your sincere enthusiasm encouraged me greatly and I was able to make changes on the basis of your insightful comments. Thanks to: Tegan McTaggart (best wishes in your writing career), Tyler Wood, Langdon Dorval, Michael Nykolishen, Davis Hersberger, and Lacey Kinley.

Best wishes and many thanks to Carmen Wittmeier (author, editor and teacher, cwittmeier@gmail.com) for your two thorough readings and many helpful comments. Without your help the novel would not be nearly as good as it is.

Many thanks to Joyce Burns, Parksville, for the cover illustration. I told you what I wanted the picture to convey and you nailed it. Fabulous.

To my support team at **Pursuit of Excellence** (www.excellenceseminars.com) headed up by master motivator Terry Marquis, a large thank you to each of you.

Particular thanks to my 'big sister' Meritta McKenna who has been there for me with encouragement and no doubt prayers, throughout my life.

To all my friends both of recent acquaintance and from ages ago, I appreciate each of you being in my life. And while none of you are a character in **Before the Dawn** you may notice a fleeting glimpse of yourself or a passage of dialogue that was once yours.

Best wishes,
Paul Colver,